THE
BACHELORETTES
OF THE BIBLE

THERESA V. WILSON

Writers in the Marketplace™ Press Subsidiary of VMAssociates, Inc.

The Bachelorettes of the Bible by Theresa V. Wilson Copyright ©2021

www.theresawilsonbooks.com

ISBN: [Ebook] 978-1-7356409-1-4
ISBN: [Trade Paperback] 978-1-7356409-2-1

Cover Designed by: J.L. Woodson, Woodson Creative Studios
Book Editing by: JL Campbell
Interior Design & Formatting: DHBonner Virtual Solutions, LLC

THE BACHELORETTES OF THE BIBLE

THERESA V. WILSON

THERESA WILSON BOOKS
MOVING FROM VISION TO PRINT

To the unsung heroines of the Bible.

CONTENTS

ACKNOWLEDGMENTS

Giving all glory and honor to my God, the big "G," the Source of all the resources needed to complete this fictional work.

Special appreciation to Writers in the Marketplace Christian Consumer Readers (CCR) group members, my husband, Doug (JD), Leslie Butler, and daughter Donielle Rooks. The value of your opinions, critique, feedback, written commentaries and prayers cannot be measured. To Robert Delaney Rooks, my son-in-law, who's a strong supporter of whatever I seek to accomplish. To my Mom, Ireatha, for her example of strength and encouragement to never stop.

Thank you to J.L. Woodson, Woodson Creative Studio for hearing my heart and creating an awesome book cover. Most special appreciation to J.L. Campbell, awesome Line and Content Editor.

NOTE TO THE READER

The Bachelorettes of the Bible is a fictional journey that explores what could have been the behind-the-scenes life of some of the most well-known single women of the Bible.

The stories in this book are speculative Christian fiction. It does not, in any way, replace or rewrite the irrefutable word of God. This means several descriptions of biblical characters, situations, and relationships were created to fit the narrative. The biblical scenery is the same, with the stories taking place on the continent of Africa focused on the people whose descendants are Israelites or families connected to the Israelites.

The story line was adapted based on authentic historical figures with some the narrative content infused with a dialogue of what could have been behind the scenes events and circumstances, that may have influenced the decisions and choices that change the course of history.

It is my sincere hope that, in addition to enjoying the stories, this book inspires you to engage the scriptures and learn more about the word of God.

STORY ONE: RAHAB: THE AMORITE HARLOT OF CANAAN

CHAPTER 1

Huge flickering orange torches illuminated the entrance of the ivy-covered archway leading to the temple. Guards with enormous deer head masks decorated with beautiful multi-colored stones, greeted the throngs of worshippers moving slowly, in unison, toward the site the pagan festival. The dome of the temple was surrounded by numerous torch lights that began from its peak down through its pentacle to a gold-framed marble base. A magnificent structure, it was the center of weekly activities for the town's inhabitants.

Rahab and her family moved with the crowd. Ammon, her brother, on one side, and her mother Hathor on the other, with her father and two other siblings not far behind.

Ammon, who took nothing serious, nudged his sister. "I wonder what weird goodies they have for us tonight?" He lifted both hands and chuckled. "I know. The gods will raise someone from the dead."

Hathor leaned forward with a scowl and snapped, "Quiet, both of you. This is a sacred event. Meditate and follow in silence."

Ammon didn't speak but shrugged, and stepped back with the others.

The Festival of Worship was a sacred event in honor of gods and goddesses, celebrating seasonal blessings by offering human sacrifice. Attendance was mandatory. "Cover your face! We're nearing the temple and everything must be in order," her mother ordered.

Tucking in her curly black hair and adjusting her shawl so that it fit closer around her face, Rahab glared at her mother. "For goodness' sake," she smirked, while shifting her skirt. "This is not my first ceremony."

Hathor stepped in front of Rahab so fast she almost stumbled face forward onto the gravel walkway. After regaining her balance, Hathor pulled her daughter close, lowered her head, and gave Rahab a penetrating stare that made Rahab shift on her feet. "Let's try this again," Hathor whispered. "You are about to enter the temple, and you are of age to be an asset to our family."

Rahab started to speak but remained silent as cold, calloused, work-abused fingers pressed against her lips, indicating silence.

Still holding her daughter's arm with a firm grip, Hathor smoothed the stands of hair using slow deliberate motions, to ensure they were tucked neatly and no longer visible beyond the veil. She sighed and spoke in a softer tone. "You are a striking beauty, my Rahab. You could be highly favored by the temple priest. This would not only be good for you, but good for the entire family. I need you to enter the temple as the princess you are."

At any other time, Rahab would have been warmed by her mother's kind words, but these comments were conveyed without emotion. This was a directive, pure and simple—strictly business. Favor from the high priest would elevate her family in the town, resulting in more customers for their hostel "boarding house."

Rahab pulled out of her mother's firm grip, propped both hands on her hips, and leaned to one side, eyeing her with a raised brow. "So, I'm a show plate to dangle before the high priest," she hissed. "Mother, you never cease to amaze me. All this time you pressed me to study the ways, practice the rituals, and attend services. Here I thought you were a believer but all the while it was a set-up. I was part of a business plan."

Before Hathor could respond, someone gripped her elbow. "My dear," Rahab's father said as his gaze burned with disapproval. "Enough." Waving for his daughter to move inside, Koren guided his wife to follow. "Calm yourself, my dear. You will not get Rahab to do what you want through anger and threats. She is a woman now. Guide, don't push." Hathor nodded and moved forward.

Melodic sounds emanating from the building, followed by a familiar mantra rising from the crowd, suggested the ceremonies were about to begin. Rahab, her mother, and siblings, who were straggling behind, reached the entrance and were greeted by yet another set of torches mounted strategically high above the crowd. They entered the designated gateway to the presence of the god of their sun. All persons participating in the ceremonies sat in the front on sheep skin rugs, facing the statute of Ra.

The strong aroma of incense permeated the air. The priest, tall in stature—attributable to his ancestry of Rephaim giants—stood before the congregation, prepared to perform the black art rituals to appease Amurru, the lord of the mountain, and his wife Belit-Seri, Lady of the Desert. Holding clay tablets, they walked slowly, in rhythm with the chanting, laying hands on the worshippers in the first two rows.

Rahab, seated in the rear with her family, shifted in the uncomfortable chair, and anchored her attention on the priest pacing slowly at the front of the room. As he moved, repeating the mantra for the day, he gazed in her direction several times. His piercing eyes made her swallow to relieve the constriction that tightened her throat. She turned to her mother, Hathor, pleading, "May I be excused? I don't feel well."

Hathor whirled and grabbed Rahab's arm, squeezing tight. "Surely

5

you can't be serious. I won't hear of it." She whispered. Her eyes revealed her irritation. "You will sit here attentive and quiet," she commanded. "This is a sacred ceremony. To move now would anger the gods and bring severe punishment on our family. You are of age to attend these rituals and I expect you to be obedient to whatever you're directed to do."

Rahab stiffened. "Yes mother," she replied, wishing she could control the quiver in her voice. She had never been angrier with her mother than at that moment. It wasn't enough that she had to ignore the pinching and inappropriate patting from their frequent "house guests" at the *family tavern*, because it was good for business. Now she was expected to attend these rituals in honor of a god she wasn't sure she fully understood.

The priest paused, holding the torch light high above the covered throne of Ra. His long, blue and red silk robe—accented by a wide belt decorated with tassels laced in rubies and diamonds—glistened in the light. As the worship mantras continued, he advanced toward the front row, taking slow deliberate steps, while lighting additional candles held by congregants who bowed each time he approached. Though impressive, the scene was overshadowed by large torch lights mounted on massive pillars surrounding the throne of Ra.

At every reverent bow to the statute of Ra, the priest turned slowly, in a robotic motion, and waved the censor, with fragrant burning incense, over the gathering. Everyone was required to bow when the censor was offered in worship. Each time this task was performed, he paused briefly and looked in Rahab's direction. She felt his eyes observing her response to the instructions to perform the required bowing and swaying responses. Shifting uncomfortably, she avoided his gaze whenever possible. *"What's that all about,"* she thought.

For what seemed like hours, the designated "anointed servants" segment of the ceremony proceeded with each member of the front row rising, walking slowing to the throne of Ra, while bowing and swaying in time with the rhythm the minstrels played on enormous string instruments. Turning from the front rows, the priest walked the aisle stopping once or twice to speak directly to individuals he chose at random.

Hathor had been giving instructions to Koren when she noticed the priest walking toward them. She nudged Rahab with her elbow. "Sit straight and mind your movements. The high priest is coming this way."

Rahab gave her mother a side-eyed glance, followed by a dismissive wave of the hand. "Mother," she sighed, "please stop. He has no interest in me." Yanking her arm tight, Hathor spoke with increased urgency and anger. "You listen to me. The high priest has shown favor toward you. I've been watching this night. Favor from him, means prosperity for the family. Eyes down, Rahab," her mother chided. "And mind what I say. Here he comes."

Rahab breathed deep and lowered her chin. While her eyes were closed, a warm hand caressed her face. She looked up and locked gazes with the priest. The room was quiet, the music stopped, no one moved. He seemed much taller close up and his smile showed a mouth full of pure white teeth cut close together. His eyes, however, disturbed her the most. Their penetrating gaze was full of what Rahab could only describe as unmasked evil. Stroking her cheek, he leaned closer, before breaking the silence. "Your destiny is set." He sneered. "So be it."

Rahab stiffened. Goose bumps immediately appeared on her arms as his hot breath bathed her ear. She froze, closed her eyes, and lowered her head to avoid any further contact with the priest. He didn't speak again, but stood over her for what seemed like an eternity. Barely touching her head, he chanted softly in her ear. Rahab tried to regain her composure but couldn't ignore his whispering. She wanted to move but, frightened, remained motionless. Suddenly, the room seemed to spin. Desperate to escape, Rahab reached for her mother, "Mom, I don't feel well, help me," she pleaded, as her eyes rolled back in her head. Before Hathor could respond, Rahab fell forward and slid to the floor.

"Ra, Ra, wake and see what the gods have in store for thee." Rahab woke to the sound of her siblings chanting outside her bedroom door. Irritated by their revelry at an inappropriate time, she jumped out of the bed and opened the door with such force her two sisters, Keket and Anippe fell, face forward, on the floor inside the room. She leveled a look of contempt in their direction. "This is far from funny," she shouted.

Gripping both girls by their elbows, she guided them to their feet. "You need to take care how the name of Ra is used." With a disdainful attitude, she leaned on the door frame. "Now, if I'm not mistaken, you have chores to finish before father returns from his meeting. You best get to them." Her sisters eased quietly out of the room and proceeded down the corridor toward the kitchen. Before turning the corner, Keket, the second oldest, looked over her shoulder. "No problem, Sis," she smirked. "Oh, special one."

Rahab breathed a sigh, shut the door, and plopped on the bed, surrounded by goose feather pillows. She spread her arms wide, stretched, and flipped on her stomach. The scent of baked honey buns and roasted lamb had already reached her nostrils, but she ignored the aroma. She wanted to be alone, with her thoughts, in the sanctity of her room. As the oldest girl, and her father's favorite, she was allowed the corner of the large rooming house. Her window, at the back of the house, overlooked the desert. Despite the limited vegetation, Rahab enjoyed the beauty of the cactus plants and the vastness of the land.

Other than periodic caravans, her view was rarely disrupted because of the rock formations that inhibited comfort for travelers moving through the area. She closed her eyes and enjoyed the cool early morning breeze, and the few moments of quiet time in her personal space. Before she could return to the pleasant visions of her last dream, Ammon, her brother, banged firmly on the bedroom door. "Hey princess, time to get up. Our Mother's got some things for you to do in preparation for the sun worship celebration at noonday."

Rahab didn't respond, but turned slowly toward the door. As she scanned the room, her gaze fell on the large statue of a falcon sitting beside her wash basin. It was a "present" from the priest last night. She was uneasy having received the gift, and shuddered at the thought of what it might mean for her future. She shook her head at how elated her mother and father were at the attention their daughter was getting. *"They haven't a clue,"* she mumbled. Favor from the high priest guaranteed a stronger position of influence for them in the community, but it also meant loss of freedom, rigid requirements, and more responsibility for her.

Ammon interrupted her thoughts. "Ra," he shouted, while knocking a second time, "come on girl, get out of that bed and get ready. Your days of doing as you please have ended, so let's get these events going, so I can get favor in my business dealings," he said, then laughed.

Rahab, threw the covers to the side, rose and swung open the door. Clasping both hands in front of her chest and a feigning look of innocence, she fluttered her eyelashes and swayed side to side. "Why, brother dear, whatever do you mean?" She smiled. "I fully intend to continue doing as I please. In fact, I suspect I will have my way even more after all the attention I received last night." Smoothing the hair away from her face, she winked. "I think the priest is weird, but I know his attention can only be good for us."

Ammon shrugged and chuckled. Though always into questionable adventures, he was dependable when she needed him and hand a good command of business. "Whatever kiddo," he responded. "But, to be clear, you have some new responsibilities and they begin this afternoon, so get dressed and come down to eat. It's going to be a full day."

Rahab raised one brow. "New responsibilities? We'll see. I have not agreed to anything." Ammon crossed his arms and shifted from one foot to the other. "You didn't have to. Mom and Dad were called to the temple and had a long meeting with the high priest this morning at sunrise. They shared a bit of that conversation with me."

Rahab grabbed her brother's arm and pulled him into the room. "Come in. Talk to me while I pick out my outfit for the day." He hesitated, looked quickly down the corridor, then stepped inside. "I'm not going to stay long. Mom and Dad want to talk to you themselves. It's not my place to discuss what they plan to share with you, Ra. Just know it's good for all of us that you are favored."

Not happy with the response, she glared at her brother. "That's nice, but I hope they didn't make promises they can't keep. I'm not a temple girl. I don't want to enter that rigid environment." Ammon touched his sister's arm and raised her chin so their eyes met. "Whatever it is, you can handle it." He approached the door and gave her a brilliant smile over his shoulder. At the doorway, he turned and smiled. "Now baby sis, get dressed and I'll see you downstairs."

Sitting on the edge of the bed, Rahab ran her fingers along the silk threads of her sheath dress. Everyone knew she and Ammon were close and that he was one of the few people who could influence her to conform to decisions that involved her. He had done it many times, so it was no surprise that he had been sent to set the tone of what she was about to hear. At the thought of what might be demanded from her, Rahab's peace fled. Gathering her toiletries to refresh before dressing, she took one last look out the window to absorb the peaceful scenery.

One last moment of calm before I meet this challenge.

* * *

Rahab walked slowly toward the noise and chatter on the lower level of the house. In spite of the pleasant odors of fresh baked bread and lamb roast she knew would be smothered in pungent spices and vegetables to delight the tongue; she wasn't looking forward to the crowd.

"Get a move on, girl!" The squeaky voice of her baby Sis, Keket, resounded while she stomped several steps behind. "You made a mess of things last night. Mom and Dad were furious when you fainted. They had to leave before the ceremonial sacrifice to Ra." Keket, who was now in step with Rahab, grabbed her favorite sister's arm, tugging lightly. Whispering now, for fear her voice would carry, Keket stepped in front of her sister bringing them to an abrupt stop. Laying both hands on her sister's shoulder, Keket glared at her. "You know the priest had identified you to assist last night in the sacrificial ritual, don't you?"

Rahab cocked a brow in surprise, but said nothing. They had reached the top of the staircase, and were about to descend. Before continuing, Keket inspected their surroundings. "Look, it's not just about you, Sis. What happens to you paves the way for the rest of us. You know, whatever happens to one, happens to us all."

Laughing, Rahab squared her shoulders and descended the stairs. "I don't know what the family has discussed, nor do I care." She sneered. "I am not going to play into any attempt to transition me to the temple to serve the priest. I understand this may be a great disappointment to you, Keket, but I have other plans. You can disagree with me, as is your right, but that will not change the fact that my future does not include life behind those walls. Besides, I am not sure I'm comfortable with everything they do."

Keket's skin blanched and her eyes went wide. Her words had left her sister speechless. Feeling empathetic, Rahab stopped at the bottom of the staircase, turned, and wrapped her arms around Keket, who still hadn't said a word. "Don't be concerned my sweet. I will take care of you. In fact, I will take care of all of us if necessary, and we won't need the favor of the priest to be secure."

Keket pushed away from her sister and threw her hands in the air in surrender. "Tell me, how do you plan to take care of us?" Bitterness filled her mouth. "Oh yes, you have a secret pot of gold stored for the lean times ahead." Rahab gave her a frosty look, walked ahead, then looked over her shoulder. "Whatever I decide, you will make the adjustment. You'll have no choice." With a half-smile, Keket followed Rahab into the dining room.

In addition to the regular lodgers congregating for the midday meal, neighbors were already stopping by to "visit and chat." Actually, they were focused on positioning themselves to ensure a special connection with Rahab's family. Ammon and Anippe, her brother and other sister, acknowledged her entrance with a nod—Ammon smiling and Anippe conveying a look of disapproval. Before reaching her siblings, someone shoved a tray into Rahab's hands. She looked up to see her mother glaring at her.

"Take these drinks to the table in the corner," Hathor said through clenched teeth. "You're late, and our lodgers are hungry." Rahab rolled her eyes upward, gave a half shrug, and delivered the tray to the table. This process went on for hours. It seemed like the entire town had decided to visit and chat, sing and dance. Midday meal turned into evening repast. The kitchen never closed. The helpers from the morning shift changed, but Rahab and her sisters maintained their assignments to serve and register "guests" for short term use of the rooms.

Keket was in a better mood than when they first entered the dining area earlier that day. Waving and smiling at several guests, then licking her tongue at Ammon who was in the corner flirting with one of the waitresses, she escorted a man toward her mother. The tall stranger seemed out of place, as his posture was stiff, almost stately. The grey, hooded cloak he wore fit so closely around his face, she could not distinguish his features.

What an odd creature. I wouldn't want to meet him on a dark road. Rahab chuckled at her thought, spent a few moments talking to several guests, then gathered dirty dishes from the empty tables. As she turned toward the kitchen, she noticed the look of horror on her sister's face before she screamed. "Mother!"

Rahab rushed between the tables, knocking into chairs, and pushing through the crowd until she reached where Keket had been standing. Her mother was lying in a pool of blood, while Koren kneeled, cradling his wife's head. "What happened?" Rahab asked.

No one answered at first. Her father looked up and whispered. "I think ... I think she slipped or something. Her head hit the floor. I was in the doorway. She was talking to the representative from the temple then turned to walk away. Suddenly, she fell." Shaking his head, Koren looked in his daughter's direction. He seemed fearful to speak, eyes wandering in every direction. With a deep sigh, he continued, voice quivering, "After the temple representative spoke to her, she just took one step and fell."

During the chaos, someone sent for the physician and Hathor was carried to her bedroom. Rahab search the room for the temple representative, only to find he had left the scene. Ammon was busy working the crowd, calming the guests and trying to establish some normalcy while Keket and Anippe continued serving food and drinks. The family business had to keep running. It was their livelihood and they were trained to let nothing get in the way. The evening continued without further incident. Several neighbors hung around waiting for news on

Hathor's condition so they'd have something to gossip about; others sincerely wanted to assist where needed.

Rahab was registering a new lodger when the physician, who had been attending Hathor, appeared and asked to speak with her. They entered the back-room office. The physician closed the door, crossed the floor, and leaned on the desk. He rubbed his hands as if to remove invisible dirt, adjusted his sheepskin covering, paced the floor for a few seconds, then sat on one of the cushioned chairs near her mother's desk. Rehab stood near the door, arms folded, waiting for the physician to speak.

Clearing his throat, he studied her with concern. "Your mother is very ill. It was a nasty fall that seemed to have triggered a malady that affects her speech and memory. I believe it's temporary." He squeezed his eyes shut and gritted his teeth. "Actually, I am not sure what to make of it. There was a bump on her head from the fall, but the bleeding came from an unexplained cut on her upper arm."

Rahab gave him a penetrating gaze before shooting rapid-fire questions at him. "I'm afraid I don't know what you mean. What happened to my mother? What ailment are you suggesting? Will she be alright? What do you mean *unexplained cut*? Was she stabbed? I need answers."

The physician stood, raised his hands as if to calm the atmosphere and stepped closer to Rahab. "Your mother specifically asked that I speak to you directly," he said, with his brows knitted together in a frown. "She will need you to step into the role of running the Inn and managing the books until she can take over again. Your father will care for your mother. They will speak to you shortly, but I wanted you to understand that your mother will look and act different from when you last saw her, so be prepared. Her condition is temporary, but for now she's unable to move her right arm and will speak more slowly."

The physician paced the floor again, appearing nervous. "Her mind is clear and I am sure, in due course, she will return to normal. I just need time to study this case more closely, so I can be of more help. Do you understand what I'm saying?"

Rahab nodded, but remained silent as she walked the physician to the front entrance. There was something he left unsaid, but his facial expression made it clear she was not to ask. After seeing the physician out, she checked on Keket and Anippe at the front desk, then headed to her parent's room to check on her mother. After two gentle knocks, she opened the door and entered. Her parents' suite included two spacious rooms and a balcony overlooking a private courtyard. Rahab smiled at the thought of her mother's creativity. She took great pride in selecting beautiful decorations that normally created a welcoming living area. The atmosphere was different this time.

Though the decorations were attractive as usual, the room was dimly lit. She inhaled the pungent medicine the physician had used to clean her mother's wound, and noticed a scrap of cloth with dried blood-stains on the floor near her bed.

Koren was seated at Hathor's bedside, holding his wife's hand and staring into space. Rahab shivered as she scanned the room. *Why is it so dark? So many shadows, she thought. Must get more torch lights in here.* As she approached, Koren looked up and smiled, but his eyes betrayed his true feelings. He was afraid.

"Father," she said in a hushed tone. "Go. Get something to eat. I will sit with mother until you return." He nodded and started to stand, but sat in silence and cupped his head in both hands.

Rahab approached, took her father's hand and pulled him gently. "Please go, I will be here. Get some food." Koren forced a smile, kissed his wife gently on the forehead and left the room without a word.

Eyes still closed, Hathor groaned, shifted her position in bed and called to her daughter. "He can't take over managing the business. He is a good man, but I need you, Rahab, to take over running the affairs of the Inn and managing the guests who use our rooms for short-term visits." Hathor opened her eyes, staring fixedly at her oldest daughter. "We do fairly well with the restaurant and travelers, but our money is made through our special visitors who enjoy the company of our ladies, a good meal, and drinks. Do you understand me, daughter?" Her tone was gentle but firm.

Rahab sat in the chair near the bed, leaned forward, and rubbed her hands together. "Mother, I don't understand what happened to you. The doctor said something about a cut on your arm. I don't know if you were stabbed or what. On top of that, you had a nasty fall, too."

With a deep sigh, she rubbed her mother's forehead. "I am very clear what we do here and you know it. We offer rooms for travelers but we also sell rooms nightly for rogue customers—most married—who need a place to stay while they satisfy their needs with *their* ladies or with the ones we provide." Rahab leaned closer and extended her index finger toward her mother. "Don't you think I know Ammon is our in-house pimp?" She chuckled and rested her hand on her hip. "And he does a good job."

Hathor started to respond, but Rahab threw her hands in the air in frustration. "Mother, for goodness' sake, don't. Please don't attempt to lie to me about this situation. I'm no fool, and frankly, I have a better way than this current arrangement, which I feel will reap an even greater gain in this family business. I will discuss this with you in more detail later."

Hathor turned her head to the wall and fell silent. At that moment, Koren entered the room. Concern for his wife still showed in his eyes. After scanning their faces, he asked Hathor, "Did you tell her? Silence fell over the room. Rahab felt the intensity of the dark shadows again. Her gaze darted from one parent to the other before they narrowed on her father. "Tell me what?"

Koren helped to lift Hathor higher on the pillow. She was leaning severely to one side. The pain from the shift showed as she winced with every movement. Rahab approached to assist, but Hathor waved her aside. "Sit daughter. Sit down and listen. Please, please don't judge me in what I am about to say. Just listen that we may move forward beyond this incident."

Clutching her husband's hand, she continued, "There are things moving in our lives here in Jericho that are beyond our power to influence. It has been going on for many years, and we have had to make choices to enable us to survive and thrive as a family. I am not making excuses. I just want you to know the way it is."

Koren turned to his daughter. Fighting back tears, he grabbed her hand, and squeezed hard. "Believe us Rahab, anything we did was so the family could survive, and live with them in unity and peace in this town. We were mandated to obey, or face the penalty. This we did, but this one time we failed." Rahab's eyes flickered with curiosity. She peered at her mother. "Tell me, what is this thing that has you so upset?"

Hathor smiled, glanced at her husband and began to explain the secret they have been holding from her. "You were promised to the temple years ago, so that we could prosper in this business. We have been favored, and negotiated that you could stay with us as long as we ensured your presence at all ceremonies and that we instilled certain teachings so that, when the time came, you would have been ready and willing to enter the service of the temple."

Rahab stiffened, squeezed her eyes shut, then opened them to glare at her mother with contempt. "You sold me to the temple!" she shouted as she jumped from the chair and paced the floor. "You bartered my life for prosperity? I wonder how could you have thought to create such a conspiracy, and what did you offer—my body for sex, my blood? Just what did you sell?"

Koren covered his face and shook his head. "I told you, Hathor, I told you she wouldn't understand. This is bad. It is all a terrible thing. We lost our way in this thing. We made a pact with the devil, and look," he said, while pointing at his wife. "Now, we pay."

Hathor was silent for the moment as tears ran down her cheeks. She turned her attention to Rahab, who by this time was standing near the bedroom door prepared to leave. "My daughter, wait. Please sit and hear what I have to say. You need to know it all."

Rahab smoothed the hair away from her face and pressed both hands to her cheeks. She scanned the room again. This time, the dark shadows seemed to fit the heavy mood that overcame the peace she had enjoyed in her life. This time, she felt she was preparing for war. Without responding, she returned to the chair near the bed, crossed her arms defiantly, and waited.

With a weak smile, Hathor continued. "We did all they wanted us to do but provide you with the continuous temple teachings. You see, I was the intermediary. I went to the temple and represented the tradition with the plan that I instill these teachings to you. When you and your siblings were younger, I served by assisting with several of the rituals, and had been able to deceive the temple priest during times of the 'transition of power,' and the new priests take over. It worked well because temple leadership changed several times through the years, and we were able to keep hidden from most of the various new priests the agreement we made when we moved here."

Hathor shifted, winced in pain, then continued. "Unfortunately, things have changed. This new priest is different. We have been butting heads for the last few months. He's a much more wicked one, this priestly man. No negotiations with him. He was determined that I meet the requirements for your obedience to the temple or pay in another way." Hathor dropped her head and tightened her fists.

Koren gently patted his wife's hand. "It's alright, my love. You did the best you could to delay the path this has taken. You were dealing with a man with no heart, with one who mocked the family and worked to smear his filth and venom among the people, while stealing the children to offer as sacrifice to the gods."

He turned to his daughter; brow furrowed as his mouth turned grim. "So, you see, my child, the impatience and harshness you experienced periodically from your mother these past years was but a residual effect of what she was experiencing while fighting to keep the temple priests at bay. Yes, we gained much benefit and favor, but the tradeoff was what she sacrificed while working in the temple."

Without a word, Rahab arose and walked to the window. The courtyard was quiet, except for the few men paid to manage the shrubbery and maintain the pool. These men also doubled as enforcers when things became too rowdy in the tavern. The marketplace stalls were shut. All the people had congregated in their homes or had gone to several of the local taverns down the road. Their courtyard was now quiet, with only a few friends of Hathor and Koren, waiting to hear news of Hathor's condition.

The sky was clear, with a full moon periodically covered by dark clouds passing over. Rahab breathed deeply as a soft breeze flowed through the open window in her mother's room, moving the sheer blue curtains trimmed in white ribbon her mother had created to drape the wide window frame. She turned from the view and anchored her attention on the woman she called mother—the one she trusted to protect and guide her.

"So that's it. The other night in the temple. Was that the big pay off?" Rahab said, stepping closer to her parents. She grabbed the large candle at her mother's bedside and held it high, so both their faces were illuminated. "Let me look at you, she shouted while fighting back tears. "Tell me, Mother. Was I supposed to be turned over to the priest as part of some ceremony? Was last night supposed to be some kind of pay off?"

Koren stood while holding her mother's hand. "Yes. There was supposed to be a beginning of an exchange, but something happened when the priest approached you. He has a powerful influence and you know this. We, your mother and I, felt you were strong enough to be chosen to serve in the temple and not be fully overcome by its practices." Rahab lowered the candle and sat quietly in the chair but her heart raced. Her father's revelation was unexpected.

Koren waved his hand high overhead in wide circular motions. "We knew you could, well, we hoped you would serve in the temple like your mother, and that would meet the requirements of the promise she made. After a time—a "season," they would release you from this commitment and we would move forward with our lives and prosper in business."

Hathor interrupted; tears shimmered in her eyes. "But it didn't happen. When the priest approached you to begin the incantations, something prevented him from continuing. He was repelled and said something like "so be it." Before I could figure out what was going on, you fainted. Your father and I knew the temple priest was angry, and we decided to get you out of there as soon as possible, in spite of the disruption we knew it would cause. We decided to deal with the consequences later. I guess later was tonight."

Hathor brushed her palms together. "You see, I sent word that you would appear at the midday ceremony today. Remember, I sent Ammon to wake you. I was going to go with you, but we got busy and were doing so well, I didn't make the effort to attend the event. Instead, I decided to wait and put it off for another time."

Crying uncontrollably, her mother described the contact with the visitor. "He seemed to float toward me. I heard Keket call my name and I turned as she escorted him in my direction. The only thing I remember was hearing him say was 'you failed; you pay.' I felt a painful prick on my arm and was instantly paralyzed for a moment before I fell to the floor."

Rahab listened in silence. Leaning forward, she made a steeple of her fingers as she fell into deep thought. *This all seems so surreal; it couldn't be happening. I've been a pawn in an evil game controlled by the temple priest gone rogue.*

Sitting straight, she removed the hair ribbon, and tossed her hair from side to side, as if to relieve the pressure moving through her head and down the back of her neck. After a few moments, she spoke directly to Hathor.

"Mother, I must admit I don't understand everything going on here but I am clear about one thing, I will take over from here. You rest and don't worry. We will be alright."

With that last comment, Rahab rose from the chair, kissed them both gently and left the room. She walked down the few short steps, and moved along the back corridor toward the main dining hall. Music and laughter floated from the main room. She recognized the strong deep voice, singing a love song. Ammon was in rare form, the consummate showman, determined to keep things moving as usual. Rahab made a note to hug him later for his warrior attitude.

At the entrance to the main room, she paused, looked back toward her parents' suite and sighed before moving forward. With her next few steps, Rahab entered the new era of her life as owner and operator of one of the most popular hostel/brothels, in Jericho.

CHAPTER 2

"**W**hat do you mean I'm in charge of the maid service?" Anippe stomped around the family room, eyes crossed in exasperation, throwing pillows before slumping in a large cushioned chair near the opening to the family courtyard. At the opposite side of the room, Ammon—oblivious to his sister's ranting—was enjoying several of the afternoon delicacies prepared for the family meeting. The tasty treats included fresh bread, dried figs, sweet grapes, fish soup, roast lamb, and a platter of mixed vegetables. Still making his selection, he responded to Anippe's outburst.

"My dear sister Nippe." His voice dripped with sarcasm. "Can we have a little calm, please? What's the real big deal here? The bottom line is we need to keep the business going, and we all have to do our part. You were given what you handle best. It's an important management task. Learn the business and maybe you can grow up to be in charge."

He popped another fig in his mouth, and eased into a chair near the desk. Flashing a brilliant smile at his favorite sister, Ammon stretched, leaned back and spoke very slowly, "Okay now, madam sister in charge, what's next?"

Rahab ignored Ammon's comments and Anippe's emotional display and continued delegating the duties her siblings would follow. A little over ten months had passed since her mother was incapacitated. Apparently, whatever attack the priest ordered as a penalty for Hathor's disobedience had resolved the issue. Her mother had no further visits from the stranger, whom they were sure had been a messenger from the temple. The family had not returned to the temple since the incident. Despite the decrease in popularity of their business with the immediate neighborhood—who feared displeasing the temple priest—their establishment was prospering.

Rahab finished counting receipts from the reception desk cash drawer and handed the container to Anippe. "I get that you may not like it, but you have a dual role, Anippe. You will continue to oversee the check-in processes at the front desk, with Keket assisting, and you will oversee the maintenance—that is, the cleaning of our guest rooms. The cleaning staff also have their schedule for assisting regular lodgers and the lodging night crew in the west wing have their assignments for our special guests.

"Humph, special guests?" Anippe said as she rolled her eyes skyward. "You mean our special team will handle the filth left by these men in heat needing a sexual fix." Rahab slammed her fist on the desk and shoved her chair so hard it flipped on its side, as she moved quickly across the room to her sister.

Before Anippe could avoid contact, Rebab grabbed a handful of her hair and held tight. "Listen to me, you pampered wretch. I'm trying to keep this business afloat so your rump doesn't land in the street along with the rest of us. I'm sick of your whining and complaining about the work you have to do. In a full day, the most difficult task you have is clocking the girls in and out, and collecting dues from the guest they served after their evening romp with them."

While Anippe whimpered, Rahab leaned even closer and hissed, "Don't think I don't know you've been trading favors with our guests for extra talents you stuff in your skirts until you can add them to your stash behind the bed boards in your room."

Rahab loosened her grip on Anippe's hair, and continued, "I have no time or patience catering to your wants, wishes, or opinions. Get on board with the business plan, and I'll let you keep the proceeds from your side job, without sharing the percentage of what you earn by sleeping around on the side. Are we clear?"

Anippe sniffed, wiped her eyes, and nodded. Feeling a dash of sympathy, Rahab smoothed her sister's hair. "Please don't force me to battle with you about this again. I really don't like confronting family. We have to work together. Your time will come to lead in the family business. This, I promise." Leaning forward, while continuing to stroke her hair, Rahab lifted her sister's chin and kissed her on the cheek.

"Go. Clean up and get ready to welcome our evening guests. You can even go to my room and borrow my blue sheath dress with the shimmer trim that you always liked, and wear it tonight."

Anippe jumped from the chair, hugged her sister, and headed for the door with the cash container under one arm. At the exit, she stopped and swung around while holding the door handle.

"Sometimes, you are one hard witch." Leaning on the door, Anippe sighed. "But I know you are trying to do your best for us, and I'll try to do my part, oh wise one," she said with a grin. With that last statement, her sister bowed deeply, and left the room.

* * *

Ammon chuckled. "Now that was smart, Sis. Beat them up, then give them a gift. I still say you would have done well in the temple." Rahab ignored the comment and returned to counting the afternoon proceeds from the midday meals. Ammon started to leave, but hesitated in the doorway and looked over his shoulder. "So, have you heard the rumors of about war brewing for our little Jericho?"

Rahab shrugged. "When aren't we hearing about some conflict? People travel here from all over with stories about disruption in the region, so what? I think they start this stuff as a distraction when the people get bored."

Ammon closed the door, grabbed a chair and moved closer to his sister. "Yeah, I know there's always chatter about some conflict or the other, but this time it seems different. There's lots of talk about the Israelites moving in this direction. So, I hear even the temple folks have increased their security and protection detail, and we know how secretive they can be."

Still preoccupied with tallying the lunch proceeds and planning for the next day's activities, Rahab was only half listening to her brother's warnings of gloom and doom. A few moments slipped by before she noticed he'd stopped talking. When she looked up, Ammon had leaned back in his chair and was staring through the window. Moving in slow motion, Ammon clasped his hands behind his neck and rocked the chair back and forth.

"Strange isn't it how this room, like yours, Sis, is part of the mountain wall facing the desert? In case we are attacked, you will be able to see them coming. Who would have thought this old structure, built out of a mountain, would give a perfect view of the enemy's invasion?"

Rahab shook her head and chuckled. "You never cease to amaze me. Always a story with you. Why don't you try this one? Our certified house pimp needs to recruit some more girls for the increased traffic we're getting. Variety is our focus here, my dear brother. I need you to use your charm and corral additional beauties to expand our available selections for the customers. I need them dressed and positioned in various locations, including the courtyard and entrance. Do you get my meaning?"

Ammon arose from his seat and tapped his sister on the cheek. "Okay, Okay, I'm moving. I'll get your girls, but don't forget I told you something is coming." He opened the door and paused. "You need to awaken to the reality that things are going to change, and your choosing to disregard my information won't change that, baby girl."

Rahab looked up and responded with an edge irritation. "We've been through a lot these last few months. I am not going to allow myself to be consumed by thoughts about something that may never happen. That serves no purpose for any of us. I've gotta keep this business moving, so the only change I am focused on right now is the change you, dear brother, will make by bringing fresh faces and gorgeous bodies in here for our customers to enjoy."

Ammon threw his hands in the air, forced a laugh, then left the room. Rahab paused to watch him leave, then walked over to the window. Warm, dry evening air brushed her face as she leaned over the window ledge to view the expanse of the mountain. The pink-shaded stone, jutting from the wall, glistened in the sun setting over the horizon. In the far distance she saw a large caravan traveling away from the city of Jericho. *Heading where?* Rahab allowed herself to daydream about being one of the travelers in the caravan. Suddenly, she longed to be somewhere else.

Just beyond the horizon, a meeting was taking place on the other side of the Jordan. Joshua, the new leader of the Israeli people after the death of Moses, sat in the meeting tent with his troops. "It is time to cross the Jordan and go to the place the Lord has promised us. It is our time. We will look neither left nor right, but remain focused on that which is to be ours."

Joshua addressed the commanders of the people. "Within three days, we will pass over the Jordan and go to possess the land of Jericho." Voices rose in the crowd expressing concern, doubt, and questions about how his plan was going to happen. Joshua stood and raised his hand to silence the crowd.

"Enough." He shouted. "I will no longer tolerate this mumbling and complaining. This incessant doubt and hesitation must cease. We must be strong and courageous. If we continue to keep the law of Moses in our hearts, we will not fail, for God is with us." Pointing to the heavens, Joshua continued, "He will not forsake us in this endeavor. Go now. Prepare your food and store your belongings, because we will cross over the Jordan and go to possess the land of Jericho in the next three days. We have been promised this land as our inheritance."

The crowd dispersed, with all the soldiers leaving except his high command. Pacing the area, Joshua stopped at the tent entrance, then turned to face his leaders and announced, "I need watchful eyes over the people in the next few days. Root out the naysayers and separate them from the crowd. All those who rebel against this commandment and do not obey this decree must be put to death. I will not have the minds of the people contaminated. We will cross the Jordan and enter Jericho. In order to be successful, we need like-minded people. In preparation, I need two spies to enter the city and report back with details of what we can expect."

As silence fell over the group, Joshua sat before his men. "I thought carefully and chose two people I trust to accomplish this task." Pointing to the far corner of the tent, he motioned to two men standing in the shadows. "Pinchas and Salmon, come and join us."

Pinchas and Salmon immediately approached and stepped into the circle with the commanders. Joshua gestured toward the two men. "Their role will be to move through the town quickly, scouting passageways seeking the best ways to enter, look for every possible means of escape, observe and gather details, and assess the people.

Joshua anchored his attention on Pinchas and Salmon. "I want you to melt into the scenery and connect with and study their lifestyle, while learning as much as you can about their agriculture and other natural resources. Remember, everything you gather will be shared with the people, so they enter battle with good thoughts about what they can expect once this land is conquered. You see, the focus is preparing the people for battle."

Pinchas and Salmon listened attentively to the instructions provided. They were dressed for travel, with goat skinned satchels packed.

"Sir," Pinchas offered, "we are ready to leave immediately."

Joshua smiled. "Good. Because I will organize the tribe to cross the Jordan in three days. It will take another ten days of moving this large group before our arrival in Jericho. This should give you time to canvas and collect the information we need."

Pinchas and Salmon gathered their things, bowed briefly to Joshua, who nodded and waved. Without another word or acknowledgement to any of the other commanders, they were gone. Joshua stared at the tent exit as he prayed. "May God protect and keep them safe on their journey."

"Exactly when do these chores end," Keket asked Rahab, as she dragged one of the baskets to the next stall in the marketplace. "I've got the welcome desk duty, the maid service monitoring, and babysitting Mom and Dad. It's impossible to have a life."

Rahab pinched and tapped several fruits before making a selection, and rechecked the list of items they still needed to gather in preparation for the special celebration planned for her parents that night. While strolling, she glanced sideways to point her sister to some foodstuff. Before she could stop herself, Rahab bumped into someone in her path.

"Oh! Sorry." She stopped mid-speech. Standing before her a tall, strikingly handsome, dark-haired man stared down at her. Though his mouth was set, unmoving, his eyes seemed to smile, as he appraised her with interest. Keket giggled and shook her head. "Rahab, you're so clumsy," she quipped.

Ignoring her sister's outburst, Rahab decided to turn on the charm. *Customers are always welcomed.* "Please excuse me," she mumbled. "I should have watched where I was going. My name is Rahab. You're new to our region, right?" She purred while smiling seductively. "I'm the inn keeper of one of our better establishments." The stranger didn't respond.

Pointing to the surrounding stalls, she continued, "We were gathering delicacies in preparation for a delightful meal for our guests tonight." Touching his hand lightly, she smiled. "Come join us. No one leaves my establishment unhappy."

The man narrowed his eyes in a disapproving look, bowed briefly, and walked away, leaving Rahab flustered. Keket eased alongside her sister, bumped her hip to hip as she chuckled then whispered. "Who was that you were flirting with? I've never seen him before." Rahab turned, grabbed a container from one of the stalls, and studied the contents while ignoring Keket's sly tone.

"My goodness girrrl," she said with an edge of irritation. "I have no idea who that man was. I just bumped into him. Nothing more and nothing less. He's just a stranger wandering in the market." Rahab shrugged, then signaled to the proprietor that she was ready to make a purchase, and continued fingering silk material on a nearby bolt. "He means nothing to me. Now, focus on the job at hand. I've got to get back to the tavern."

Keket threw her head back and laughed while pointing. "Well, you certainly mean something to him. He's turned around several times since he walked away with his friend."

* * *

Pinchas and Salmon continued their stroll through the marketplace, absorbing the sights, sounds, and the way they did business, as Joshua had commanded them to do. They separated earlier to cover a wider area to gain as much information as possible.

"What have you discovered so far," Salmon asked as he took one final look at the woman. Rahab. The woman with her had revealed her name. He tested the sound of it on his lips.

Meanwhile, Pinchas pulled the papyrus he kept hidden in his robe sleeve, and spent a few moments reviewing the notes he wrote about what he had learned so far touring Jericho. Salmon listened intently. As he finished the update, Pinchas followed Salmon's gaze, and asked, "So what's new with you?"

Salman paused and inspected their surroundings before responding. "I've been moving about, having breakfast and midday meals in various locations for the last few days. There's lots of discussion about our people coming and the pending invasion. Some of the people here are anxious, while others scoff at the news."

Pinchas raised his hand in caution, and walked to a nearby vegetable stall, picking several figs and oranges for purchase. After scanning the crowd, he continued. "On a positive note, there are rich resources in this land. It has great potential to be a lucrative benefit as our new home. One particular enterprise mentioned often is an establishment owned by a woman called Rahab." Salmon repeated her name, "Ah, Rahab, I just met her."

Pinchas smiled, "So I see. Well, from what I hear, many foreign merchants frequent and stay in this place on a regular basis. It appears to be the information center of the town. This Rahab woman was favored by their temple leaders some time ago, but something happened. Perhaps we need to visit her place of business, at some point, before we leave."

Before Salmon could respond, they were interrupted. "Who are you? Why have you come to Jericho?" The voice spoke with authority, then fell silent.

Pinchas and Salmon turned to the man standing behind them. He was dressed in a long, hooded gray robe and his face was barely visible. He held his head straight and erect, and his countenance had the appearance of royalty. Both hands were cupped firmly across his chest. The only movement was the sway of his robe, prompted by a warm breeze that brushed the hem revealing a well-made pair of sandals, trimmed in gold threads, strapped securely around his feet.

Pinchas cleared his throat as he noticed several people watching the scene, pointing, and whispering. Salmon interrupted the silence by acknowledging the visitor's presence. "May I ask who you are and why you question our presence? Have we done something wrong?"

The stranger moved closer. "You have been observed for several days moving around our town, staying in several locations. I hear you've been walking the streets late at night going nowhere in particular."

The stranger dropped his hood exposing icy blue eyes and unsmiling lips covered by a heavy beard. His braided black hair emanated from a crown of matted, bushy strands around his face. His rugged features suggested a man who had seen much battle. This was no ordinary person. He studied Pinchas and Salmon with an unnerving thoroughness.

"There is talk of enemies sending spies to our town before their planned invasion. I represent the group searching for these spies. I question everyone without connection to someone in the town. Do you have a relationship with a family or business here?" Stepping closer, he cocked his head to one side. "If not, why are you here?"

Pinchas pulled a pouch full of gold coins from his sleeve and smiled. "Sir, my brother and I are merchants, canvassing to determine whether this might be a good place to settle and perhaps open our own establishment. If you or your people need further proof, we won't be able to provide that until a few days from now when our caravan of merchandise arrives."

The stranger didn't respond, but tracked Salmon's gaze before returning his attention to Pinchas. In a low voice, full of contempt, the stranger stepped closer.

"Since the rumors started, we have been sending messengers out daily to canvas the roads and bring word of any movement. Strange there's been no mention of a caravan heading in this direction, only news of a large army moving toward Jericho." He curled his lip above his teeth. "So perhaps your caravan is delayed?"

Pinchas nodded, as Salmon shifted from side to side. "Of course, that may be the case. If so, it isn't the first time and it's something we will look into."

After a moment of uncomfortable silence, Salmon stepped forward. "So, if you could let us know how to reach you, we will provide an update as soon as we can assess the situation. People travel here daily and may be able to tell us if they have seen our people."

The stranger rubbed his hands together and smiled. "We shall see. No need to seek me out. I will find you." He bowed, gave them one last intense glare, replaced the hood over his head, and walked into the throng. Pinchas and Salmon watched until he was no longer visible. The crowd that had gathered was still watching and whispering.

"We need to get moving. This place is no longer safe," Salmon said.

"Let's return to our rooms and stay out of sight for a day or so until the curiosity about us dies down."

As they moved in the direction of their lodgings, they heard conversations about the movement of the enemy getting closer to Jericho. A townsman commented in a loud voice out of the crowd. "They're coming! They're going to storm our gates. Some are here already. We need to get ready for the siege." The group of people milled around talking to one another about the best way to prepare for this challenge.

Pinchas and Salmon didn't pause to listen to the chatter but, with casual and deliberate steps, moved out of area. They needed to finish exploring the town and leave Jericho as soon as possible. Their presence created too much attention, discussion, and curiosity—all of which spelled danger.

Looking over his shoulder, while keeping a steady pace, Pinchas pointed toward an empty alcove. "Let's head for your room since it's closer. We'll stay out of sight until later tonight."

CHAPTER 3

In spite of the loud music and incessant laughter at a distance, Rahab was relaxed in her favorite place—her room. It was the largest area on the back side of the house. Since she took over management of the business, she also inherited the overflow area that used to be their "play space" as children. That part of the building could be accessed from this room, and included an attic. All of this led to a secluded area at the end of a long corridor.

Having just washed her hair, Rahab walked to the window to let the breeze help her dry the long locks. She scanned the mountainous terrain and noticed a large orange glow. "Oh crap, what is that," she mumbled. "It can't be the sun. Not this late in the evening. Good grief, that's a huge fire so close to town. I wonder who could be setting up camp that far out and why don't they just come into town? This could be a big night. We're going to be busy. We may need more girls on hand."

Rahab continued gazing out the window momentarily lost in thought. Then she heard heavy footsteps moving quickly along the corridor leading to her room. Before she could cross the floor, Ammon burst into the room, leaving the door wide open. Eyes wide and puffing, he exclaimed, "I told you. I told you the invaders were coming, and now they're here!" He pulled her to the window, while waving his arm, then pointing. "Come, see for yourself. Look over the horizon. Can you see that glow? That's a camp fire. Hundreds of them, in fact," he shouted, with clenched hands above his head. "And they're coming our way."

"They sure are!" Keket chimed in, as she entered the room. "I was just listening to a couple of travelers—a pair of chatty big mouths—who were in the tavern acting like they were experts on what's about to happen. They say they passed a large group of people moving this way a few days ago. They weren't hostile, but they weren't friendly either. Though they were offered food, the men were not encouraged to stay but went on their way immediately after a brief repast." With a slight closed-lipped smile, she looked directly at her big sister. "So, what are we going to do? How do we prepare for this?"

Rahab narrowed her eyes, frowned, and tightened her lips. "One thing we are not going to do," she snapped. "We are not going to panic about something we cannot control, or fret over the unknown reason why these people are coming to this area. What if they are just seeking a new home or, better yet, just passing through to some other part of the region, and, if that's the case, why are we standing here?"

While tying her hair with a ribbon and shouting orders, she walked to the closet to get dressed. "Look, instead of wringing your hands in fear, help me plan to take advantage of an opportunity to benefit from what might be our biggest event. In fact, I'm even thinking about opening a stall in the marketplace." Smiling at her siblings, Rahab whirled around holding her most decorative outfit. "Come on, let's get started. Focus on the business, not the people."

"No, that won't do," came a soft familiar voice from the doorway. They all turned to see their mother, Hathor, leaning on the door frame fully dressed, wrapped in a long shawl. Koren, her father, stood close behind.

Rahab approached her parents cautiously. "Mother, why are you dressed like that? Where are you going this late in the day?"

Hathor did not answer. She walked to the window, paused at the opening, turned, and pointed. "They *are* coming. We will be attacked, and yes, it is a military invasion. I was visited by representatives of the temple earlier today." She threw her hands in the air.

"My dear children, you must hear me as I speak. The invasion is imminent. No one is just passing through, and they don't want to join us. They want to capture Jericho and make this land their own."

Ignoring Rahab's look of disbelief, Hathor gripped her husband's arm for support. "The priests, our prophetic guides, shared this news based on good authority. Spies are already in our town. They are looking for them now. In the meantime, we must join the ceremony of sacrifice tonight to evoke the protection of Ra." She looked directly at Rabab. "All of us are commanded to appear and join the ceremonies to pray for the defeat of the enemy, or face the wrath of the king of Ai." Ammon and Keket looked at one another, but didn't speak.

Rahab could not contain her frustration with yet another plan to visit the temple. "So, this is the result of my relenting to your plea to continue worshipping at the temple." She smacked her palm against her forehead. "I should have known. Despite what they did to you, I didn't try to prevent you from attending services. I didn't even argue when you tried to get me to join your sojourn for these special ceremonies, even after that violent encounter that nearly put you in the grave."

As her mother looked away, Rahab approached and shouted. "Do you think I didn't know you were sneaking away to attend those repulsive human sacrifices and blood rituals performed by these barbaric people?" Hathor looked down but didn't speak.

"Yes mother. I knew all about it, but I let it happen, because I didn't want you to be threatened again."

She kicked her cushioned chair, flopped down and covered her face with both hands.

"So, I tolerated these activities to pacify you and the temple priests. Now they expect us to drop everything, believe the cries of fear, and join the ritual of protection that will save us from an invasion."

Ammon stood beside his mother and father. "Do what you like, Sis. I am going to the temple." Before Rahab could respond, Anippe entered the room.

"Hey, what is this? A convention? We've got people coming in, the girl at the front desk needs help, and half the crowd down there are cowering in fear. No one is buying drinks, so the girls are down there pushing it, trying to get them upstairs so they can get paid. And what's this talk about an army coming to storm the gates and take over our town?" she shouted while flailing her arms.

In the moment of silence, Rahab took charge. "Ammon, you and Keket stay here. Don't entertain any discussions about any invasion. Keep the people eating and drinking. Ammon, encourage the girls to do their business. We need the upper rooms busy." She turned to her mother, pressed her hands to her withered cheeks. "You win mother. Anippe and I will go with you and father to the temple."

* * *

"Man, I'm glad it's getting dark. Let's keep moving. We can't afford to stay in one place for long. The people are curious. We've been identified as people to watch," Pinchas said and pulled his hood closer around his face.

"Still, there's one last observation I think we should make. We need to confirm what we've heard about how their worship. When I've asked what

THE BACHELORETTES OF THE BIBLE

it's like, people have hesitated respond. A lot of folks appear frightened and have challenged me with questions, especially those who have young children."

Salmon nodded in agreement. "I've heard people will be gathering at sunset. We should make our way to the temple. Come, let's mingling with the crowd up ahead," he said pointing to the large group of townspeople in the center of the street.

Salmon and Pinchas accelerated their pace until they were in the center of the throng, which moved at a slow, steady pace toward the temple. The chatter in the group was useful to them. Joshua and their people were within one hundred kilometers of Jericho. They expected to be in sight of the city by daybreak. As they entered the temple, Pinchas noticed the girl from the marketplace. She recognized him, and their eyes locked briefly before she turned away.

Once they entered the temple, people scurried for seating. Pinchas and Salmon found a spot in the shadows near the exit. Attention to them seemed to have died down, as people focused on their fear of the enemy approaching.

"Silence," the priest said and raised one hand over the crowd. "This is a sacred place. You are here to worship and learn. Our god Ra is not pleased and seeks that we be punished for lack of consistent respect and reverent worship. The enemy at the gates is part of this punishment. We must give sacrifice to Ra, so that we are protected against any disaster."

The priest turned his back to the crowd. With a tip of his head, two temple maids held both sides of a long drape, positioned at the front of the room. The priest walked to the center and pulled a diamond-studded, gold-handled knife from the inside cuff of his robe. After several slashing motions, he ripped the curtain at the bottom then stepped back while his servants pulled the fabric so that it separated. The females walked in opposite directions, pulling the cloth until the silk material was torn from the floor to the top of the temple.

The crowd roared as the gold table behind the curtain revealed a basket. Something moved inside the basket. At first Rahab was certain it was an animal but, as she looked closer, noticed it was an infant. She gasped and put a hand to her chest. Surely, they were not about to sacrifice the innocent babe. Two women, dressed in beautiful red robes, stood behind the table, arms raised, waiting. The minstrels played string instruments, prompting the women to dance around the table in slow, rhymical movements.

While the crowd sat swaying to the music, Rahab's eyes widened and she jumped to her feet, stiff as a board. Before anyone acknowledged her lapse, Hathor yanked her daughter back in place. "Be still. Do you hear me? Be still. It will be alright; they're just dancing the praise of Ra."

Rahab looked around and saw the man from the marketplace observing her movements. Avoiding his eyes, she glared at her mother. "This is the sacrifice they planned? This is the favor we're offering to the gods to keep us safe from the enemy?"

With a firm grip, she raised her mother's chin, so they were face to face. "No wonder men have been sent to destroy us," she said with as much disgust as she could muster from the depths of her emotions.

Rahab grabbed her satchel, glared at her brother and sister, then announced in a way that somehow made her whisper sound like a shout, "I am leaving. You can stay and watch this spectacle if you like, but I have a business to run."

Hathor panicked and tugged at Rahab's hem, but she was able to escape her mother's hold and rushed to the exit. Their hostile exchange was barely noticed as it was interrupted by the loud outbursts of several men, who barged into the temple. "They're here," one of them blurted, while pointing. "The enemy's here!"

Another man jumped out of his seat. "I knew it, and their spies have been here for days." The crowd rumbled as high-pitched voices filled the air with panic. "That's right," a woman added and gestured toward a corner of the room. "I saw them in here tonight over there."

The crowd turned to the specified area she indicated, but the space was empty. "Find them," the priest announced. "We will use them as hostages for negotiation. Divide in groups and locate these men."

The people left the temple in all directions. Behind them the priest shouted, "Do not kill them. Do you hear me! Do not kill these spies. Bring them to me." The priest then turned to his two female assistants, and commanded, "Take the sacrifice back to its original location and remain with it until I send for you."

While lifting the baby, one of the women gazed at the little victim with her amber, cat-like eyes and smiled. "Come little one." She cooed. "It seems you have a little more time to live." Wrapping the bundle gently, she laughed. "Mustn't damage you. At least not yet." She smiled, as she licked her lips. While walking away, she turned and directed the other priestess. "Bring the bassinet. We will stay in the waiting room as the priest instructed." They disappeared behind the drapes.

Koren, Hathor, and Anippe sat in place for several minutes as the people cleared the temple. They observed the priestess and her assistant until they were out of sight. "Good grief," Ammon whispered to his parents. "Those folks are creepy. Look at them. Instead of walking, they almost glide down the corridor."

Koren glanced sideways to make sure no one overheard the comment, then put his arms around his wife and lifted her from the seat. "Let's get out of here."

Pinchas and Salmon observed the hostile exchange between Rahab and her parents, then left the temple, moving at a slow pace. They waited, hoping to follow her when she left. It wasn't long after that they noticed movement at the side exit, and saw the young woman emerge. Using caution, they waited until she was in a secluded area, before making their approach. Keeping pace with Salmon, Pinchas asked, "Do you think she's heading home?"

Salmon pressed a finger to his lips, signaling caution and waved him forward. When they were close enough to their subject to speak without causing attention, Salmon whispered.

"Rahab, may we talk to you?"

Startled, she turned in the direction of the voice, and gazed in the shadows. When he called her name again, Salmon stepped forward.

"Rahab, we need to speak to you and there's very little time."

Recognition filled her eyes. She looked around then approached the strangers with caution. "Who are you and what do you want of me, sir. I have no money."

Salmon moved closer and beckoned Pinchas to follow. "I think you know we are not from this region. I also believe you're aware we are part of the group that is approaching your city. I have observed you and feel you do not agree with the practices of your people. Well, neither do we."

Suddenly, they heard loud voices and observed several townspeople moving in their direction, searching building to building. Though still some distance away, Salmon stepped closer, urgency in his voice. "We are the spies they seek, and we need a place to hide until we can escape."

While speaking, Salmon stepped closer and closer to Rahab until he was close enough to touch her arm. She didn't move, but studied his face, before responding.

"First," she said, with a quiver in her voice, "other than my immediate family, these are not my people. Next, they would kill us for helping the enemy. But, most importantly, why should I take such a risk?" She had continued her walk toward home and left the two men to follow.

Pinchas and Salmon maintained a short distance between them, and continued to look over their shoulders. "We represent a contingent of warriors who will overtake Jericho. There is no hope for this town but, right now, we are trapped with no way out of the city. Any attempt to escape would result in our capture." Touching her arm gently, Salmon paused, then added, "Rahab, under no circumstance can we be captured."

Rahab, whirled around to face Pinchas and Salmon. "Okay. If I do this, will your people spare my family? We want nothing to do with this conflict."

Before Salmon could respond, loud voices grew closer with several townspeople moving in and out of the shadows. Rahab leaned sideways to look around him, then waved them forward. "Come. Follow me. We can enter my establishment, unseen, using our lower side entrance. This area is near my parents' suite. They aren't home, which makes it easier. Once we enter, I can take you across to the upper level of the building, which is my area, without your being seen."

Moving quickly, they reached the isolated entrance to Rahab's home. Before turning the knob to open the door, she faced the two spies again. Arms crossed, she looked from one to the other, her suspicion and concern evident. "Look, I need an answer. Do I have your word that my family will be saved, if I help you escape and you return to your people?"

Salmon moved in close and pulled back the hood of his robe so his face could be clearly seen by moonlight. "We declare to you, if we are able to escape without harm, you and your family will be spared during the invasion of Jericho."

She stared at him for a few seconds as if trying to find truth in his eyes. With a tight-lipped smile, Rahab opened the door, pressed a finger to her lips, and led the two spies into her home.

CHAPTER 4

Tossing his satchel on the floor and leaning back on the old, dusty wooden chair, Salmon sighed then smiled. He and Pinchas were now situated in a small, windowless attic, which was their new living quarters. "I think we can count this as the completion of a successful assignment. We'll have much valuable information to share with Joshua."

Pinchas shoved his satchel in the corner, and sat on the pallet he made from sack cloth, old pillows, and scraps of material. "I agree we have been successful up to now, but it's not over. It's true we've gathered a great deal of information that will be useful to our people. However, ideally, we should have been able to clear out of this town before being discovered."

Salmon leaned on his elbow, stroking an imaginary beard, while glancing sideways. "Yeah, you're right. I get your point. The information will be of little use if we can't share it before the siege takes place."

Pinchas put both hands behind his neck and studied the ceiling. "So, it will be important for us to remember that everything we do from this point forward will either enhance or destroy our chances of getting out of here.

For example, throwing your satchel on the floor creates noise. We need to remember where we are at all times, so our presence is not exposed. Keep this in mind."

* * *

Rahab left the visitors to settle in their small space. *"This is crazy. What have I gotten myself into? Breathe, just breathe. Gotta get them some food up there to last a few days. Then wait until I can find a way to get them out of here."*

Entering the kitchen, she grabbed a basket and began to load it with fresh baked honey bread, fruit, dried figs, grapes, and roast leg of lamb. She covered the basket with a large kitchen cloth, entered the back corridor, and climbed the steps leading to her rooms. At the top of the landing, she stopped as soon as she heard Ammon's voice behind her near the base of the staircase. He was giving orders to several of the girls.

"Okay," he shouted. "Whoever they are, they won't enter the town tonight, and that's for sure, so get back to work and keep the patrons eating, ordering wine, and ready for your services." Laughing loud, he continued. "Now, has anyone seen Rahab?" he shouted before he started climbing the stairs.

Rahab's eyes widened in fear as she set the basket down. There was no way she could explain why she had a basketful of food, and wasn't ready or willing to share that she was hiding spies in the attic. Thankful that the stairway was dark, she shouted to her brother. "Ammon, hey brother dear, would you fix me a quick tray of food? As a matter of fact, add some extra food and wine and come join me for a meal in my room. We need to talk."

Tilting his head in the gloom, Ammon responded with an edge of agitation. "Good grief, girl, I am mentally and physically beat. Now you want me to serve you."

Rahab laughed. "Come on, brother. Grab the food and join me. I'll be waiting," she sang."

Ammon, grunted. "All right. You win," and backed down the stairs, while calling one of the girls to help him prepare their meal.

Rahab, grabbed the basket and moved as fast as she could through her room to the side door leading to their former play area. She pulled on the long red cord hidden behind the curtain and dragged the staircase leading to the attic until it landed gently on the floor. Climbing halfway up, she called to her hidden guests. "Come, please. Help me with this basket of food. Move quickly, as my brother will be here soon."

Salmon descended the stairs with Pinchas close behind. Rahab moved from one foot to the other, frantic to get the stairs back in place. "I will bring water in a little while, but I must get back to my room now. My brother will be there to dine with me shortly. In the meantime, there are several bottles of wine hidden on the top shelf above the cot in the room. That will have to do until I return."

After assisting Salmon with moving the basket over the last few steps into the attic, Pinchas, paused and touched Rahab's arm. "Thank you for the food and for helping us to stay hidden."

She blushed and avoided his eyes. "Please, hurry. My brother will be here soon."

Pinchas climbed the stairs, and pulled from his side as Rahab pushed them back into position. Just before closing the attic entrance, she reminded them again how important it was that they remain quiet. "My brother has keen ears, and prides himself on being alert to any potential danger."

Back in her room, Rahab poured a basin of water and refreshed her face. While brushing her hair, she walked to the window and was amazed at the sight that met her. The sky was bright, lit not more than fifty kilometers outside the wall with what appeared to be huge fires. As far as she could see, tents with hundreds, no, at least a thousand people positioned outside. They were moving toward the town, but seemed to be settling in place.

Her door opened, and in walked Ammon followed by Keket. "It's quite a spectacle, huh?" Lots of potential business out there, you think?" Ammon said.

Rahab shook her head but continued staring at the lights in the distance.

Keket stood next to her and pointed. "They aren't friendly visitors. The word is, the king sent his representatives out there and they returned with demands that we surrender. Did you hear me? These people have demanded that we surrender or die.

Ammon sucked on a lamb bone, and tossed it aside. "Calm down kid, have you noticed our walls. They're impenetrable. They can sit out there as long as they like. The food and water are plenteous here, and the king probably already had a plan to ensure we win, should they even think to attack."

Rahab threw her brush down and pulled her chair close to the tray of food. "Keket, calm yourself. Let's eat. Like your brother said, we're safe. They won't be able to enter our gates."

Keket tapped her feet and responded in a high-pitched voice. "Won't get in, huh? What about the spies they've been looking for? They certainly made it in." Neither Ammon nor Rahab responded.

Koren burst into the room. "They're moving toward the city—hundreds of them. Look," he said as he moved toward the open window. The siblings watched as what seemed like thousands of people marched toward Jericho in the flickering light from the flames.

* * *

A short distance away, outside the walls of Jericho, Joshua held a final battle strategy meeting with his leaders.

"Sir, there's still no word from Pinchas or Salmon."

Joshua nodded to his attendant, held his shoulders back, and returned to giving instructions. "Nothing has changed. We will follow the plan as discussed. I have no doubt our spies will return unharmed. The people will march and position themselves around the city. Beginning at dawn, they will follow the orders as we discussed. The tribes will march around Jericho once a day for seven days. At the end of each day, each tribe must stay together, in place, and make camp until the dawn of a new day then march again."

Joshua walked through the meeting tent, stopping to pray for individual tribe leaders, and assigning hierarchy positions in preparation for the next day's march. "My orders are to be followed in detail, and without question. Remember, the men are to march around the city, *in silence*, once a day for seven days."

With a fixed gaze, he emphasized, "This daily march must be done as I have directed, in order to assure our victory in this battle." Joshua fell silent for several moments, walked to the opening of the tent, and rubbed his beard, while watching the women prepare the evening meal. One of the men broke the silence with a question.

"Sir, we're preparing to storm the gates of Jericho without knowledge of what to expect. Should we not wait for Pinchas and Salmon to return?"

Joshua sighed and returned to the circle of elders. "Hear me. As your leader, I have the plan for our victory. We will proceed as discussed. Pinchas and Salmon will arrive at the appointed time. I have no doubt we will have what we need when we need it. In the meantime, stay focused on the issue at hand. Am I clear?" He said with a flash of anger.

All were silent.

"Now, back to the subject at hand. The most important day is the seventh day. That will be different," he said, with the veins in his neck throbbing. On this day, we will march around this city seven times. At the beginning of the seventh time marching, assigned leaders will give the signal for all to shout, and we will see the glory of the Lord come forth to make a path to our victory."

The men looked at each other, then one of the leaders spoke. "Sir, on this seventh day, we are to walk around Jericho seven times, then shout. Do we then take up our weapons and storm the gates?"

Joshua, faced his men, and pumped a fist in the air. "We will carry no weapons. The Ark of the Covenant will go before us. The people march in silence until, as I have commanded, they shout to victory." Slapping his hands together with a powerful force, Joshua announced, "We will conquer this place, Jericho."

One elder gave his friend a side-eye glance, but made no comment. An unusual silence fell as the group dispersed, leaving the meeting to issue instructions to their men. Joshua was their commander-in-chief and they would follow his orders without question.

Three days had passed since the invaders began their march around the city, and Rahab had agreed to allow the spies to hide in her attic. Other than a few comments from family about her spending so much time in her room, the days were uneventful. She quieted their curiosity about her seclusion by telling them she was maintaining a watchful view of the events outside the wall and her room provided that advantage. From her vantage point, she would have enough time to warn the family, empty the tavern of its occupants, and initiate the "lock down" process.

People were frantic the first day or so, but seemed calmer by the third day because there was no aggression from the enemy. Once a day, the invaders walked around the walls of Jericho in silence, then and made camp each night. King Ai convinced many of the townspeople that the enemy was too afraid to attack, and that they would go away in due time.

Rahab knew differently. In her daily delivery of food, she spoke with the spies several times, enjoying lengthy, late-night discussions.

The man named Salmon spent time sharing details about the tribe called Israel and the God they served. She was drawn to his gentle nature and sincerity about his beliefs. Rahab was also attracted to his kindness and lack of condemnation about her chosen profession as an inn keeper, a manager of harlots.

A strong, yet soft-spoken man, he chose to share information about his life. He knew who she was, but it didn't seem to matter. Salmon told her that their leader, Joshua, had shared the entire plan to invade Jericho, and confirmed Jericho would be destroyed.

Rahab didn't understand why this had to happen, but was clear it would come to pass, and she needed to be prepared.

Having ensured her 'guests' were comfortable for the afternoon, Rahab decided to attend to her inn-keeper duties. Rather than go directly to her office, located in the front lower level of the building, she decided to detour through the kitchen and grab a quick meal. While descending the stairs that would bring her to the backside entrance, she heard the raised voices.

"I don't know what happened to the bread and any of the other junk you're screaming about. I didn't take it, and I don't know who did. Get off my back, Keket!"

When Rahab reached the bottom of the stairs, Keket was throwing pots and pans around and cursing. "Working in the kitchen doesn't give any of you the right to take food when you want," she shouted, with a smirk playing across her face.

"This is business and when there's a shortage of food, it affects what we can put on the menu." Waving her arms and pacing between the stove and pantry, she narrowed her eyes and studied each person in the kitchen.

"When we don't have the ingredients for our popular fish stew or honey bread and side dish of figs to serve, we don't make a sale and people look for someplace else to eat. Do you people hear me?"

She whirled around, as if she had regained energy. "Now get this," she continued with one hand on her hip, and the other holding an empty pot. "With the next missing item I discover, everybody will share the penalty of reduced wages the end of the week. Do you hear me?"

No one in the group answered, or offered explanation, but continued with their duties in silence.

Rahab entered the kitchen, nodded to the group, and approached Keket. "Baby Sis, I need to talk to you." Before Keket could object, Rahab interrupted. "I need to talk to you now."

The sisters left the kitchen and entered the small room behind the front reception area, just beyond the dining hall. Rahab closed the door, leaned on the frame, and closed her eyes. *This had better be good. I've gotta convince my sister that I've all of the sudden either become a pig for honey bread, figs, and everything else, or I've been having a secret party for the last few days.*

Avoiding eye contact, Rahab announced, "Actually Baby Sis, I took the food."

Keket's hazel-brown eyes widened in disbelief. "You what?" She clasped her arms behind her back and continued, "You mean you let me rant on and on about them being thieves, and even almost smacked one or two of them, while all this time you were the one stealing? What the heck, Rahab? I feel like a damn fool. Why did you do it? Where is the food?"

Before Rahab could respond, Keket slammed her fist on the table. "So now, not only do I have to apologize to the kitchen staff, I have to go to the marketplace and try to replenish the food supplies in time for the meals this evening."

"Okay, Keket. I get it." Rahab offered. "Calm down. I'll do the shopping. As for why I did it," she shrugged. "Well, when I left the temple the other evening, I was approached by two women begging for food. They told me they were going to try to leave the city before the attack. I tried to tell them they were being ridiculous, but I let them follow me and supplied them with food."

Keket looked at her sister, confused by the answer. "You supplied them with food for two or three days?"

Rahab, scanned the room as if looking for a response, then snapped, "Look, some people needed food, so I made sure they had it. I will go to the marketplace and replenish our supplies. Enough about this. Go back to the kitchen and tell the girls I'll be in shortly. I'll handle it like I always do."

Keket studied her sister for a moment, but before she could question her any further, a loud crash came from the front entrance and they heard Ammon's raised voice, protesting.

"What do you think you are doing?" Ammon said with authority. "You can't just barge in here and roam our place of business."

Rahab and Keket arrived on the scene in time to see Ammon confronting the men who had climbed the stairs to their private quarters. "What is going on here?" Rahab asked the man issuing orders. "Why have you invaded my place of business and my home?"

The man seemed familiar but she couldn't remember where she had seen him before. His smile made her feel uncomfortable, and she hoped it didn't show.

"I am the investigator sent by the king via the temple," he smiled. "You befriended the spies, did you not?" He asked with a look that seemed to pierce her very soul. "It has been said you, and perhaps one or two others, spoke to the strangers in the marketplace. You were also seen with them the night of the temple ceremony. We are certain they are still in the town. No one saw them leave. So, we continue our search."

Rahab threw her head back so her curly hair shook loose, slapped her thigh, and smiled sensually at her unwelcome visitor. "Sir, you do know what kind of establishment I run here, don't you? We serve food and entertainment. Whenever I am in the marketplace, I am always canvassing for new customers. If I was seen with any male strangers, it was to increase the traffic for my business. That is always my focus, even now."

As she spoke, the sound of several of her ladies squealing in terror traveled through the upper-level corridors. "Do you hear that? Your men are disturbing my customers while looking for your mystery men." Turning quickly to Keket, she commanded, "Go calm our customers in the dining area. I will check on mother and father." Flashing an angry look at the intruder, she continued to speak to her sister. "I'm sure Ammon is handling things with our guests in the upper level."

Rahab turned to leave, but was interrupted by a firm hand on her shoulder. She stiffened, looked at the hand, then glared at the man who gripped so hard she wanted to scream. He stepped in close, towering over her. His eyes were large, black and bloodshot. After staring at her for a moment, he smiled. He was standing so close she smelled his stale breath.

With his eyes narrowed in a sinister expression, the stranger pointed a finger, with long, curled nails, at the door. "I think I'll walk with you, as you check on the well-being of your dear mother and father," he sneered. "Lead the way."

Rahab yanked away from the stranger's grip, held her head high, and mustered the strength to walk ahead of this evil that had entered her home. *Gotta play this right. If they find those spies, me and my family are dead. Distraction. That's it. I need a distraction. I could sure use the help of that invisible God Salmon had been talking to me about in these past few days.*

Salmon and Pinchas removed their sandals and sat still on the floor of the attic while listening to the movements below as a group of men searched the family rooms.

"There's nobody here," a male voice shouted. "This is a business, we are innkeepers. Our rooms are not a refuge for criminals and spies. If they don't pay, they don't stay."

Pinchas chuckled and shook his head. "That must be her brother, Ammon. That's some guy," he whispered.

With a finger to his lips, Salmon frowned. Pinchas fell silent and continued to listen. After several minutes, the loud voices faded and they both relaxed. Salmon slowly rose from the floor, stood and stretched, then stopped suddenly. Tapping his ear and pointing, he gave a cautious wave to Pinchas. Footsteps approached along the corridor near their location. They heard several voices in conversation.

"It's Rahab," Salmon whispered, "and she's not alone."

"You and your men have been through every room in the inn," Rahab said loudly. "There's nothing else to see."

The lead investigator for the spy hunt walked closely behind Rahab. "Perhaps," he snapped. By the way, which room belongs to you?"

Rahab ignored the comment and walked to the stairs leading to the back of the building. "I think your tour is over." She hoped he couldn't see the anger flooding through her. "Your men have already investigated this level. When you go down these stairs, you'll find the exit door."

The investigator grabbed her arm and squeezed firmly. "I said, which room belongs to you?"

Trying to maintain a calm demeanor, Rahab pointed to the door leading to her bedroom. "Here; I live here."

With a vicious laugh and quick movements, he dragged her into the room.

"You're an inn keeper, right?" A vicious leer grew on his lips, while he pushed her closer to the bed. "Well, tonight you will keep me." He laughed.

Grabbing Rahab's hair, he pressed his lips hard on hers and fondled her breast while breathing heavily.

"Please stop," she shouted while struggling to escape from his grip. The harder she tried, the more he resisted her attempt to get away. Just as he groped beneath her sheath dress, a loud thump came from the room with the attic.

Her attacker stopped moving.

"What was that?" He asked suspiciously.

Rahab went stiff in his hold. *This can't be happening. We've been discovered. How am I going to explain this?*

With a flash of anger, Rahab responded, "What? It's nothing." Then she smiled and moved closer to the repulsive man to distract him, but he pushed her away.

"Let's go see this nothing, shall we?" He yanked her from the bed and pushed her forward. "Open the door," he said, in a threatening tone.

Rahab turned the knob and step into the room. Relieved, she held in a sigh, then smiled at the sight of her sister. "Keket, what are you doing here?" she said softly, as she tossed her head, eyeing the investigator with a smirk.

Keket rose from where she sat, looked directly at her sister as she said, "I needed to escape the invasion of our property." She continued while giving the stranger an icy look, "I see it's not over."

Rahab turned to face the investigator. "Like I said. We are not hiding the spies. You and your men have searched the entire building. You have seen all there is on the property. You should leave now."

Scanning the room, the investigator walked to the window where he looked over the ledge, then turned and pushed past both women, tossing them an angry look as he left.

Rahab dropped into one of the cushioned chairs and covered her face with both hands.

As the footsteps receded, Keket crossed the floor, sat on the arm of chair, and hugged her sister tight. Still hugging Rahab, she whispered, "Now tell me something, Sis. Who's in the attic?"

Rahab stiffened but didn't look up. "How did you know?"

Keket released Rahab, looked out the window at the fires lit by the intruders who had been walking around Jericho the last four days, then turned to face her sister.

"With all the people congregating in front of the tavern, I decided to come up the back stairs while looking for you. I passed the attic, heading to your room, and heard a noise. I came in here to investigate." Keket looked at Rahab with worried eyes. "I wasn't in here more than two minutes before you and that slimy excuse for a man barged in, investigating because *he heard a noise.*"

Rahab avoided Keket's eyes, then looked at the attic cover above their heads. "Keket, you have to hear their story and trust I know what's best."

Letting out a ragged sigh, she reached for her sister's hand. "You have to help me keep this a secret, so our family can be saved when they attack."

Pulling her sister to the window, she pointed to the hundreds of camp fires stretching as far as the horizon. "Look out there. They are a tribe that follows a powerful God, more powerful than Ra and any other God. We've already heard a little about them through stories from our travelers. Though we shrugged it off as rumors, believe me I know now it is true."

Keket pressed her lips together and rolled her eyes. "Why did you keep this from us? We should have had a choice to decide if we wanted to be involved. We've always been able to keep out of politics and war. What do you think this will do to our business if they find out we were hiding spies? And for the love of Ra, what do you think Anippe will do with this news?'

Rahab raised her hands, pleading. "Hear me. Knowledge of their existence must remain between us. This is day four of their hiding, and I have a plan. The king's men have stopped searching this end of town. They've searched our home from top to bottom and found nothing. Our guests will be gone before this night ends. Believe me."

Keket was silent for several minutes, then took a deep breath and shook her head. "Girl, you got us in a mess but I'm going to let you get us out of it." As if continuing a conversation, she shook her head and stared beyond Rahab. "I don't want to meet them. I don't want to hear anything they have to say. I just want you to get them out of here, so we can get on with our lives."

At the door, she studied the ceiling as if she was trying to see the spies, then chuckled. "Sista girl, you never cease to amaze me."

Without another word, she closed the door.

CHAPTER 5

Salmon and Pinchas sat quiet, listening. The attic allowed them great opportunity to hear the conversations in Rahab's room and the adjacent old family room leading to their hide out. This night, they also heard the clamor of feet and loud voices of men in the corridor, and those moving in and out of the guest rooms.

"You exposed our presence," Pinchas snapped as they listened to Rahab and Keket conversing below. "No point in raising your hand for me to be silent again. She knows we're here. Just listen. Your Rahab is trying to convince her sister not to turn us in."

With a sour expression, Pinchas shifted his position so he could have a more direct view of Salmon. "Look man, you lost sight of our mission. I've noticed the way you look at her and how you've shared details of our culture and lives." He threw his hands in the air. "But tonight, when the guy attacked her, I couldn't believe you considered going down there, exposing our presence just to save an inn keeper. You know what inn keepers are, so having a man in her room and providing favors is certainly not foreign to her."

Pinchas listened as the door closed in the room below. He shook his head and looked at Salmon with disgust. "So now we have Rahab *and* her sister who know we're sitting up here like sheep ready for the slaughter. Look, she seems like a good person, and I certainly appreciate the help she's given, but the focus remains our getting information back to Joshua before the attack on day seven. We can't lose sight of that fact."

Salmon closed his eyes, nodded in silence, then leaned forward with unblinking focused eyesight. The candlelight illuminated the anger in his face. "I am well aware of our mission. Decisions about strategies and movement in this town have been mine. In fact, all this stuff we've been doing, since our arrival, is the result of recommendations I offered including the approach to Rahab." Before Salmon could continue, someone called his name.

Salmon stood near the attic opening, prepared to drop the stair chain ladder. He looked at Pinchas who sat in the corner, still agitated by their conversation. "Before she comes up here, I want to make something clear. You're right, I had no intention of letting that man rape Rahab. I had faith that God would not allow us to be discovered before we could get away. Even so, she saved our lives and we owe her."

Pinchas gave a slight smile. "I understand."

As soon as Keket closed the door, Rahab jumped up, went behind the window curtains, and unhooked the long red cord she used to release the attic cover. Salmon and Pinchas' mumbled conversation carried to her, and Rahab wanted to update her warning that they soften their tones in case someone unexpected visited her room. She also decided it was time to help the spies escape.

She lowered the stairs and climbed into the small space.

"You have to leave. It has become too dangerous for you here. The temple investigators just left. They seemed satisfied, but I have no idea when they will return. They know you're in the town and are determined to expose you."

Wringing her hands, she peeped into the lower room and cocked her head to listen for footsteps in the corridor. As she returned her attention to her two visitors, she grasped Salmon's arm. "My sister now knows you're here. Seems she heard a noise and my visitor also heard you moving about and entered the room almost at the same time. Thanks to my sister, the visitor thought she created the noise." Studying Salmon's face, Rahab continued, you'll have to leave, and I have a way out."

Rahab spent the next several minutes explaining the escape route for Salmon and Pinchas. Using a long cord, they could lower themselves to the ground. If done as soon as possible, that would limit the possibility of them being seen since the searchers were focused elsewhere. Rahab suggested they take the remaining food supplies and hide among the rocks on the mountain's edge for a day or so before crossing the sands to the Israelite's campsite.

"The journey to return to your people will be dangerous. The spies are very active right now and could still capture you at the short flatland crossing before you connect to your group. There are different pathways to your destination, but only one or two are safe." She touched his arm. "I will draw a map that will lead you to the safety of the caves where you can hide. With any luck, you'll be back with your people in two days."

Salmon put both hands on her shoulders. "Sit for a moment, and hear what I have to say. We've had many talks about the difference between my beliefs and yours. I am not anxious about the outcome of this situation. You have been surrounded by people who pray and worship many gods, yet they are running around anxious and fearful." He raised his arm toward heaven, palm upward. "Join me now, and believe in the God who made the universe."

A long silence followed his statement while he held her close, then Salmon helped Rahab descend the attic steps. She reached the bottom, looked up, and smiled. "I'll be back."

Salmon acknowledged her statement with an answering smile as the attic cover closed.

Rahab moved through the corridor quickly. Time was of the essence. She loved her sister, but wasn't confident she would be strong if under stress. Should the temple investigators return and interrogate the family again, she was likely to reveal what she knew. Keket and Ammon were talking in the food prep area. When Rahab approached, they stopped.

"Okay, let's put it all on the table," she said and grabbed a straw basket to load with food supplies. "Our guests will leave tonight. I just need you both to be quiet and follow your regular routine, except for one thing." She leaned on the counter, and faced her siblings.

"I need the two of you to swear your knowledge about the spies we're hiding in the attic will go no further. I don't want Anippe or Mother and Father to hear this information until after I get them safely away."

Keket started to speak, but Rahab cut her off with a dismissive wave. "Don't even think about saying another word. How long did it take you? Ten, maybe twenty minutes, and you're already running your mouth."

Ammon interjected, "Unfortunately, neither of you can hide much. Rahab, your behavior has been incredibly wacky for the last few days. You haven't concentrated on your inn-keeper duties, which is totally unlike you." Stepping closer, he hugged Rahab.

"Baby girl, I also observed your agitation, and how you pressed to change the subject each time these men were mentioned. I knew whatever was going on, you knew the details. I just didn't know the depths of your involvement. You walked in as I completed my interrogation of Keket." He chuckled and dragging Rahab closer, he grabbed both their hands. "She was really upset at breaking her promise, but she was afraid."

Rahab, shook her head and sighed. "Okay, but I hope you both realize we are in a war and need to be clear that our only role in this is survival. Those two people hiding in our attic are our key to surviving this inevitable invasion."

Moving away from them, Rahab picked up the basket and loaded it with more food. "We are at the end of the fourth day watching the Israelites march around Jericho in silence. There are hundreds, if not thousands of them out there. The good thing is, I have an agreement with them that when the invasion begins, our house will be spared if we help them escape."

With the last of the food stuffed into the basket, Rahab lifted the bundle and went to the back stairs. She stopped and smiled. "I believe them. I just need you to believe me."

Ammon, walked to the stairs and took the basket. "I believe you. Let's go help these guys get out of here."

Rahab started to protest, but realized her brother was determined to join the effort to remove their unwelcomed guests. Besides, she realized she needed help.

Keket shouted to them, "I'll handle things here. Don't worry. When Mother and Dad return from the neighbors, I'll keep them busy here with me, and you know Anippe is swamped. In addition to dining room activities and the front desk duties, she'll manage the evening girls."

Salmon and Pinchas were packed and ready to move when Ammon and Rahab arrived at the attic room. Again, she pulled the red cord from behind the curtains and the attic was opened. Rahab put a finger to her lips for Ammon to be silent as she climbed the steps. She stopped midway and called to Salmon, who appeared with a smile of welcome.

Rahab's cheeks warmed from the way he looked at her. "I'm back, and brought my brother with me. He will help in your escape."

Salmon looked beyond Rahab and frowned, then smiled. "Thank you," he said while studying Ammon's face.

Ammon didn't smile. "Yeah, well, let's just get this over with." He walked to the closet, pulled out a satchel, and packed the food they brought from the kitchen. Rachel ignored her brother's rude actions, and eased a parchment from the basket.

Salmon and Pinchas gathered their things and descended the attic ladder. Pinchas stood guard at the door, and watched Ammon's movements. The tension in the room increased. "Come," Rahab waved and guided Salmon and Pinchas to the window opening.

"My brother and I are going to help you descend the mountain from this window. It is the only way to escape. Any other choice would result in your capture and death. Here, let me show you." Rahab spent several minutes reviewing the drawings with them. She showed them how they could reach the caves and hide until it was safe for them to cross the divide to reach their people.

Salmon covered her hands with his. Rahab felt the rough calluses of a man who worked hard with his hands during his entire life. He gently squeezed. "Thank you again, Rahab, for everything."

Rahab looked deep into the eyes of this strong, yet gentle man. "You have promised our safety. You gave your word that we will not be harmed when you attack the city. Please, confirm this promise to me in the sight and hearing of my brother."

Salmon, still holding Rahab's hands, affirmed to her and her brother. "I promise you, when we invade, you and your family will be saved. Now listen to me, this is important for you both to remember. The day you hear we have stormed the gates, leave a marker outside this window and our men will know to leave your home untouched."

Rahab asked, "What marker?"

Salmon looked around and found excess red cord similar to that used for pulling the attic cover in the folds of the curtains. He handed it to her. "Let this cord hang from the window. My people will be told to look for this symbol so that you and your family will be saved from their wrath."

Ammon grabbed rope from the closet then threw two satchels loaded with food in front of Salmon and Pinchas. "We need to move if this is to happen tonight. It will get busy up here soon. Our parents have been looking for Rahab. Are you people ready?" he said with an edge of hostility.

Pinchas hurried forward and said, "Ready."

Salmon ignored his comment. Never taking his eyes off Rahab, he responded in a soft tone. "Ready."

Ammon moved toward the window. "One of you will descend, then we will send the food satchels. After that, the next one will climb down. I've anchored the rope. Let's move it now." I am thinking that it should be noted earlier that Ammon brings the rope with him so then it doesn't simply appear at this point in the scene.

Pinchas tied the rope around his waist and lowered himself over the edge of the window with Ammon guiding the process. Salmon stood behind, ensuring the anchor was holding.

With Pinchas safely on the rock below, Salmon grabbed one of the satchels and secured it with the rope. Ammon lowered the second bundle in succession. He looked over the window ledge then turned to Salmon. "Okay, it's your turn."

Salmon turned to Rahab, touched her cheek, and smiled. "I will be back for you." Rahab returned the smile, but didn't respond. Salmon turned to Ammon and said, "I thank you for supporting your sister. You will not regret it."

Ammon nodded, but didn't speak. Salmon grabbed the rope and disappeared over the edge of the window. As Rahab watched the man who touched her heart disappear, Ammon planted his feet to ensure the rope remained anchored.

Darkness had fallen, so she lost sight of the men in the shadows of the mountain. As she stood gazing over the rough terrain, she experienced a moment of clarity. Salmon intended to be a part of her life. She had no idea how their story would end, but her heart melted at the thought of life with him.

"Get a grip ole girl. Listen, your mother and father are coming. Get away from that window and leave here. In fact, go to your room. Let them find you there. Ammon pointed to attic steps. "I'll close the attic and hide the rope before I take this basket back to the kitchen. Go now and close the door." Rahab took one last look at the window, hugged her brother, then ran to her room.

She closed the door and slid onto her cushioned lounge chair near the bed. From a distance, she heard her parents' laughter as they walked down the corridor toward her bedroom. On the other side of the door, Ammon dragged the last of the furnishings back in place, replaced the staircase to the attic, and left the room. She leaned on the soft pillows, closed her eyes, and reflected on events of the last few days.

Suddenly, she sat erect and smiled as she scanned the area. Everything in her room was the same, yet she was keenly aware her life would never be the same.

COMMENTARY

R ahab's story is proof that God will use ordinary people to do extra-ordinary things. In this story a Canaanite woman, who operated the town brothel promoted as an inn for travelers, was instrumental in saving the lives of two spies important to the Israelites' plan for an invasion of her town.

In the period of time Rahab hid the spies, she had time to interact with them, with the conversations resulting in her interest and eventual fondness for one of the spies, Salmon.

As noted, on the orders of Joshua, the Israeli warriors walked around Jericho guided by the covenant of the Lord carried by the Levites. Their commitment to follow, as commanded, resulted in the walls of Jericho tumbling down, leaving the town defenseless. Jericho was conquered, her family saved, and Rahab eventually entered a new life as the wife of Salmon.

God blessed this union, as the son of Rahab and Salmon was Boaz who married Ruth (See Book of Ruth). From this union was born Obed.

Obed was the father of Jesse, and Jesse was the father of David, who would eventually become king of Israel.

STORY TWO: THE EMPOWERED CONCUBINE OF GIBEAH

CHAPTER 6

In the cool of the evening, several young adults had already gathered for food, wine, music, and fun in the upper courtyard of the large, well-manicured estate home of Isaac and Rebecca. Large round tables were prepared in readiness for the evening gathering hosted by Esau and his wife. Each table was stacked with household fine linen and utensils so they are easily accessible to the large number of guests expected.

Rizpah entered the reception area, paused in the archway opening, and scanned the room in search of her cousin. A striking beauty, she didn't go unnoticed. Her deep, hazel-brown eyes were accented by distinct arched eyebrows and long eyelashes that captivated the observer. Though small in stature, her body was strong, shapely, and well-proportioned to her height. For a moment, rage flashed through her when she remembered why she was there.

King Saul had been attracted to her during his brief visit with her father some months earlier. Without considering her wishes, and in her absence, decisions were reached and she and her father were ending their visit of several days before continuing their journey to Gibeah where she would live, as a concubine to King Saul, Israel's first king. Filtering the crowd, she recognized the woman waving in her direction as her cousin, Judith. When Rizpah reached the table, an attendant pulled out a chair for her to be seated.

"Hey, I thought you weren't coming," Judith teased as her mouth twitched. "Here, I've been holding this cup of wine just for you."

Rizpah adjusted her seat and gave her cousin the once-over. It was clear, from her slow-motion rock from side to side with eyes half-open, she had been drinking for some time. She leaned forward to get Judith's attention but was interrupted.

"Excuse me, ma'am," one of the maidservants interrupted, "I believe your father was looking for you."

Rizpah nodded but didn't respond. The servant bowed and left the ladies alone.

Judith laughed. "You know your father will search until he finds you."

Rizpah stood and grabbed her wine. "Let's not make it easy for him." Gathering their things, the two ladies moved through the crowd and found a table in the far corner of the outer patio. "It's the last night of our visit. Let's just have girl talk."

The two ladies sat still for a few moments observing while the servants transferred several platters of the food and wine to their table far from the music and party goers inside the congested room. The torch lights shimmered over the nearby pool, creating a crystal multicolored reflection on its stone interior.

The servants finished their preparation duties, bowed, and left them alone to continue their conversation. As soon as they were out of sight, Rizpah rested her chin on her palm and quivered with indignation. "I can't believe I'm being forced to live a life not of my choosing.

"Look, lady, are you serious?" Judith laughed, rolled her eyes, and drained her third cup of wine. "I married Esau, who brought me to live in the home of his parents, but you're going to be a royal concubine to King Saul." She pulled her chair closer and gave a side-eyed glance. "Tell me, cousin, my clever girl," she chuckled, "just how did you manage to pull that one off, hmmm? It's no secret that being chosen by the king is no easy trick."

Rizpah tapped her fingers in a steady rhythm on the table top, shrugged, but didn't speak. The three-day visit with her cousin Isaac and his wife Rebecca's was a welcomed break in her journey. This was the last evening before she was scheduled to begin a new life in the household of King Saul, a prospect she was not particularly enthusiastic about. In the silence, Judith poured more wine in her cup and raised it as a salute. "To you, my dear, for creating a sweet deal."

Rizpah glared at her relative and clenched her teeth to prevent smacking the cup from her hand.

"Look, there were no tricks in this arrangement. I had no choice in this matter; you must know that." Rizpah stood and walked to the edge of the patio, hands behind her back, then faced Judith. "My Father and I have been in the king's court several times and, after their discussions, the decision was made that I would become part of the king's family. The difference between your marriage to Esau and my preplanned arrangement as a concubine is that you had a choice. I didn't have that luxury."

Judith chuckled, then nodded. "True, no argument there, but at least you don't have to deal with a mother-in-law complaining when you have a few guests over or whining if cushion pillows are out of order."

Rizpah came back and leaned across the table, positioned so close to her cousin she could smell her breath. "Let's be honest, shall we? You chose Esau because of the potential luxury you saw in this estate, and the status of the family in the community." She smoothed her dress, then glared at Judith, whose eyes gleamed with disapproval. "Despite all of this, cousin, you've been well cared for and I'm sure you will survive the choices you made."

The balcony door opened and Aiah, Rizpah's father, entered the balcony followed by Esau. Aiah waved at his daughter to signal it was time for them to leave.

Esau drained his goblet and staggered over to his wife. "It's always good to have your Uncle Aiah and cousin Rizpah favor us with a visit. Perhaps we will return the favor soon," he commented while hugging Judith.

Rizpah rose from her chair and joined her father. She squared her shoulders and slid her cousin a guarded look before responding to Esau's comment. "I enjoyed our visit and thank you for the invitation. My future, however, has been predetermined so opportunities for family visits will be very limited. God's blessing to you and yours. Be well." She curtsied to Esau and nodded to her cousin, then followed her father back inside. The pungent scent of incense hit her almost immediately, and the crowd was much more reckless and noisier than earlier that evening.

As they maneuvered through the packed room toward the guest quarters, Aiah held her hand with a firm grip while guiding them through the crowd. Several times he raised his other arm, in a blocking motion, to clear a path.

"It's almost over," he shouted over the noise. "In a few days, we'll be in Gibeah, the home of the king."

When they reached the exit, Rizpah yanked her hand from her father's grip. "Do you understand what's going on here, Father? You are delivering me to become *the woman* who lives with a man as if she is his wife, without having the proper status and respect of a wife," she said, pointing at him. "For a few weeks now, since King Saul's brief visit to our home, you have been trying to impress me with how favored I am to be chosen to be his concubine—a second class rank. I am a human being who has been turned over to a man to be his slave woman but not his wife."

With tears in her eyes, her temples throbbed with rage. She shoved past her father, rushed down the corridor and across a small courtyard behind the house to her guest room door. The faint sounds of festive music and laughter could still be heard in the distance. She paused, took a deep beath, and gazed at the clear sky. It seemed thousands of stars surrounded the bright full moon. The warm breeze brushed the loose strands of her hair around her face.

Turning the knob, she looked over her shoulder at her father, who watched her in silence. She stepped inside. Before closing the door, she flashed him an angry look, her throat thickened with sobs.

"This night, my last night of freedom, will be forever burned in my memory."

Rizpah and her father arose early, said their goodbyes, and continued their journey. In the late afternoon, near the end of the two-day trip to Gibeah, they braved an enormous sandstorm that arose unexpectedly. Despite the pain from brittle pellets striking her face from the force of the wind, she was happy for the event, as it provided solitude from the incessant, "oh how lucky you are, be happy" conversations with her father.

As quickly as the storm arose, it ended. Out of the blazing hot sun, rising over the sand, stood tall, marble post fencing, which surrounded a large castle. On the other side of the fence, close to where the caravan approached, stood oakwood stalls that housed several camels and horses. The workmen paid little or no attention to the small caravan approaching the gates. Rizpah quivered with indignation. *Wow, what a warm welcome. I can barely wait to meet the rest of this group.*

"Well, we've finally arrived," her father announced as his camel pulled up next to her. He cleared his throat, moved closer, and continued to talk using slow, deliberate words. "The household of King Saul awaits you, my dear." An attendant, assigned to assist the travelers, approached and awaited instructions.

Rizpah touched his shoulder, her body locked up with rage. "Father, I know you are trying to make this a pleasant exchange, and I don't want our separation to be hostile, so please don't speak about this situation again. Let's just say our goodbyes here."

Tears of remorse flooded Aiah's eyes. "Be well. my daughter, be well." He kicked the camel and moved away; head down, shoulders slumped.

Rizpah watched her father disappear into the crowd. With a deep breath and a half shrug, she beckoned the attendant for assistance. He grabbed the reins, the camel kneeled and she dismounted. He pointed to her new home.

"You will enter through the side door beyond the gate."

Rizpah grabbed her small satchel, and walked the cobblestone path leading to a side entrance. Midway through her approach, a huge mahogany door swung open and a small older woman appeared, draped in a beautiful, long sheath dress with a matching blue shawl. With quick, deliberate steps, she walked past Rizpah, barely acknowledging her presence. The old woman pulled Rizpah's camel from the group and led it to attendants waiting at the side entrance. Waving Rizpah forward, she commanded, "Come this way."

After directing household attendants to unpack her remaining things from the camel, she turned to Rizpah and pointed to the entrance.

"You will enter here," she said in a low, almost inaudible voice. "I am Myra of the household of King Saul and my duties are to ensure your comfort," she said with a stiff smile. "Welcome."

Rizpah ignored the cool reception and followed Myra inside the building and down a long hallway. The walls on both sides were made of wood, the floor was layered in red cobblestone. Several torch lights lined both sides of the interior walls. Myra led her toward tall, wide oakwood doors and grabbed the handles. Then she pressed her lips with a slight frown, and looked over her shoulder. "We are about to enter the chamber leading to the royal wives' quarters. No one speaks unless addressed directly. You may, of course, nod and smile but conversations are restricted until you are permitted."

An uncomfortable silence followed Myra's comment. Rizpah adjusted her shawl, smoothed the creases in her travel robe, and stepped closer to her escort. She dropped her satchel and curled her lip. "Until I am permitted?" She chuckled. "You mean I am not allowed to speak to the wives of the king because I am not a wife of the king, right?"

Myra withdrew her hands from the door and stepped forward so she could be seen under the torch light. She was not smiling, but her eyes were soft, almost sad. "Hear me child. I am here to help. You are not welcome here, so make the best of it. King Saul chose you, but the wives will not accept you. To them you are, and always will be, a slave. The sooner you accept your role, the better it will be for both of us."

Myra lifted Rizpah's satchel and a faint smile crossed her face. "Now, I will open these doors and guide you through this area to your room. Again, for now, it's best to look neither left nor right. Just follow in silence."

Rizpah's face contorted in a frown, and her eyes flashed with anger. She crossed her arms and tapped her foot.

"I appreciate your honesty about how unwelcome I am in this household, but it's not like I was given a choice in the matter." She spread her arms wide.

"Look at this. After a long, uncomfortable journey, including trekking through a sand storm, I reached my destination only to be directed to a side gate where I walk down a dark corridor like someone who appeared unexpectedly."

Myra ignored the emotional outburst, grabbed both handles, and opened the door wide. She walked inside and pointed Rizpah toward the entrance. "Follow me and keep pace."

Rizpah did as she asked without comment, while rage flashed through her. They walked through the suite of rooms full of colorful sheer drapes, lounge chairs trimmed with lamb skin, all accented by small oakwood table. Though well decorated, she was surprised at the more rustic design. Dark mahogany walls with multi-colored tapestry covered both sides, accented by sturdy oakwood tables and chairs covered in lamb skin. When they approached what appeared to be a gathering space, a group of women observed their presence.

"Are these women the royal wives?" she whispered.

Myra didn't respond, but gave her a look of disapproval.

Rizpah fell silent and followed as they entered the room. All eyes were on her as she moved through the maze of chairs and large pillows strewn in their path as they moved across the floor.

"So that's the king's concubine," one of the wives snickered while sucking a ripe plum. "Do you suppose she can wash clothes too?"

Everyone laughed.

Rizpah swung around in time to catch the eye of the spokesperson, but Myra grabbed her around the waist with a firm grip. The small woman pushed her through another set of double doors, closed them securely, then held up one finger. "You will do well to curb your temper, young lady," Myra warned.

"On the contrary. I will do well to establish who I am," Rizpah retorted. *As soon as I can establish exactly what that means, that is.*

Increasing her pace, Myra was steps ahead as they continued down yet another long corridor that ended with them facing a small balcony overlooking a beautiful garden. To the left of the balcony's entrance, Myra opened a large mahogany door and left Rizpah's satchel inside.

Myra rubbed her shoulder and gave a bitter laugh. "This is your suite. Not bad for an unexpected guest, don't you think?"

Rizpah tucked a lock of hair behind her ears and avoided eye contact.

The small woman continued, "all other items from the caravan, that belong to you, will be delivered shortly." She walked to the double doors leading to the balcony that connected to the one in the hall and pulled the sheer curtains, then fluffed the pillows on the beautiful royal blue and white silk draped canopy bed. "In the meantime, I will send a maidservant with your midday meal, wine, and water for your bath. It is required that you remain clean and refreshed at all times, should the king require your presence."

Myra, moved quickly to finish her final welcome duties then stopped at the door, removed her shawl, untied the ribbon holding her pony tail, and exhaled. "I'll leave you now to rest, calm down, and think about how you intend to spend your life here. It could be comfortable and good, or miserable. You decide." She gave her one last look of disapproval and closed the door, leaving Rizpah quivering with anger.

It was hours before Rizpah was sent word to prepare to attend to the king. As directed, she bathed in the fragrant soap and sweet oils, brushed her long, curly reddish-brown hair, and applied face cream using one of a variety of large selections provided.

Pleased with the results, she sat and waited for what seemed hours for the attendant to return and escort her to the king. Impatient with the lapse in time, she opened her room door and stepped into the hall. As before, she noticed the opening to the balcony connected to her suite. To the right was the torch-lit corridor leading to the suite of rooms of the king's wives, but straight ahead was another corridor lined with several white doors trimmed in gold on one side and beautiful arched white pillars surrounding a small courtyard on the opposite side.

She trembled a little and stepped into the corridor, looking over her shoulder periodically, expecting the attendant to appear at her room door. When she reached the courtyard, a loud, stern voice rose from behind one of the white doors.

"When I give an order, I expect results. We only have a short time to interrupt our enemy's resources and foil their plans. Go! Return to me with news of success." Rizpah trembled, cringed, and eased away from the door. After several steps, she felt a presence behind her and whirled around.

"What are you doing?" Myra snapped. "You are not permitted to roam the halls until you have been provided the proper tour and rules of movement." Before Rizpah could respond, one of the white doors opened. Myra immediately bowed, and Rizpah froze when she recognized the face of King Saul.

Though she saw the king briefly, at a distance, on the occasion of his visit to her father's home, this was the first time seeing him up close and personal. She shivered when his striking dark-brown eyes met hers. His thick eyebrows accented a handsome face covered by a short, well-kept beard. The loose-fitting robe covered broad shoulders. Stepping forward, he towered over them.

Oh my God, he's gorgeous.

King Saul stroked his beard and stared, which made her skin flush. "Welcome, Rizpah," he smiled and cocked his head. "Learning your way around?"

Her knees wobbled.

"My king," Myra interjected. "I thought it would be helpful to provide a tour of the courtyard area before bringing her to your rooms, so she would be familiar when returning."

King Saul clasped his arms behind his body and dissatisfaction plowed his brow. "Myra, I appreciate your thinking, but would prefer you maintain the established protocol." He massaged the back of his neck, then pointed to the courtyard. "This area is off-limits, not open for a tour at any time by anyone but me." He looked over his shoulder and waved an attendant forward and pointed. "Escort this young lady back to her rooms. I have other matters to attend and will meet with her another day."

The attendant bowed, turned to the two women, and pointed the way up the corridor toward the rooms. Rizpah and Myra followed. Halfway to their destination, one of the maid servants rushed down the corridor.

"Ms. Myra," she stuttered while avoiding eye contact. "King Saul commanded that you return to his suite. He wants to review some additional instructions with you."

Myra flashed Rizpah an angry glance, reversed direction, and followed the servant back to the king's chambers.

Rizpah closed her bedroom door and scanned the area. *It's a prison, a beautiful well-landscaped prison.* Hearing the sound of a shofar, she rushed to her entrance to the balcony. At a distance, just beyond the ridge of several tall dunes, was a caravan traveling in the direction she had come from earlier that day with her father. The sun was high on the horizon, at its brightest before setting. Foolishly Rizpah squinted to see if she could recognize her father in the group, but her vision was clouded by the tears that welled in her eyes. "Goodbye, Father. I'm sorry I was so cruel." She whispered words he would never hear.

Rizpah sat on the balcony until nightfall. The maidservants left her evening meal on the side table but, at the instruction of Myra, did not disturb their new household member with questions or conversation.

CHAPTER 7

S everal weeks passed before Rizpah was commanded once again to prepare to visit the king's quarters. During that time, she, along with the king's wives stood by the windows of the upper-level suites or on adjacent balconies and watched the king leave for and return from various campaigns. Myra spent very little time with her, providing only essential information and direction. When Rizpah approached her to determine the issue or details about her future, Myra responded with quick, angry statements.

"You wouldn't listen to me when I tried to help by providing the best way to adjust to the rules and the way things are done. I advised that there were limitations because of your status here, but that life could be good if you followed the rules and made the necessary adjustments."

She folded her arms and rolled her eyes skyward. "Instead of listening to me and following simple instructions, you violated a rule the first day, forcing me to create a story that put me in a bad position with the king and members of this household."

Following her unfriendly exchange with Myra, the new member of the household spent the last few weeks eating alone, wandering the *permitted* area of the grounds by herself, and having only limited communication with the servants of the household. Her status as a concubine was reinforced over and over again. She was to live with a man, in a slave status, performing as a wife without the status and benefits of a wife. During the weeks of seclusion, she was assigned a guide who taught her acceptable protocol and the history of the region. Most importantly, she learned what it meant to live a sub-status existence.

One evening, Rizpah was lounging on her balcony after dinner when Myra entered, followed by several maids with towels, fragrant oils, incense, and water for a bath.

"The king requires your presence," Myra announced while scanning through several dresses before putting a blue and white sheath dress on the bed for her to wear. "We need to prepare you for the visit."

Rizpah's shoulders tensed, but she didn't speak. Preparations for entering the king's chambers were extensive. She was bathed and pampered from head to toe. It was the most attention Rizpah had ever experienced. When the preparation was complete, Myra dismissed the servants, closed the door, and faced her charge.

"This is your opportunity to step into a role of favor with the king. He has been away for some time and is challenged with many responsibilities. He is here for rest, refreshment, and escape from the rigors of war. Make no mistake, this is a great opportunity for you to be chosen to be in his presence."

Myra took a deep breath, gave Rizpah a frosty look, and wagged her fingers. "I took a hit for you, young lady, because I thought you'd be good for him. Tonight, you need to enter the king's chambers and secure your future." She brushed her palms together. "Make no doubt, this is your most important meeting. It could establish your position of favor, no matter what label you were assigned in this household. It's up to you to make it work."

Rizpah smiled, rubbed her temples, and studied the woman who had been consistent in showing her what she needed to do to be successful. "I know you don't think it possible, but I appreciate what you have done for me. In the last few weeks, I have learned a lot and am prepared to accept my assigned role."

A knock at the door interrupted their exchange. In a rapid motion, Myra ran her fingers through Rizpah's hair to reposition several loose strands and jerked her head in the direction of the sound.

"That must be the royal eunuch. He is assigned to escort you, and all the wives, to the chambers when your presence is commanded by the king." She smiled and gave Rizpah a warm hug. "Go. I will have your room ready with refreshments and handmaids waiting to care for you upon your return."

Myra opened the door and faced the eunuch, who didn't speak or make eye contact. He bowed and pointed in the direction of the hallway with the white doors.

They walked in silence. Rizpah was preoccupied with thoughts of what might be expected of her for the evening. She had never been with a man before, and had no interest in a stranger's hands being on her body, even if it was a good-looking king. "Which door are we entering?" she asked while looking over her shoulder, hoping Myra would appear and state that the king had changed his mind.

The eunuch didn't respond but jerked his head toward the courtyard. When Rizpah followed his direction, she gasped. The secluded garden area across from the king's rooms shimmered from the moonbeams streaking through the trees. In the center of the courtyard, surrounded by serving tables draped in white linen, stood a round table with two tall, thin candles at its center, accented by silver plates and matching long-stemmed goblets. It was the most beautiful scene she had ever laid eyes on.

Several maids and attendants acknowledged her presence with a smile and a nod, then continued preparing the serving tables with lamb, fish, and beef platters, in addition to the complimentary vegetable and fruit side dishes. Joy overwhelmed her at the thought that the wonderful preparation included her. Before she could speak, the eunuch pointed, directing her to the table. "You will sit here and await the king."

Once she was seated, the eunuch bowed, and his brow furrowed as his mouth turned grim. "The king will be with you when he is ready. In the meantime, do not roam about." Without awaiting a response, he crossed the courtyard and disappeared behind one of the tall, white doors leading to the king's rooms.

Rizpah sat motionless, observing the servers checking and rechecking the food and items on the table. She scanned the area, thoroughly enjoying the view until her eyes fell on the bubbling fountain in the garden just beyond the courtyard area. After a few moments of waiting, she stood, looked around, then walked to the fountain and sat on the marble overhang to enjoy the sounds of the water flowing over the jagged rocks. She was so lost in thought, focused on enjoying the calming atmosphere from the waterfall, she did not hear anyone approaching.

"You are an inquisitive, self-directed young lady," came a quiet but firm voice from behind. She jumped, put her hand to her throat, and took in a sharp breath. Her eyes flickered with embarrassment. "Sire, please accept my apologies. I was just enjoying the scenery while waiting."

King Saul moved closer and reached for her hand. "Yes, well, I had planned to take you on tour after we dined." He guided her back to the table. "Come, sit with me. I am hungry and we can talk."

Though it seemed like a short time, King Saul and Rizpah talked for hours, interrupted only once by a servant to confirm if there was any other food or wine-related requests. The evening ended with their walking the gardens, followed by Rizpah returning to her rooms, escorted by the eunuch.

Myra was seated near the bed. She jolted from the chair when Rizpah stepped inside the suite.

"Is everything alright? You're back early." Rizpah laughed.

"You mean I didn't end up in bed? No, he was wonderful and very patient. I feel special." She glided around the room, bouncing on her toes and flapping the shawl above her head. "He made me feel as if I *was* his wife." She tugged at her hair and stuck out her chest. "He even told me I wouldn't be treated less than a wife in this position. I didn't ask why, but I've truly accepted this concubine status." She stopped moving and held out her hand. "Myra, thanks to you, I know I will be happy and feel blessed to begin this journey."

Myra held her hand and gave an appraising glance. "I could be wrong, but I believe you will be a blessing not only to the king, but to this household."

Weeks, then months passed with Rizpah and the king meeting regularly, sealing each connection with intimate moments. After one such evening, they talked long into the night. "You have taught me so much in our time together," she whispered while moving closer under his arm. I am so impressed by how important your faith is to you and understand why you were chosen to be king."

King Saul kissed her, tucked a lock of hair behind her ear, and smiled. "When we first met, I thought you were cute but extremely shy. I was initially concerned that living in this household would be too much for you."

He adjusted the silk covers so they fit snug around them. "I can see now, however, that I was wrong. You are a strong woman and this connection between us is good."

He leaned on one elbow and stroked the area below her neckline. "Because of the challenges in the region, I will have to be away in the coming days for long periods, and you will need to depend on that strength in the future."

Rizpah attempted to respond, but he pressed his fingers to her lips. "No more talk for now." In the silence, desire radiated between them. After they made love that night, the king fell into a relaxed sleep, but Rizpah lay awake thinking about what he had said to her and decided to learn more about the life of this man she had grown to love. It wasn't easy, since she had very few people to ask besides Myra and the eunuch. Everyone else remained distant, providing only information needed to move her from one location to the other.

After weeks of constant questions and prying, with no success, she found a way to corner her assigned servant and guide for details. Following close behind Myra during the room cleaning inspection visit, Rizpah pulled her to the private balcony. "Sit. Be still for a moment. I need to know more about my king, and you're the best source for details."

She laughed, pulled one of the lounge chairs closer and sat. Then she leaned forward, fingers interlocked below her chin, and waited.

Myra shifted and looked around, but didn't speak. She was clearly uncomfortable about being forced to share information.

"Look," Rizpah stiffened, "I'm getting sick and tired of this avoidance game. I asked a simple question and I need an honest response. What's the problem? Why can't you answer me?"

"The king is the king," Myra snapped while scanning the area to ensure the handmaids had cleaned it properly.

"The people loved him and wanted a king who was a strong warrior, to ensure the defense of the nation. King Saul was that man. He has conquered many of our enemies and is a feared man of God."

She paused, her mouth set in a hard line, and rubbed her cheeks.

"He has been known to be strong-willed and difficult. I've heard stories that he and our prophet, Samuel, have had a strained relationship at times."

Myra gripped the arm of her chair and stood. She smiled and gave a dismissive wave. "Perhaps your relationship with him will soften his responses and change that situation too."

She brushed invisible lint from her skirt, as she said, "Now that you know more about the king, let's get your midday meal."

Rizpah chuckled and nodded, conceding that she would not be able to pull any more information from Myra that day. "Well, that was helpful, and, yes, I'm hungry and ready to eat. We'll talk again later."

At Rizpah's request, the king often allowed her to be in his presence, seated quietly in a far corner of the chamber. This happened more than once, while he dictated non-confidential messages to kingdom representatives, studied scrolls, or accepted requests from the other wives or family members for an audience with him. One such relative was Ahinoam, his first wife. It was the occasion of her announcement that he would be a father. She passed the concubine, acknowledging her with an angry gaze, then directed a warm smile at the king and curtsied before him.

"Sire, I hope you are well," she said, smiling. "I bring you great news. I am pregnant. We shall welcome our fourth bundle in the Spring."

Saul nodded and smiled, while massaging the back of his head. "Well, this is very good news."

The king rose from his desk, walked past his wife, and waved Rizpah forward. Grabbing her around the waist, he raised Rizpah's chin and looked into her eyes. "Increasing the size of our household will always be cause for celebration. I look forward to better news from the fertile fields of this family."

Ahinoam's lower lip trembled as her annoyance flared. "Surely, Sire, you distinguish your wife's children from all others?"

King Saul ignored the comment and pulled Rizpah closer. "My family includes everyone connected to me in this household, which means no one member is more important in ranking or favoritism than the other." He puffed out his chest. "There is no need to battle over differences. I want all members reconciled to each other so there is no unnecessary division. Am I clear?"

Ahinoam nodded, bowed, and kissed the king on the cheek. "Understood," she responded in a sweet, cheerful tone then turned to glare at Rizpah.

"We will be planning a celebration of the baby in a few months. I would welcome your participation in the events," Ahinoam offered as she reached for Rizpah's hand.

The two women smiled, both fully aware it wasn't genuine.

"Well, I'm glad the ice is finally broken and the battle won," Rizpah commented as she strolled to the door. I look forward to participating in your baby celebration event and will pray blessings for a healthy delivery." With one last knowing glance at Ahinoam, and a loving look at Saul, Rizpah closed the door and returned to her suite.

Myra, who was busy directing the staff with the weekly cleaning and changing of linens and curtains in the bedroom, barely noticed her entrance.

"They all hate me so," Rizpah shouted and slammed a pillow against the room door.

"But none more than Ahinoam. Just now, she pranced in the chamber to announce she is pregnant. It's obvious she plans to milk as much attention from this situation as possible."

She threw her shawl on the chair near her dressing stand, and flopped on the bed, fighting back tears. "All of the wives and sons of wives have children," she yelled as her lips drew back in a snarl.

Despite her efforts to remain calm, she jumped up and paced the room, simmering in anger. "Though they periodically let me into their circle of chatter and gossip, I can tell they laugh and talk about me, the king's concubine, behind my back." She glanced at the ceiling and toyed with a lock of her hair as she lay flat on the bed. "I've gotta get pregnant. I must have King Saul's child."

Myra chuckled, pinched her nose, and tilted her head to one side. "Well, that shouldn't be a problem considering the amount of time you both seem to spend in his chambers. Just don't focus on it so much that you get yourself all stressed out."

Rizpah nodded and tugged at her earlobe. "I won't," she said while taking inventory of her surroundings. "We'll need to make room for the little bundle when it arrives."

"Sure," Myra chided while pausing at the door holding an armload of linen to be cleaned. "But let's get you pregnant first," she said over her shoulder and grabbed the handle.

"Wait! Wait!" Rizpah jolted upright and raised her hand for Myra to stop. "Before you leave, tell me more about Ahinoam." She leaned forward.

"She's the king's first wife, which she never fails to remind us, but 'I've had minimal interactions with her." Rizpath shrugged. "Whatever the exchange, she is often hostile and rude. In fact, the only person I have ever had any pleasant exchange with is Saul's oldest daughter Merab."

Myra dropped the bundle of linen and sat on the sheepskin cushioned chair by the bedside. It was a warm day, with little or no breeze, so the heat stained her cheeks with red blotches. The fine lines on her face signaled a woman who had been through years of hard living. "I suggest you measure your battles, my dear. Don't forget, despite your position, you have been allowed a great deal of wiggle room."

Rizpah didn't respond but rolled her eyes, then inspected her nails as a somber expression crossed her face.

Myra rubbed her forehead and pursed her lips. "And one more thing, don't be too concerned about getting to know any of the king's wives, especially Ahinoam. She will never allow you in the circle, so don't put your hopes on that plan."

Though silent, she pinned Myra with her eyes. Finally, she said, "Look, let's be clear. It hasn't gone unnoticed by these wives that my presence when they are in the king's chambers, has reinforced my position of favor in this household. With that understanding, several of the wives have changed their attitudes dramatically and have been comfortable including me in their group excursions and discussions."

Rizpah paused, breathed deeply, and plucked her nails for several uncomfortable moments to keep the atmosphere calm. "Look, Myra, you and I both know Ahinoam has been a constant source of aggravation with her pompous attitude and snide remarks. She is determined to set herself apart like the queen bee, and I'm determined to see that it doesn't happen when it comes to me."

Myra shook her head, slapped her lap with both hands, then stood and gathered the linen. "Okay, little lady," she said as the corner of her mouth lifted. "I suggest you measure your battles. You see, it doesn't matter the favor upon you that has allowed a great deal of freedom in this household. But remember this, in the end, you are still a concubine."

Rizpah walked to the side table, poured a cup of wine, and chuckled. "The way I see it," she offered, voice dripping with sarcasm, "I am much more than a concubine, at least in the king's eyes, and I intend to maintain that position." She slammed the cup on the table so hard, fruit from one of the small platters fell to the floor. "Yes," she snapped and tossed her head, "I will most certainly have the king's babies, and they will be treated royally. You'll see."

Myra clicked her tongue and shook her head. "Look here young lady, you tend to forget your place and spend much to much time battling for a position." She held up her palms in frustration. "I thought by now you would have been satisfied with your status. Instead, you continue to create impossible situations." Myra opened the door and paused. "It's unfortunate that's not the case." She left the room without another word.

CHAPTER 8

At the end of her second year in King Saul's household, Rizpah gave birth to her first son, Armoni. As was the custom, she spent several days confined to her bedroom suite.

"Such a perfect child," Myra commented while wrapping him in swaddling cloth.

Rizpah rubbed the back of her neck as her face glistened with sweat. "That little bundle didn't make a smooth entry into this world, but I'm happy he's here," she chuckled while stretching her arms to retrieve the baby.

"Sit a minute," she coaxed and patted the edge of the bed. "Keep me company while I feed my hungry little newborn. With the king gone, other than you and Amir here, I don't get much company and it's a bit lonely."

Rizpah hummed for a few moments, while her son drank his mother's milk. Just outside, below the balcony, they heard what appeared to be the sound of a man shoveling dirt, with another giving orders about cuttings to be done. Careful not to disturb the baby lying comfortably on her bosom, Rizpah cleared her throat and heaved a sigh. "So, I hear the king's grandson, Mephibosheth, *the royal grandson*, (why is he a grandson if he's the king's son? If this has a physical condition that has made him lame. I'm sure Jonathan's wife was upset, considering how she prides herself as the perfect wife among all the wives."

Myra offered a stern look as she stroked the baby in his mother's arms. "Be careful with your sentiments, my dear. Being joyful over the sorrows of another can produce pain and misery in your future. Right now, you are the king's only concubine. Make yourself happy with that fact and forget the petty jealousy of others over whom you have no influence or power."

"You know what?" Rizpah smiled. "You're right. As far as I am concerned, the envy is on their side. There is no competition for the king's favor but, just to be sure, I think I'll give him another son—a perfect specimen—and he will be named Mephibosheth."

"What are you saying?" Myra snapped with her eyes wide. "You lie there with a beautiful, healthy gift from God while plotting how you will have yet another son, just so you can embarrass your competitor by highlighting the imperfections of her child?" She rose from her seat next to the bed and gave a bitter laugh. "You can't be serious."

Before Rizpah could respond, the door opened and the king entered unannounced. Though happy to see him, Rizpah pretended she didn't notice him and maintained her focus on the baby.

Myra jumped, curtsied, and pulled a cushioned chair closer to the bedside near Rizpah and her baby. "Sire, I will have midday refreshments delivered," she said, while backing toward the door.

Without waiting for a response, Myra left the room. Rizpah stuck her nose in the air as her mouth curved in a smile. "My love and my king, you've been gone from us for days and your son has missed his father's presence."

King Saul laughed, sat on the edge of the bed, and rubbed her leg. "My son, *our son*, isn't even old enough to acknowledge my existence."

He leaned forward and kissed her on the mouth long and hard. "The fact is, my son's mom is pouting in my absence, and needs to know I still think she is special to me." His expression sobered. "And yes, she is."

Two years later, Rizpah gave birth to a second male child whom she named Mephibosheth. He was a strong, healthy baby with no physical challenges. King Saul spent many hours with his sons and concubine, to the dismay of the other wives. Not to be outdone, within three years of Mephibosheth's birth by Rizpah, however, Jonathan's wife gave birth to yet another son whom she also named Mephibosheth.

"Can you believe it? This can't be happening," Rizpah screamed as she stormed into her bedroom and slammed the door. "That miserable piece of dung had the nerve to name her baby Mephibosheth." She threw several pillows across the floor and rubbed her temples. "That woman is stealing something very significant, more priceless than gold. A person's name is an identity that sets them apart from all the others. She didn't even have more imagination than to take my child's name and place it on her newborn boy, acting like there was nothing to it."

Myra finished overseeing the evening bath for the boys. It was warmer than normal for the time of year so she directed several maidservants, who were on standby, to fan the children as they prepared to retire for the night. The nursery was located just beyond Rizpah's suite of rooms. Considering the agitation of the boys' mother, Myra rushed the servants to get the children out of the way and settled.

"Let me finish this task and deliver the children to the attendants. In the meantime, you need to calm down and put everything in perspective,"

Myra retorted. "Besides, what can you do? She is the wife of the king's son and you are only one step above a slave, no matter what the king says."

Rizpah ignored the comment, grabbed her shawl, and stormed out of the room. She paused, unsure of which direction to take.

The corridor leading to the king's chambers appeared cold and unwelcoming, different than any of her other visits through that area. Still hesitating, uncertain of where she wanted to go, she gazed at beyond the balcony. In the distance, at the edge of the dunes, a dust storm churned. She stretched her neck and squinted in time to notice a group of men, on camels, moving through the whirling sand following a chariot with horses. Rizpah walked closer to the edge of the balcony to get a better view and noticed three men, as opposed to the normal two riding the chariot. One man was in charge of steering the horses, with the other two riding as passengers.

As they drew near the castle gates, Rizpah realized one passenger was leaning forward, supported by the other. Her heart drummed when she recognized that King Saul was injured. Without hesitating, she whirled around and bolted down the hall. Taking a shortcut, she pushed the doors and ran through the wives' area, bumping into tables and leaving a mess behind her.

Focused on reaching the rear corridor at the opposite end of the room without interruption, she ignored their questions and agitated outbursts of concern. The passage leading to the back entrance wasn't well lit, so she stumbled several times over the uneven cobblestones. She rushed past the soldiers as they dismounted and removed their equipment until she reached the chariot.

The king grimaced as the color drained from his face. "My dear lady Rizpah, you are out of order." He laughed, winced in pain, then fell forward. Before Rizpah could speak, someone tugged her arm.

"You cannot be here," said a heavy, deep voice behind her. She yanked her arm, but the man wouldn't release her. When she turned, a tall, well-built stranger in soldier's attire, towered over her.

"Please, come this way," he repeated and released the pressure on her arm slightly. "My name is Abner, a relative of the king. He will be fine, but you need to leave the king's men to care for him and return to your quarters." She shook her head as tears streamed from her eyes. This was the first time she had seen King Saul injured. "Please, let me help. I have cleaned and dressed wounds before, and I do it now. Let me stay with him."

Abner waved to the eunuch, who had been standing in the doorway, to come forward. "You should return to your rooms, I will send word shortly to let you know the condition of the king. In the meantime, there is nothing more you can do here."

The eunuch hurried forward, gripped Rizpah firmly by the elbow, and guided her back to the passage leading to the corridor adjacent to the wives' quarters. There was nothing gentle about his movements. His annoyance was evident with every move. Before opening the door, the eunuch stopped suddenly and yanked her forward.

"From the day you arrived, I knew you would be trouble. Don't you realize you are under my charge?" He glowered, and Rizpah was sure he would strike her if she made one move. Fear paralyzed her, but she stood her ground.

"How dare you? I am the king's ... well ..." Rizpah hesitated to finish the sentence.

The eunuch glared at her and moved so close she could feel his breath on her skin. "You are the king's what?"

Neither saw Abner approaching from behind. He cleared his throat and stepped forward. "She is the king's and that should be enough for you, don't you think?"

The eunuch immediately released Rizpah, stepped back, and bowed.

Abner did not acknowledge the gesture. He held up Rizpah's shawl. "You dropped this in all the commotion. I'm glad I decided to catch up with you to return it."

He curled his upper lip and addressed the eunuch, who avoided eye contact. "Now, with the courtesy due to her position, return the king's lady to her rooms and report back to me immediately. Is that understood?" he commanded as his eyes flashed with anger.

Without another word, Abner turned and proceeded back down the passage. The silence that followed was uncomfortable for Rizpah, but she was determined not to give her unwanted partner the satisfaction of knowing how she felt. Standing erect, with shoulders back, she smoothed her skirt and waited for the eunuch to open the door leading to the wives' area.

Staying several steps ahead of the eunuch, she hastened through the main gathering room, barely acknowledging the questions from the wives about her earlier behavior. Tears filled her eyes. She was embarrassed and angry, but determined to show strength until she reached the solitude of her room. A weight settled on her heart. *What if they are lying to me? What if he is dying and they didn't want to tell me. Who will be left for me then? I should be making friends, not enemies. I may need them. My God, help me.* She reached her room door, paused, and cleared her throat in preparation for her next words.

"I guess I should thank you for reminding me of how inappropriate it was for me to run to the courtyard unescorted. I must admit I should have considered the results of my actions, and I'm sorry." Without waiting for a response, she turned the handle and entered the room. She looked over her shoulder with a smile to thank the eunuch, only to discover he had disappeared. She didn't have any idea when he left, or whether he heard anything she said. With the door securely closed behind her and surrounded by darkness, she fell across the bed, exhausted, and cried herself to sleep.

The next morning Rizpah slept late and was undisturbed. Even the handmaids moved about the other rooms in total silence, taking the boys with them to a play area after their morning meal. Myra, on the other hand, was on a mission. Her lady had made a spectacle of herself and needed direction immediately before things got out of hand.

With a platter of breakfast in her hands, she opened the door, placed the tray on the table and opened the curtains wide. Rizpah stirred, then squinted as the bright sun beamed directly in her face. Myra poured a cup of water, placed it next to the food tray, then set her palms flat on the table and leaned forward, her face contorted.

"Well missy, you made quite a ruckus last night." She waved her arms around. "Everybody is talking about it, even the handmaids." Rizpah propped the pillows behind her shoulders and drew her knees to her chest. "I know I didn't exactly make the right moves last night, and for that, I'm truly sorry. It's just that when I saw them bringing the king and he was injured, my first thought was to go to him, to see to his care." She looked at Myra, eyes pleading for understanding. "I just wanted to be there if he needed me for any reason."

In disbelief, Myra scrunched up her face and rolled her eyes.

Rizpah jumped out of the bed and rushed to the window. "Look, I was over there, on the balcony," she pointed, "and remembered I could reach him more quickly by going through the wives communal lounge."

"Okay," she shouted, hands in the air. "It didn't occur to me they would pay attention to my urgent movements, and besides, they ignore my comments all the time—much less to acknowledge I exist. Frankly, explaining my actions was the last thing on my mind."

Myra shook her head and took a deep breath. "It was a dreadful idea, violating all protocols, and disrespecting those who are accountable to the king for maintaining what is appropriate and mandated to be followed."

Rizpah walked to the breakfast treats left by Myra from the early meal, grabbed a bunch of grapes and a slice of sweet bread, and ate in silence for a few moments. After several bites, she looked up at Myra, who stood by her side with a disapproving air. "I forgot to tell you, I did attempt to apologize to the eunuch, but I think he left before he heard what I had to say."

Myra threw her head back and laughed. "Are you surprised?" she shouted and paced the floor. "Tell me, are your feelings hurt? All these years and you have only referred to him as "the eunuch." Did you ever think to ask and use his name? Or did you not think he had one?" She sighed, softened her tone, and put her hand on Rizpah's shoulder.

"I realize you had a bumpy start with him, and because of your unique position with the king, you were allowed to skip a few steps normally considered part of the protocol for communicating and visiting with the king. But, other people are involved and you need to recognize that, and give them due respect for what they do."

Rizpah stopped chewing, tossed the food on the platter, and cleared her throat. "I'm sorry, I just didn't think. My start here was rough, and the eunuch," she said with hesitation, "was part of that rough beginning." She took a deep breath. "I will fix this Myra; I will fix it as soon as possible." She arose from the chair, hugged Myra, and whispered, "By the way, what is his name?"

Myra shook her head and laughed uncontrollably. "His name is Amir and he is my son."

Rizpah made an abrupt two-step retreat from their embrace, appraising the woman she'd known for as long as she'd lived in the palace. "What are you saying?" she said as bitterness filled her mouth. "He's your son?" She gasped and rubbed her hands together. "I just can't believe it.

Why did you keep this important information from me? All this time and all the secrets I've shared with you but you kept this significant fact from me?"

Myra's eyes flooded with tears and her expression hardened. She walked to the table and moved several unclean utensils to the tray. After a few moments, she quivered with indignation. "There are certain secrets that I chose not to share others." She raised her chin and continued. "You see, even we servants have private lives."

Dropping the tray, her legs buckled and she dropped to the nearest chair as she fought back tears. "Besides," she huffed, "Amir also wants to keep it that way. The reason is of no importance to you or anyone." She gave Rizpah a weak smile and rocked back and forth. "You are now one of the few people who know this fact, and I prefer we leave it that way."

Rizpah rushed to her faithful servant and friend, took both hands, and guided her to the entrance to the veranda. "Come, let's you and I sit on the balcony together and enjoy the sun."

Myra looked around, then pulled back. "I can't lounge on the balcony," she insisted. It isn't permitted."

Rizpah laughed. "It's my balcony. You delivered the food, so relax. The maidservants will not be around again for hours, the boys are off playing until their midday meal, and my balcony is the most secluded area of the palace because of its proximity to the king's quarters."

She grabbed the tray of food, then looked over her shoulder and directed Myra to follow. "Bring the water and cups. You will sit with me for a little while at least."

Myra shook her head but obeyed. "You will always be a little disobedient. I guess you can't help it."

As they ate and sipped, the voices of children playing could be heard in the distance. The sun was high and intense, but despite the warm temperature, a soft breeze provided comfort during their short respite. "I wonder if he is well, the king, I mean," Rizpah mumbled while she nibbled her bottom lip.

Myra shifted in her chair, still uncomfortable at the thought of being seen relaxing while she should be working. "I will ask Amir to send word to you when he's able." She leaned forward so their eyes met. "In the meantime, make no moves on your own. Do you understand?"

Rizpah went poker-faced, then laughed and nodded. "I understand. No more making decisions alone." She laughed, then added, "At least not for a little while."

CHAPTER 9

L ife for Rizpah improved through the years. The wives were more receptive, if not courteous, and life with her boys, now young men, fulfilling. Not so for the king. In the early years of his reign, he had the favor of God and the love of the people of Israel. As time passed, however, his arrogance and bad judgment led to poor decisions, placing him and his kingdom in jeopardy. The result was inevitable.

The sounds of crying and screaming were deafening. Still numbed by the news, Myra left the wives' quarters and rushed to Rizpah's suite, carrying a flask of red wine and several goblets. She eased the door open just wide enough to peer through the crack, hoping Rizpah was resting. Myra opened it wider, noticed the bed was empty and scanned the room. Plates and utensils were on the table, but the food was untouched. Piles of clothing lined the walls leading the closet and several satchels lay open on the floor. Evening shadows had already fallen, but there was no candlelight.

Myra stepped inside. "Rizpah," she whispered, "baby girl it's me."

No answer.

Myra crossed the room and lit a candle on the side table, then noticed the doors to the balcony were open. She crossed the floor, stepped onto the balcony, and studied the surrounding area. The night air was oppressive, with only a slight breeze for comfort. To her disappointment, Rizpah was not in her usual location. She anchored her attention on the outer wall. Looking both ways, she walked to the edge and leaned over. Breathing a sigh of relief when she didn't see a body on the ground below, she walked back to the bedroom entrance.

"I just can't believe it," Rizpah sobbed. "He can't be dead. It just can't be."

Myra jumped at the sound coming from a dark corner at the far end of the balcony. "What are you doing down there?" She approached with care, still unsure if Rizpah was standing on the edge, ready to jump.

"Come inside where it's cooler." Myra reached for her hand. "Come on baby, let's get you something to eat. The boys need your strength, and there's nothing you can do about the king. He's dead and that's that."

Rizpah jerked her arm away, waved both hands in the air, and screamed. "That's that? So, I just forget about the last twenty-one years, pack up my life and go where? This is all the boys have known. They had plans to join their father's army in another year. Now what?" She crumpled to the floor. My life is over."

Myra patted her shoulder. "You are a strong woman, everyone says so. This is a tragedy for sure but, by law, the household of the king will be managed during the transition, and all of the wives and, uh, well you know, concubines, will be properly cared for as is tradition." She reached into the pocket of her skirt and handed Rizpah a soft white cloth. "Never forget, just as God made a king in one day, he can also remove a king in a day. King Saul's season is over but his legacy must live, and it will, if you maintain your strength in the days ahead. Your young men will need you even more now."

* * *

Rizpah nodded, wiped her face, and held her head high, overwhelmed by the numbness that infused her body. She entered her room and sat to eat some of the food left for her. Myra poured wine then rehung the clothes that had been strewn in piles across the floor. After some time, they heard footsteps in the hallway.

Rizpah looked up smiling. "Perhaps it was a mistake. Maybe the news was wrong and they've sent a messenger to say the king was injured and not dead."

Before Myra could respond, Rizpah swung the door open, excited to greet the visitor. She didn't recognize the stranger at first glance, then remembered the incident when King Saul was brought home injured from a battle. It was this man who has intervened between her and Amir, the eunuch.

"Abner, how good of you to come." Rizpath smiled and grabbed his hand. "Please come in, have a cup of wine or some fruit." She instructed Myra to prepare a plate of refreshments, then turned her attention back to Abner. "You have good news, right?"

The king's cousin frowned, shook his head, and swayed on his feet. "No, Rizpah, I'm truly sorry for your loss. He was a good man and a great king. We will all miss him." He stepped closer and puffed out his chest. "I stopped by to let you know I'm here for you. Just send me a message at any time and I will ensure your needs are met."

Rizpah's body rocked with rage. She walked around Abner, her head tilted, and mouth curled. "Thank you," she sneered and folded her arms. "Right now, would you be good enough to just leave me alone."

Abner rubbed his chin and lifted his shoulder in a half shrug. "I understand how you must feel, but please think about it. You may find me a worthy advocate and friend." He grabbed the door handle, flashed an appraising glance over his shoulder, then left in silence.

Rizpah put her hand over her heart and breathed deep. "Can you believe this? Now that's what I call loyalty to family and friends." She tossed her hair and gnashed her teeth. "Saul's body isn't even cold and they're already dividing the spoils. He turns my stomach."

Myra gathered the dirty dishes and cleared the table. "I'll send the handmaids to prepare a bath for you and ask Amir to find your sons."

She paused and shook her head, her mouth set in a hard line. "Be cautious when rejecting support, my dear. We don't know which way the wind will blow in this situation. You should stay neutral to all offers of support until the dust clears."

The next few weeks following King Saul's death were filled with stress and uncertainty for the entire household. Rumor after rumor, internal conflict, and heightened jealousies flourished. Rizpah kept close tabs on her two young men, ensuring they were not involved in the verbal exchange among members of the household. It didn't take long, however, before the rumor cycle landed on her doorstep.

"What are you suggesting?" Rizpah said through clenched teeth.

Amir raised his hands in a calming gesture. He requested a meeting with her in the king's courtyard to discuss the rumors.

"I understand there have been unfortunate rumor of a sexual relationship between you and I even before his death."

Rizpah placed the flowers she had been carrying to decorate her room on the courtyard table. She trembled, remembering that particular table was where she sat for her first meal with King Saul. She faced Amir, bitterness filled her heart.

"You're telling me the household is talking about my going to bed with another man?"

Rizpah pushed past Amir, almost knocking over one of the tables, and walked beyond the rear entrance to the king's chambers and into the corridor access to the wives' quarters. Amir hurried behind.

He yanked her arm before she pulled the door handle.

"Nothing good will come of a confrontation with those women. Please think before you enter the wives' chambers and create a disturbance. Besides, I don't believe any of them is the source of this rumor."

She whirled around, face contorted, and smacked his face. "You liar! You know very well the source of these disgusting stories comes from the good wives of King Saul. Well, I've had enough. Today, we have a final word. Today I'll have my say, and the devil be damned. I won't be stopped."

Amir jolted forward, but stopped midway, his mouth twisted. "I've done all I can do to prevent you from making yet another misstep, but you've rejected my help as usual. Go then, make a spectacle of yourself."

He made an abrupt turn and walked away.

"I will be in the shadows observing and will clean up the pieces of your mess, again, when you're through."

Rizpah watched Amir walk away, smoothed her hair, went poker-faced and opened the door. A heavy scent of fragranced oil filled the air, combined with the odor of fresh-cut lilacs and roses. She scanned the room, packed with people chattering in small groups. Maidservants moved from cluster to cluster with loaded platters of lamb, fish stew, mixed vegetables, fruit, and sweet bread.

"May I have your attention please," she shouted and stepped into the center of the room, turning full circle to ensure she had everyone's attention.

"I'm here to announce that you are mistaken if any of you think I will spend another day here being the brunt of your insults and lies. I was faithful to my king and carried his children, who have grown to be fine young men."

She waved her fist in the air as tears shimmered in her eyes.

"Not once, do you hear me, not once was I unfaithful to him and I challenge anyone to suggest otherwise."

She moved around the room, stopped in front of Ahinoam, and leaned forward, the corner of her eyes crinkled. "He loved me more than you," she whispered, "and you know it. You never forgave him for it, but it doesn't matter now." A muscle in her jaw tightened. "What does matter, however, is the fact that I won't let you or anyone else destroy me or my boys with vicious lies."

The chamber doors opened and Abner entered, followed by Amir. Dressed in a linen cloth draped to the waist and a lambskin leather breastplate tied securely with a silk sash, his attire suggested he was preparing for battle. He walked to the far corner of the room then strolled the entire area, pausing in front of each of the wives, giving full eye contact. At each pause, the tension in the atmosphere increased. Having completed a tour of the room, he stopped in front of Rizpah, rubbed his hands together, then faced the group.

"Well, what have we here? A celebration?" He signaled Amir, who dismissed the servants and walked to the center of the room to await further instruction. "All wives are to prepare to welcome new leadership to the former house of Saul," Abner directed. He took several steps back and stood beside Rizpah, acknowledging her with a nod.

She slid him a guarded look but remained silent.

Abner cocked his head and drew in a long breath. "As you know, with the death of King Saul, major adjustments are required of everyone, as with any transition. I will assist with many of the details." He jerked his head toward the king's chambers. "In addition to addressing a few skirmishes, I will be attending regional meetings for the next few days. Until my return, you will continue to follow instructions from Amir and perform your duties as normal."

Abner narrowed his eyes, crossed both arms behind his back, and scanned the room. "A rumor has been brought to my attention and I am going to address it here and now," he shouted. His nostrils flared as he continued, "The king's wives and his concubine are untouchable by anyone, under threat of death." His expression sobered. "I was angered to learn there had been discussions that I violated any of the king's rules or took advantage of anyone in the king's household."

A hush fell over the room, with each person avoiding direct eye contact.

Flushed with anger, Rizpah pushed past Amir and ran from the room. Instead of entering her chambers, she went to the balcony, seeking escape from a potential conversation she might have if Myra was in her suite. To her surprise, both of her sons were sitting at one of the tables, engaged in conversation. Her youngest, Mephibosheth, was the first to recognize her entrance.

"Mother, what disturbs you?" he asked, with concern etched on his features. "Here, be seated."

He pulled one of the chairs forward, but Rizpah gave a dismissive wave and paced the balcony floor. "Not now, son," she snapped. "I'm too upset to sit. I must think. We are entering dangerous times and I must search for a way out of this mess."

She stopped, looked over the wall, and gazed at the mounds of sand. The sun was high over the ridge, shining over a group of travelers in the distance, heading away from the compound. Her heart dropped at the thought that she truly was a captive slave, with no way of escape.

Rizpah returned to the table, sat, and grabbed the hands of both her sons. "I believe there's a plan to place me in a negative light with the new king, whoever that's going to be. So far, it appears all hasn't gone exactly according to their plans, at least based on the meeting I just left, but I know they won't stop until they reach their goal." She turned her face away, avoiding their eyes as tears filled hers. "With so many wives, I am not fighting one but several plans. I need to come up with a counter move. Because they are wives of the king, and I am only a concubine, they have an unlimited number of resources available, which presents a huge problem for me. No matter what they try, however, I am not going to give up. They won't win."

Mephibosheth hugged his mother while Armoni went to the side table and poured her a cup of wine. "Not to worry, Mother," Mephibosheth whispered, "we will protect you." Rizpah touched her son's face. "I know you mean well, but there is very little you can do, and any effort could result in your being put in chains. Just remain still, so you will go unnoticed." She punched the air. "I will secure the favor of the new king, and we will survive this attempt to remove us from favor."

Amir appeared in the doorway, his expression sober. "Your presence is requested in the king's hall." He stepped forward. "I will escort you there."

Armoni jumped from his seat and stood between Amir and Rizpah. "We can escort our mother to the king's hall."

Rizpah placed her hand on her son's shoulder. "It is well, my son. The forces of good are on our side, and I have done nothing wrong." She stood and walked to Amir, smiling. "I know God will protect us as we continue to honor him. I will fight against these liars and maintain honesty in my actions and communications. Justice will be our guide."

* * *

An uncomfortable silence followed as Rizpah hugged her sons, adjusted her skirts, wrapped the silk shawl close to her face, and followed Amir to the king's chambers. Moving from the glow of the high sun at their backs, dark shadows greeted them when they entered the corridor. The curves and corners of the building didn't allow for openings to let in natural light, so torch lights lined the walls and remained lit in the passages. This day, however, only two of more than ten torches had been lit, giving the area a sinister appearance.

Amir stopped suddenly, touched Rizpah's arm and pressed two fingers to her lips. He pulled her into one of the hallway's corners. "You must listen to me for one moment," he said while checking both ends of the corridor.

She followed his motions in silence.

He stepped closer, stared at her for a moment, then drew a long breath and buried both hands in his hair.

"As the eunuch, I have had much freedom of movement and have heard many things." Amir moved from side to side, looked heavenward, and breathed in deeply. "Abner has always been attracted to you and made no secret of this fact often, during unguarded conversations among some of the king's people."

Rizpah stepped back, put her hands to her throat, and gasped. "I never knew," she protested. "I did nothing to encourage this feeling."

Amir raised his hands. "It makes no difference what you did or did not do, and how foolish you were to even let him in your chambers that day. Remember? My mother warned you, but you didn't listen."

Rizpah glared at Amir, then dropped her head.

"Let me continue, please," Amir said. "There's so little time for you to make this right." He leaned against the wall, rubbed his head, and continued. "It is clear that King Saul lost a great battle, and King David is now ruler over the Southern half of the kingdom. Abner, in addition to being King Saul's cousin, is also a well-respected general. Well, he and Ish-Bosheth had a good relationship, and Abner was promoting him as king."

He paused when they heard footsteps coming from the opposite direction. Before reaching their secluded section of the corridor, the individual opened a side door and walked through, shutting the door behind them. Amir gave a half-smile, wiped his forehead, and continued. "The transition of leadership was progressing well until someone told Ish-Bosheth that Abner had been sleeping with you, and he believed it. Needless to say, this was considered a major violation of all propriety functions, as the king's court belongs to the king."

Amir straightened his shoulders and exhaled. "So, you see, as of now, Abner and Ish-Bosheth are at odds because of these accusations, and Abner was forced to leave the region. Rumor has it he will switch his allegiance and loyalty to King David."

Rizpah's mouth turned dry and she fought the urge to throw up as her eyes filled. "This can't be so," she sobbed. "Why would anyone do such a thing? What did they hope to gain?"

Amir shook his head and threw his hands in the air. "Who knows, maybe they thought if they could discredit you then you'd be banished from the household and returned to your home in shame. What does it matter?"

Amir pulled Rizpah closer, so their eyes met. His chest rose and fell with rapid breaths. "Hear me, this is your opportunity to convince Ish-Bosheth that you have been a loyal concubine. You cannot fail. Both our lives depend on this." Dissatisfaction plowed his brow. "Everyone knows of Abner's visit to your rooms. For that reason, you must admit he made an unwelcomed approach, but you were never alone with him and you must emphasize that you reported his behavior to me."

Rizpah stared at him in shock. "So, you expect me to tell him that I reported the incident to you? Won't that put you in a serious situation with the new king?"

Amir nodded and took her hand. "Not to worry. It will work out for the best. Ish-Bosheth knows of my years of loyalty to his father and that I have handled many situations without disturbing him with the details. He will assume I addressed the issue directly with Abner, and he will certainly believe what I say, especially if I confirm you had already spoken to me about your discomfort with Abner's visit."

He lifted her chin and brushed a strand of hair from her face. "Now smile and come with me. Let's get this meeting over with."

CHAPTER 10

Rizpah kept to herself for weeks after the incident concerning Abner. She was relieved to learn Ish-Bosheth had made her position clear to the wives and, once again, she was afforded privileges in an elevated position as a royal concubine. Then, the peace and calm they enjoyed for several weeks were destroyed with news of Abner's death.

"Myra would you please stop moping around here, wringing your hands. What are you fretting about? He's dead and that's it," Rizpah shouted in anger. "We have to survive this turmoil, and the best way to do it is to stay out of conversations that don't concern us."

"You have no idea what this means," Myra responded. Opening the balcony door, she stepped into the sun. "So much death in one family is never good."

Rizpah walked onto the balcony, , sat on the lounge chair, and crossed her ankles in front of her. "Well, the boys tell me, from what they heard, he was likely killed by an unknown assailant while leaving King David's camp. Of course, no one knows why he had been meeting with the king or what deeds he had agreed to perform in exchange for whatever favor he was promised by the king."

She stood, strolled to the balcony ledge, leaned over, and scanned the landscape. The flowers they had planted earlier that month needed water, but the wells were dangerously low so there was little to nothing left for the vegetation and plants.

"Myra, look at this, Rizpah pointed to the area below. "The plants are dying and the land is so dry."

After peering over the edge, Myra shook her head, "this is not a good sign for the season ahead. Not a good sign at all."

Several weeks passed without incident. Ish-Bosheth expanded the men in his guard, organized, and recommissioned key officers. A celebration was scheduled and the new king sent Amir to command that both the concubine and wives attend the ceremony to observe his ascendancy over the northern tribes, scheduled as part of the evening festivities.

After hours of preparation, Rizpah entered the great hall with her sons on either side. They were excited for the invitation, as they had just recently been appointed as trainee cadets in preparation for their new assignment with the home base troops guarding the castle.

The festive nature of the celebration was larger than any they had ever seen during King Saul's reign. Music, dancers, and endless platters of every variety of roasted and boiled lamb, clay baked fish, and soup complemented by honey buns, and platters of fruit and mixed vegetables. Still avoiding unnecessary communication with the wives, Rizpah found ways to enjoy herself until she could ease her way, unnoticed, from the scene and escape to the haven of her rooms.

Myra had been assigned to oversee every detail or room décor and food preparations for the evening. In the days since Saul's death, she had been elevated as a trusted servant along with her son. She was also directed to be the eyes and ears for Ish-Bosheth in the household, reporting anything that seemed out of order immediately. Though both she and Amir had convinced Saul's son of Rizpah's innocence concerning Abner, all was not well.

"This is not good, mother," Amir whispered as he helped Myra with smoothing one of the linen coverings on a side serving table. "Look at her. Rizpah's movements are so noticeable. She looks uncomfortable and suspicious," he announced. "Something has to be done and quick. Unlike many others, she has yet to approach and congratulate our new leader, and Ish-Bosheth isn't pleased."

Myra nodded in agreement and followed Amir's gaze. "She's being careful, afraid to make a mistake, and in doing so, is making mistakes." Giving her son a broad smile, she picked up a tray of fresh fruit. "I will make my way over to her but be mindful my son, no matter what he has said, Ish-Bosheth is still very suspicious of everyone. We must be very careful." She touched her son's hand and her eyes narrowed. "I know you care about her, but if we choose to continue to help, and she falls out of favor with our newly appointed leader, we may fall with her."

Several of the wives passed by them, observing their conversation and whispering among themselves.

"Enough discussion mother," Amir said with a laugh. He bowed his head and inspected the platter. "Go, talk to Rizpah."

Myra smiled, affection glowed in her eyes. Amir nodded, returned his mother's smile, and walked away.

Moving as fast and inconspicuously as possible, Myra traveled the room offering guests items from the platter of fruit. Each pause in her tour brought her closer to Rizpah. When she finally reached her, Rizpah already had one hand on a doorknob, with the other waving at her sons.

Myra stepped in the middle of her goodbye wave, giving Rizpah look that could cut her like a knife.

"Are you crazy? Just what do you think you're you doing?" Myra challenged and jerked her head toward the door. "If you step through that opening to leave, you have sealed your fate which wouldn't be an issue for me, except you may also seal the fate of me and my son." She stepped closer and a muscle in her jawbone twitched. "So, even if you don't care about yourself or your sons, please have the decency to consider what your actions will do to others."

Rizpah bit the bottom of her lip and glanced at the ceiling. "Oh my God, I didn't think. I was just focused on making a quick entrance then staying out of the way of these people, so I don't say the wrong things." Her eyes shot sparks and the corner of her mouth lifted. "I wasn't intentionally trying to create issues for any of us."

Myra cocked her head toward the area where Ish-Bosheth sat and her expression hardened.

"Great." She responded with a forced smile. "So the best way to ensure that doesn't happen is for you to take your cute humps over to that man and be as charming and engaging as possible."

Rizpah simmered with anger at the thought of being a hypocrite. "Alright, I'll play the *be charming and nice game* for a little while, but if you think I'm going to spend the evening pretending I want to engage in chatter with these phony women then you're the crazy one."

She flipped her hair, forced a smile, and walked into the crowd.

Many people gathered for the special event recognizing Ish-Bosheth's ascension to leadership. Rizpath had been notified her presence was commanded for a meeting with the new king. Rizpah glanced over her shoulders, waved at her sons, and closed the door to the great hall. She walked the familiar path to the king's chambers.

Ish-Bosheth beckoned Rizpath forward and opened their conversation with a series of questions about her life with Saul. "You were happy with my father, this is true?"

Rizpah nodded and her eyes welled up. "Sir, I cared and was faithful to your father, yes. He was a good person and a great king."

Ish-Bosheth paused and looked away, his expression sober. "Well, he certainly was a great soldier."

His response made her uncomfortable, so she immediately changed the subject. "I am the concubine of the king. My loyalty is to the king." She ran a hand through her hair, then touched his hand. "I hope I will be allowed to remain and serve you as I have served your father."

Ish-Bosheth smiled. "I trust you are faithful, and will perform to my satisfaction. Now, let's join the festivities, they worked so hard to plan for me, with the others."

Her attendance at the celebration had a rocky start and there were so many new faces. Still, she enjoyed the festivities. At the end of the evening, she bade her sons goodnight.

Rizpah returned to her room, opened the door, and was greeted with a pleasant surprise. Her nightgown lay on the center of her bed, with several soft white candles positioned next to a flask of wine and a small platter of fruit and sweet bread on her side table. She ate several pieces of fruit and bread, then strolled onto her balcony, pulled her lounge chair close to the outer wall, and settled down to relax. It wasn't long before she drifted to sleep in the chair.

"Wake up," the soft voice spoke in her ear.

Rizpah opened her eyes and a hand covered her mouth. Her heart hammered as she tried to move but couldn't.

"It's me, Amir," he put a finger over his lips, then moved his hand.

Rizpah turned her head and saw Myra standing in the shadows, waving for her to follow.

As she arose from the chair, Amir cautioned, "please don't talk. You must be very quiet. There's danger in this house, with many strangers lurking about."

Confused and disoriented, Rizpah grabbed Amir's hand, and looked around, frantic for answers. "What are you saying? What's happening and where are my sons?"

Amir raised his hand for silence, pointed to the opening, and they both walked toward Myra on the other side of the balcony. When they reached the area, Rizpah grabbed a chair and sat. She hooked her feet around the chair legs and wagged her fingers at Myra. "Look, tell me what this is all about. Why are we whispering and sneaking about on my balcony in the middle of the night?"

Myra smacked her fingers to the side, leaned forward, and put both hands on the arms of the chair. "Keep your voice down. Do you hear me? Keep it low, or I will keep it quiet." She stood straight and smoothed her hair. "Ish-Bosheth is dead. They executed him tonight while he slept."

The sound of footsteps running, along with muffled voices interrupted their talk. They remained silent for several minutes, listening. Several times the intruders paused at Rizpah's door but no one entered. Suddenly, Amir tapped her shoulder and pointed. "Over here, come."

She followed him to the balcony ledge. One by one they peered over the edge.

When it was Rizpah's turn to observe, she leaned forward and saw four men, in black robes with weapons raised, standing near eight or nine horses. They huddled in a group talking, weapons raised, then separated in different directions, canvassing the area. It was clear their main focus was guarding the horses. With her leg throbbing, Rizpah felt the need to change position and did so without hesitation.

Unfortunately, her foot rubbed against a stone, creating a loud, scraping sound. Frantic, she looked up and Amir put his finger to her lips and warned "hush."

One of the soldiers stopped and studied the wall. Eyes wild, Rizpah froze in place, held her breath, and waited.

The intruder searched in the direction of the sound, listened for a moment, then walked the length of the wall, his eyes focused on the edges. He stopped just below her location. She cringed, pressed her hand to her throat to muffle a groan, and trembled. The man studied her section for a few more minutes, then moved on. Moments later, four other men rushed into the area, grabbed the reins, and mounted the horses. Myra and Amir joined Rizpah in time to watch the men travel to the edge of the ridge then separate in different directions and ride out of sight.

Rizpah slid to the floor in a fetal position and sobbed. "He saw me, I know it. He looked right at me. I thought I would die."

Amir lifted her to her feet and said, "It doesn't matter, they got what they came for and won't be back." After seating her in the chair, he paced the floor. "Believe me, you're safe. You must get yourself together. There's so much turmoil right now, with no one knowing what's next."

Myra poured wine for them, then sat and put her face in her hands. "There are so many strangers here. They have formed several groups, each with their own definition of loyalty, or plan to position themselves to receive favor from the next king."

Rizpah took a long sip of wine, then sneered. "King David. "Yes, it's very clear to me now. The man, David, now rules both the Northern and Southern region." She raised her cup high. "Well folks, the rule of law has taken a bad turn. We're now at the mercy of a ruthless tyrant."

Amir lowered his head, stroked his beard, and grunted. "No, that can't be true. King David is well-loved by the people. His wars are against his enemies, not friends or fellow countrymen." He slammed his wine cup on the table. "No, King David is a good man. We will do well under his rule, if that is the case."

Myra nodded in agreement. "We've had enough trauma. Let's just move forward, shall we?"

Rizpah shoved the table aside and jumped to her feet. "I can't believe this. Can it be possible that I am the only one thinking clearly? Are you people that blind? Think about it. Who stands to benefit the most from these recent deaths?"

Amir avoided eye contact and Myra continued to clear the table in silence until they heard the sound of hurried footsteps. She looked around. "What's that? It sounds like they're running in this direction."

The door burst open and Rizpah's two sons rushed in.

"Mother, are you all right?" Mephibosheth shouted he and his brother hugged her close. "We were leaving the rear courtyard and these strangers stopped us. We told them who we were, but they forced Ahinoam and me to stay in the soldiers' quarters. Even now, I hear they're dragging Ish-Bosheth from his chambers." He scratched his head and gave a mirthless laugh. "So much confusion, it makes no sense."

Rizpah hugged her sons, then gave Amir and Myra a knowing look. "So, the question for us is what happens next? I guess we shall soon see."

CHAPTER 11

Weeks turned into months, and months to years. The household, under the new leadership of King David, fell into the established routine, adapting to the rules and patterns of behavior set before them. No one mentioned Ish-Bosheth, or the circumstances surrounding his death. The diminished interest was attributed partly to concern over the dramatic change in the weather. The region had been hit by an extreme dry spell. Famine had already struck several areas and had spread to nearby towns at a rapid pace.

Myra had just returned from her weekly visit to the marketplace. Shortly after, she prepared a small platter of dates, figs, oranges, and a small container of water for Rizpah's refreshment. "The merchant stalls are almost empty and the wells are drying up all around the region." She paused, rubbed her forearms to relieve the discomfort from carrying the heavy load, and fidgeted with the table. "It seems the talk is that we've been cursed because of Saul's massacre of the Gibeonites years ago—at least that's the story according to King David, as expressed by the prophets."

Rizpah drummed her fingers on the table. "Now why is it I don't find this a surprise. Saul's been dead for several years but we are still suffering a drought because of something he did to the Gibeonites. I wonder how our great King David is going to save us from this plight we face or hasn't he figured it out yet?"

Myra folded her arms and scrunched her face. "I have warned you more than once to be careful of your tongue. The walls of this place have ears. Very little that is said goes unnoticed and there is always danger that what you say will be misunderstood." Her eyes shot sparks. "Next, King David hears from God and, because of that, he leads his people well. From his battle with the giant Goliath to now, his greatness has been proven more than once. Whatever he decides will be for the good of all." She patted Rizpah's hand. "Sit, enjoy the quiet of the day and the refreshments."

After doing as Myra suggested, Rizpah inspected the meal selection.

Myra's expression softened and she pulled up a chair and sat close to her mistress and friend. "Besides," Myra continued, "we are in a situation where, no matter what is decided, we will have to accept it and follow in obedience to the rules. We have no choice."

Amir entered the room after knocking. "Go to the balcony," he ordered. "We have guests." Without hesitation, Myra and Rizpah rushed through the opening and noticed a cloud of dust moving in the direction of the castle.

"Who is it and how many of them are coming?" Rizpah asked, tugging Amir's robe.

He turned to her and lifted her chin so their eyes met. "I've only heard rumors and didn't want to share the information until I could get confirmation. I still don't have confirmation, but from what I have heard, King David must make restitution to the Gibeonites for Saul breaking a treaty and ordering the massacre of their people years ago. What this means is still unclear."

Amir looked at his mother with a half-smile. "Keep her here. I will go attend to my duties in the wives' chambers and return just as soon as I am able."

Myra nodded, wiped her face, and stood beside Rizpah on the balcony. "Don't be anxious my dear. These things run in cycles, as kingdoms change. We are going to survive the next few days just like we survived the last three years."

The horsemen arrived at the gates, but Myra and Rizpah could only see them dismount. Half of the legion entered the castle, while the others seemed to circle the area, weapons visible. Inside the castle, the only sounds they heard were shouts and screams, cries, and pleading.

Rizpah, wringing her hands, blurted, "Where are my sons and why haven't they visited me?" With all this commotion, they should have been there by now. Myra, you know this. You know they would never allow anything to happen to me. They would be here, right now, to make sure I'm alright." She paced the length of the balcony, the dust almost choking her.

"I know this is difficult my child, but you know Amir is watching out for your sons where he can. You must endure the discomfort waiting brings. It is temporary." Myra no sooner completed her sentence before Amir burst into the room, throwing his hands in the air. "They've taken them," he shouted. "The sons and grandsons of Saul have been taken, except Mephibosheth."

Rizpah panicked at first but breathed a sigh of relief when she heard that Mephibosheth had not been taken. "Okay, Mephibosheth has been spared, but what about my other son, Armoni?"

Amir walked approached, shoulders slumped. With concern in his eyes, he held both her hands. "Rizpah, you don't understand. Your son,

Mephibosheth was taken. King Saul's grandson, Jonathan's son called Mephibosheth, was spared. The seven young men have been taken to be turned over to the Gibeonites for execution as payment for King Saul's breach of contract."

Rizpah yanked her hands from his grip, ran to the door, and rushed down the corridor, almost tripping over her feet. Amir and Myra ran close behind, calling her name. Tears gushed down her cheeks, clouding her vision. Barely able to catch her breath, she entered the wives' chambers, ignored the crying and wails of despair, and pushed her way to the side exit leading to the rear courtyard.

On reaching the door, she pushed so hard the impact knocked one of the torch lights off the wall. Without hesitation, she ran down the cobblestone path, panting and coughing from the dust. The sounds of horses moving away from the castle made her heart beat so hard, she held one hand to her chest, panting.

"Wait," she screamed as the horses moved farther away. "Wait, please wait. Let me see my sons," she shouted as loudly as she could, but to no avail. The legion of men and their prisoners had already mounted and were far beyond her reach. She gagged and coughed as the dust from the sand reached her lungs. Her knees buckled as she fell to the ground sobbing.

Rizpah felt a firm hand on her shoulders and looked up to see Amir watching with tears flooding his eyes. "I'm sorry, so very sorry."

She put both hands over her face and rocked back and forth. "I know. There's was nothing anyone could do."

Amir lifted Rizpah to her feet and they walked back to the quarters with Myra following. "Where did they go? Where did they take my babies?" She moaned as she collapsed on one of the bedroom chairs and sipped a cup of water to combat the sick feeling in the pit of her stomach.

"They're to be turned over to the Gibeonites to be executed as soon as possible," Amir said, while pacing the floor. They believe their death will bring favor and end the drought."

Rizpah bolted from the chair, ran to the closet, and searched for her satchel. "I have to go to them. I have to be with my babies." She paused and leaned on the doorframe. "Please, don't try to stop me or convince me not to go. I have to be with them to the end."

While rubbing his hands together, Amir cleared his throat. "If you must go, then I will take you."

Myra opened her mouth to protest, but her son gave her a warning look.

"It won't be a long journey to the land of the Gibeonites, but, because we still face poor weather conditions, it will be challenging." He replied. "I must leave now to negotiate the loan of several camels for a few days."

Myra shoulders tensed and she tapped her fingers on the table. "Son." She warned. "I want you to be careful not to get yourself in trouble."

Amir touched his mother's hand. "See if you can prepare some food that will last a few days." He walked to the door, then looked back and smiled. "We can trust no one now. Get some rest, I will come for you when the sun goes down. It will be best to leave here in the early evening when there's less movement." Amir smiled again, then disappeared into the hallway.

"Well, now you've done it," Myra lashed out. "Now, you have my son involved. I hope you're satisfied. She opened the door and, without looking back, stepped into the hall, slamming it shut behind her. Rizpah fell on the bed, covered her face with pillows, and cried herself into an exhausted sleep.

"Wake up please, Rizpah," Myra stood over her friend with a tray of food. "You must get your things ready for the trip. Sit up. Here, I brought you some food."

Rizpah stretched and rubbed her eyes. At first, she didn't recognize the voice calling her out of sleep.

As she set the tray on the table, Myra said, "I'm sorry about my outburst earlier. I was frustrated and scared that, by helping you, I might lose my son. It was so selfish of me. I didn't think about your loss."

After a weak smile, Rizpah said, "No need for apologies. I understand," she replied and patted a space on the bed, making room for her to sit. "Amir discovered where they've taken the young men to be, *huh, uh*, to their final destination." Myra shifted on the bed and brushed her palms together. "The *event* will take place at the sanctuary in Gibeah."

Rizpah breathed deeply, moved the food around the plate, and stared into space. "I feel like I'm living a nightmare and I'm waiting for someone to wake me up."

Myra pulled Rizpah's satchel from the closet. "Let me help you pack since you'll be gone for several days."

"Pack whatever you want. I don't care." Rizpah jump out of bed and walked to the window. "I'm ready for this journey." She held back a sob as her eyes burned. "I need to see my babies, and will be there for them, no matter what."

* * *

Amir and Rizpah left at dawn, reaching Gibeah by noonday. The town was bustling with travelers arriving for the sanctuary event.

"My God," Rizpah shouted, "they act like this is a festival. Look at them!" She waved her arms high above her head. "I can't believe they chose to be here just to watch people be murdered."

"Quiet, please." Amir cautioned. "You must control yourself. We are strangers here and must not do anything to risk a conflict that would inhibit your being with your sons. Our goal is to blend in with the crowd, work our way to the sanctuary, and wait."

Rizpah nodded and allowed Amir to help her dismount. "How will we find the sanctuary?" she asked looking around for some clue to the direction they should follow. Amir took her arm with one hand and the reins of the camels with the other. "Let's walk through the marketplace, listen, and observe."

He looked around them with distaste. "I suspect it won't be difficult to find. The key is that we remain unnoticed, and attract as little attention as possible."

Amir and Rizpah were successful in reaching the sanctuary of Gibeah, but not in time for them to see the seven sons of Saul alive. Several merchants pointed them in the right direction, which made their journey easier, but all suggested the executions may be well over before they arrived. As they rounded the corner leading to the sanctuary, the scenery changed. The cobblestone walk disappeared, replaced by a dirt-filled, sharp-edged winding stone path. At the top of the path was a flat landing carved out of the ledge of a rocky mountain. There, secured in mounds of dirt, were seven crosses of splintered wood with seven men hanging, lifeless.

Rizpah stumbled over several tree stumps, running up the path to the bodies.

After securing the camels, Amir followed with water and food. He found Rizpah sprawled face down on the dirt between both her sons, sobbing and tearing at her clothes.

"They killed my babies," she sobbed. "The dirty, worthless pieces of donkey dung killed my sons." She looked up, wiped her face with her shawl, and dug the sand with her nails. "There's nothing left for me now.

"Look," she screamed, "see how they left them unguarded for the vultures to devour? I could curse King David," she shouted, "do you hear me? I curse the King of Israel for what he's done to me and my sons."

Amir grabbed her around the waist and placed his hand firmly over her mouth. "It does no good for you to create a spectacle that could bring trouble to us both. You must be calm. Grieve if you must, and you should, but remember it would be wise to remember your place."

Rizpah touched Amir's cheek it a gentle stroke. "You have been so good to me. I will never forget your kindness, but you must go now. I have work to do and I must do it alone." She pushed away from his embrace. "I am going to stay and protect the bodies of my babies and these other sons of Saul." She straightened her shoulders and dried her eyes. "If they are to hang here by orders of the king, I will watch over them as a memory of this deed. They will not disappear into the stomachs of the vultures who even now lurk high in the sky."

Amir recoiled and his nostrils flared, as he paced back and forth the length of the sanctuary, kicking dirt and rocks along the way. "You can't be serious. It could be weeks that these bodies will hang here. Where will you sleep, what will you eat? Be reasonable and let me take you home."

"Home? I don't have a home. I lived in a fancy cage in a position that was just above a slave," she responded with a bitter laugh then covered her eyes and sobbed. "Please leave me Amir," she pleaded in between the sobs. "Don't you see? This is my destiny. I will guard my sons, and protect their bodies from harm. Just go."

Several curious observers had gathered below the hill watching their exchange. Amir left Rizpah, went to the bottom of the hill, and pulled one of the camels loaded with water, a small tent, food, and her satchel up the path to the base of the rock with the seven crosses. "I would be lying if I said I agreed with you, or with your decision to stay. You do have a home and a family in Myra and me. Don't ever forget that."

Amir tied the camel to a tree stump and pitched the tent nearby. When finished, he placed her satchel and several sacks of food and containers of water inside. "You're well supplied for at least a week, maybe a little more. After that, you're in danger of starving."

Rizpah avoided Amir's eyes. "Thank you. Thank you for everything. I will never forget your kindness."

Amir didn't acknowledge the comment. "I will stay here the night, Rizpah," he cautioned, "but must leave in the morning to return home. I still have duties there." He cleared his throat and scratched his head. "I guess there isn't much else for me to say. You are dead set on this mission, so I guess I have to accept the decision and move on."

Rizpah only heard half his comment. Focused on her assignment, she grabbed her shawl, rushed to the far end of the path, and chased a vulture that had perched on one of the crosses. Amir shook his head and concentrated on building a fire for the evening.

Rizpah awoke to the sun streaming through the small openings of her tent. She stretched a bit, hesitating to move while listening to the breeze hitting the sides of the tent. Her throat tightened as she remembered her sons hung on the cross. *I will never hear their voice, enjoy their company, or hold them again. My God, my God, this is more than I can bear. Please give me the strength to bear this pain.*

The previous evening, after securing supplies, Amir said goodnight and made his bed near the campfire to ensure night beasts kept their distance. Affection glowed in her eyes. She smiled at the thought of his care and kindness.

"Amir," she called. "I bet you didn't know I do my best cooking over an open fire." Without waiting for a response, she rose, folded the covers, and brushed and tied her hair. "Hey, are you awake? Did you hear me? I'm going to fix you the best outdoor meal you've ever had," she laughed.

A soft breeze hit the tent, moving the canvas flap at its opening. She grabbed a clean cloth from her satchel, wet it with water from the pouch hanging nearby, and washed her face. Convinced she had tidied herself enough to be presentable, she left the tent to prepare Amir's meal. As she stepped through the opening, she looked at the smoldering wood of the campfire. To her surprise, the space was empty. She was alone.

Rizpah bit her lip, squeezed her eyes shut, and breathed deep. Amir had gone without saying a word, leaving her with one of the camels. She walked from one end of the sanctuary to the other, hoping this was a temporary condition, and found additional supplies stored out of sight. He had even gathered a stockpile of wood she could use to build fires for several days. Rizpah scanned the area then sat on a rock as tears filled her eyes. *He didn't even say goodbye.* After a moment of feeling sorry for herself, she lifted her chin. *Shake yourself girl, have courage, he got you here. Stay focused. You've got work to do.*

Rizpah had no time to dwell on her feelings. Two vultures had already perched on one of crosses. She grabbed her shawl and rushed forward, waving the cloth and shouting. The birds hesitated, then flew away. Panting, she sat at the base of the crosses, watching and waiting. This was the beginning of her assignment for many days to come.

CHAPTER 12

Weeks passed with Rizpah maintaining vigilance over the bodies, as promised. Day after day she awoke earlier, refreshed her body, and took her position in front of the seven crosses. Her nights were not peaceful. She was no longer able to sleep in the tent, because wolves and stray dogs began to congregate just below the ridge where she kept watch over her sons and the other sons of Saul. Only staying awake and vigilant, and maintaining the fires at night, kept the animals away.

Many people came out of their way to pass by. Some asked her what she was doing and why. Others brought food, water, and even wood for the fire. Early one evening, just before sunset, she observed a man standing in the shadows. Rizpah, having already gathered wood for the daily fire paused, adjusted her clothing, and descended from the rock. She approached the stranger, carrying the sturdy piece of wood she had been using for protection against the stray animals. Before she was halfway to her goal, the man stepped forward and raised both hands. "I mean you no harm. My king sent me to inquire of your well-being."

Rizpah stopped, clutched her throat, and took two steps back. "Your king? Who is your king and why is he seeking after my well-being?" The man came closer as he spoke. "There's been talk in the region about your living here, protecting the bodies of these men from various beasts and birds of prey for several months. You are to be admired."

The man cleared his throat, reached under his robe, and withdrew a small pouch. Then, he extended his hand toward her in slow motion. "Here are several coins to cover any needs you may have during the remainder of your stay. I sent my men for supplies to replenish your food and water. They should be here shortly."

Rizpah smiled but rejected the offer. "I didn't do this to be admired," she responded, pinning him with her eyes.

"Look, up there," she pointed. "My sons, my only family, are hanging over there." Sweat beaded her forehead as she stepped closer, swinging her stick. "I will never hear them call me mom, yet, every day and every night I am here and will be here to ensure they are not devoured and defiled by beasts of the air or land."

She surveyed the area, then gave the stranger a side-eyed glance. "Yes, keep your gold. I appreciate the offer. Thank you, and thank your king, but God has kept me thus far. He will take me the rest of the way or," she stared him in the eyes, "I will join them."

Without another word, she turned and climbed back onto the rock to stroke the fires around the men slumped forward on their cross.

Once again, she kept the night beasts away.

For four months Rizpah continued her vigil over the dead bodies. Though several people checked on her periodically, only one person brought supplies during his visits to check on her. "You are so kind," she offered while accepting her latest package. "With the drought and shortage of food, your sacrifice is so very much appreciated."

The old man smiled, shifted his feet, and nodded. He started down the hill, then stopped. "It isn't me," he mumbled. "I haven't supplied the food these many months." He rubbed his chin then continued. "A young man travels here, I don't know where he's from, but he always arrives with coins or supplies. Says he wants them brought to you." The old man looked at the ground, and, kicked a few stones from the path. "He pays me to do this for him. I wish I could do it myself but I'm a poor man of little means, you see."

Rizpah approached the old man and touched him on the shoulder. "Thank you for making these deliveries."

He nodded and continued down the path.

She followed him until he was out of sight. Night had fallen, and a stronger than usual breeze traveled across the sanctuary. She noticed it was cooler than usual. Rizpah wrapped herself snugly in her travel robe and shawl then curled up under the ridge of the rock to block the splinters of sand from her face. She remained close enough to watch any vicious beast that attempted to come closer.

It must have been Amir keeping me supplied. He's come here all this time, but never once to visit. It makes no sense. Why did he not want to see me?

Several more weeks passed until she reached the end of a five-month mission. Rizpah had lost much weight, but her spirits remained high. After a longer than usual night in the elements, she decided to spend the early morning in the tent. There was little remaining of the bodies, so the vultures had long since given up.

Rizpah performed her morning routine to refresh her body, prepare a quick meal, then smoothed the covers on her makeshift bed, and lay down. Moments into her rest, the ground trembled so hard, her body shook. She jumped to her feet, grabbed the shawl and stick, and rushed to the tent entrance. Overwhelmed at the sight that met her, she took a step back, put both hands to her face, and gasped. At least twenty horsemen and two chariots were gathered at the base of the rock. Two of the soldiers dismounted and approached, followed by another man whose face was only too familiar.

"Amir," she screamed and ran down the hill into his arms. "I can't believe it. You're here. I can't believe it." He held her tight, then kissed her cheeks so hard, she pulled back breathless and laughing. "Who are these men? Why are you here?"

The lead soldier, ignoring their embrace, stepped forward. "We have been sent by King David to retrieve what remains of the bodies of these men and take them for proper burial in Zelah, to rest with the remains of Jonathan and King Saul."

Overwhelmed with gratitude and relief, Rizpah fell to her knees, too weak to respond, and covered her eyes with her hands. "My babies," she wailed, "my babies will finally receive their proper burial. Thank God for His grace and mercy."

Amir prepared a meal and helped Rizpah gather her things, then for the next few hours, she watched as the remains of her sons and the other sons of Saul were removed for delivery to their final resting place.

When the task was completed, she stood below the rock and watched the soldiers leave, her heart heavy with grief. "It is done. My babies will be laid to rest with the dignity they deserve."

Amir hugged her close and nodded. "You, my sweet, have been a faithful mother." She searched his eyes. "Can we go to Zelah? I want to see where they will be placed."

He nodded, then laughed. "We will go."

When evening approached and the troops long gone, only Amir and Rizpah remained. The wind increased and they noticed dark clouds gathering. The old man, who brought supplies during her stay, approached and offered his home for them to rest overnight before their journey. "I don't have the best accommodations, but it will keep you well protected. See," he pointed with a smile, "looks like it's going to rain."

Amir and Rizpah rushed to finish loading her belonging, lodged the camels for the night, and hurried to their guest lodging. Already hit with several drops of rain, they reached their destination just in time. As soon as they entered the home and closed the door, the sky opened and rain pelted the earth.

"The drought has ended," the old man shouted, then laughed. He danced about the room with his wife on his arm. Amir followed Rizpah to the window. "The rain will wash away all evidence of my time on the rock," she whispered.

Amir opened the shutters to let some of the raindrops touch their faces. "The rain will also bring forth new growth of a new day and we will see this together." Rizpah rested her head on his shoulders and they watched the rain in silence.

The next morning, they said their goodbyes and journeyed to Zelah where they visited the burial site of Saul and her sons. During their brief stay, they were approached by the king's representative with a parchment scroll that had been prepared for each of them. When Amir and Rizpah opened them, the decree informed them that they had been released from their commitment and responsibilities, and were free to live as they pleased. Amir had an additional surprise, as his mother had also received the same royal decree from the king in recognition for their loyalty in service.

In the weeks that followed, Amir and Rizpah joined Myra and, with a small financial recompense from the king, started their new life as a family.

COMMENTARY

A concubine, from a biblical perspective, was a woman whose main purpose was to bear children. Not married in the traditional sense, she was considered a step above a slave. Wealthy men often acquired these women when their wives were barren (unable to have children), or to increase the family's workforce while, at the same time, satisfying the man's sexual desires. As a concubine, Rizpah became the mother of two of King Saul's sons, with the expectation that she would follow the same path of servitude. Her story, however, took a different turn at the death of her sons—a death that took place to avenge the wrongs of their father.

The twist in this story is the fact that King David, after becoming aware of her faithfulness and tenacity in protecting the bodies of the dead for such a long period, responded to her act of loyalty and ensured the remains of these men received proper burial. Her story, outlined in 2 Samuel 3:7-1 suggests (though still argued) she slept with Saul's cousin, Abner, after Saul's death, thereby creating a division in the family so that one member transferred loyalty to the enemy, only to eventually lose his own life.

Rizpah was a survivor who learned to make the best of her situation. When her sons were taken, she decided to make a bold step, the results of which ensured that all the young men—her two sons and five other sons of Saul—received the proper respect and dignity due them at their death. There is no discussion of what life was like for this strong woman after this incident, but this story is one worth remembering.

STORY THREE: DELILAH: THE WOMAN WHO CONQUERED SAMSON

CHAPTER 13

A warm breeze moved along the expansive one-story, beige, and brown cobblestone building in the Valley of Sorek. Located near the channel brook waters, this land separated Judah from Philistine. Known primarily for its vines, beautiful vegetation surrounded the home on a hill overlooking miles of lush greenery.

Steffi, a trusted handmaid for many years, carried the basket of grapes, melons, berries, and sliced apples to the veranda for her mistress and several friends sunning by the pool. She joined two other servants pouring wine and serving from platters of cheese and fresh baked bread.

Delilah lounged on her favorite goat skin lounge chair, soaking in the sun, while the warm breeze brushed the sheer material covering her skin. Her long slender legs, still wet from the recent dip in the pool, glistened from the oil, specially prepared to protect her body from the sun. "You're heading where and with who?" She shouted to her brother as she shook her curly black hair of excess water. With an angry gaze, she swung her legs to one side of the lounge chair and sat straight. "We had an agreement that when you planned a journey out of the area, you'd prepare me in advance. Instead, you're standing there, last minute, with your satchel packed ready for an overnight excursion with your guys to Philistine."

Jared rolled his eyes skyward. "You really must relax, Sis. Remember, I'm your younger brother, not your child. Besides, you worry too much, he said with a chuckle."

One of Delilah's friends, joined the conversation. "Hey girl," she chided. "Let him live a little. It's just one night. He'll be back." She threw Jared a sideways glance and laughed. "He always comes back." This time everyone laughed.

Delilah ignored the comment, shrugged, grabbed the jar of oil, and tossed it to her brother. "Here," she commanded with a half-laugh. "Before you leave, rub my back and tell me again why you're heading to the festivities across the river."

Jared grabbed his satchel and tossed the jar in her lap. He gave her a quick kiss and whispered, "get one of your girls to oil your back baby girl. I'm meeting the guys and heading across the river. There's a lot going on, including a big wedding celebration, and I don't want to miss the festivities."

He strolled across the patio to the steps. "If it is as good as they say, you may not see me until mid-afternoon tomorrow, since might be too late, or I might be too drunk," he chuckled, "to head back tonight."

Delilah stretched, raised a brow, and cocked her head to one side. "So, you're chasing the pretty women again," she teased. "Our local girls aren't good enough, uh?" She pulled her hair back exposing long lashes, and arched brows accenting hazel brown eyes and paused, a looked of concern on her face.

"Okay," she said with brows knitted in a frown. "Just make sure you're back here in time for my birthday party tomorrow evening," she winked. "And don't think I don't know your journey also includes last minute shopping for my gift, she smiled."

Jared paused, looked over his shoulder, frowned, then blew her a kiss. "See you sometime tomorrow, Sis."

Delilah forced a smile, waved, and watched him walk down the path out of sight. She's never been happy when he explores territories beyond their borders, and she wasn't pleased with his choice of friends. Since their parents' death, Jared was her only family. At twenty-seven, she was only five years his senior, but she became his self-identified mother figure. She sighed. *I should have made him promise to return home tonight.*

* * *

Samson, a tall, stately-looking man, towered over the men helping him dress for the wedding ceremony. His skin glistened over the well-proportioned muscular physic that could not be compared to any man in the region. His massive hands grabbed yet another goblet of wine that he guzzled without pause, while his groomsmen worked to get him dressed before he was too drunk to stand.

"Man," one of his groomsmen commented. "If you don't slow the drinking, you're going to need one of us to flank you to get down the aisle."

Samson belched then laughed, his voice booming so loud several guests in the outer court jumped from the vibration.

"My condition doesn't matter; this little girl will be happy to take me no matter what. You see, I'm her, Samson." The men shook their heads but didn't speak.

Helping him dress, one of the attendants straighten his collar and smooth his hair.

Samson grabbed the man's hand firmly and leveled a glowering look. "Only I touch the hair," he scowled and pushed him aside. "Enough. I'm done with this preparation and bored with this event. I already *dipped in the pool* of her luscious body," he said with a laugh. "Now I've got to play this game of marriage to save face for her and please the family." No sooner had he finished the statement, his betroths' father appeared at the entrance and overheard the comment.

"My daughter is ready, Sir, the father snapped. It is not by my choice that you marry, but I expect your decency in this situation."

The room was quiet. Samson stood and stretched, wine goblet in hand. He did not acknowledge his future father-in-law until he had taken a long drink. After a belch, he smiled. "Your daughter will be my wife this day. I promised you and her this would be so. However, it is your daughter who benefits from this union. I think you know she's aware of this fact." Samson threw the goblet to the floor, massaged his hands and gritted his teeth. "Though I will give respect as my wife, she will learn to live the life I choose for her. She will follow me and benefit from my presence."

The father of the bride stepped forward; his eyes glazed with anger.

"There are no words to describe how arrogant and self-absorbed any one single person could be. It is incredible to listen how you plan for my daughter to serve your needs, how grateful she should be as *your wife*, and the needs she will fulfill *for you*." Throwing the endowment to the floor, the bride's father squeezed his fist and narrowed his eyes. "I came here to give you the promised exchange to complete the monetary transition of my daughter as your wife. You don't deserve this offering or my daughter, but let it be so." Without another word, the father turned, brushed past the groomsmen, and left the tent.

Samson chuckled, smoothed his hair, grabbed another wine goblet, then turned to the groomsmen. "Wow! What an emotional man." He grabbed his vest, walked to the exit, turned, and grinned. "Let us go get me married, shall we?"

When he arrived, the guests were seated and waiting. Samson stepped into place, and the ceremonies began. His bride and her father entered and walked down the aisle. Samson affected, by the wine, leaned to one side but was righted by a groomsman. Adjusting, he slapped his knee and stood firm.

The bride moved slow, almost gliding, as she approached the man who would be her husband. With only a few steps left to the altar, she paused, and faced Samson. The crowd gasped in shock, then mumbled as she waved her father to be seated then stood in silence. Her father remained seated in place, rigid and unsmiling. After several moments, the guest whispered and chuckled. Sampson frowned, shifted from side to side, and adjusted his attire.

The priest cleared his throat and stepped forward to compensate the distance between the couple and began the ceremonies.

Suddenly, the bride threw her bouquet at Samson's feet, and lifted her veil. "No need to continue," she announced and stepped closer Samson, arms crossed eyes glazed with anger, and lips curled. "Look at you," she smirked. "You are one poor excuse for a man, and the funny thing is you don't even know it." She faced the guests and she announced, "there will be no wedding ceremony here today. I made a mistake. I thought I would marry a man of quality but found that he was just a tall, muscular body, with empty heart and head."

The bride brushed her palms together as if removing dirt. "This man," she said over her shoulder while pointing at Samson, "can lift boulders, destroy ferocious animals, and overpower men in a fight. What a pity he has no clue what it means to be a man with dignity and respect for others."

The bride turned her back to Samson, faced the crowd, jerked her thumb in his direction, and laughed. "I wouldn't marry this man if he crawled before me on his hands and knees and begged my forgiveness for his unruly behavior and arrogant blow-hard attitude."

The audience roared with laughter. The bride continued her tirade for several minutes, throwing insults at the thought of marrying him.

Samson, still under the heavy influence of wine, and outraged at the insults, trembled with fury.

* * *

Delilah's brother and friends arrived in Philistine to revelry from several events occurring at the same time. The massive crowds that greeted them were boisterous, lively, and drunk of wine. They spent most of the evening moving from one celebration event to another, eating and drinking, flirting, and dancing. Strolling through the marketplace, one of the local displays caught Jared's attention. "Hey, stop a minute," he shouted before stepping into the merchant's stall. "Delilah will like this," he said, reaching for a long red silk scarf with fine gold floral design.

His friend laughed, "Yeh, you can add that to the ruby studded ring you bought her earlier today. Everything must match, right?"

Jared nodded. "Yep, my sister coordinates everything and it must be top quality." Jared handed the items to the merchant. "Take care to wrap this securely. It won't due for me to lose these gifts on the way home," he laughed then glanced toward the center of town. The sun was setting over the horizon shining over thousands of people, primarily men, in the congested street. The path to the road leading home was a short distance away. He turned to his buddies with a slight smile.

"Let's head home, guys. We had a full day. If we start now, I'll be sure to arrive early in the morning in time to get some sleep before Delilah's birthday celebration. You know she likes to celebrate big, and there'll be plenty of girls for more fun."

Two of his buddies, who resisted the idea of leaving, waved goodbye and entered another tavern. Jared and the remaining companion started for Sorek, moving through the congested marketplace, toward the road home. Smiling, eyes focused on the road ahead, Jared hugged his satchel close and pushed through the throng, knowing he had one of the best surprises for his sister.

Samson continued listening to the rantings and insults of the woman who was to be his betrothed. The crowd's roar of laughter grew louder and louder. Though very quiet, his eyes were glazed with anger. Without warning, he bolted across the aisle, and lifted and threw the bride's father across the room. With a scowl he rushed down the aisle. Throwing a menacing glare at his nearest groomsmen, he shouted "stand clear."

Pushing past guests and knocking over empty chairs, he noticed a man standing at the temple exit grinning. With a loud shout, he grabbed the man by the throat, broke his neck, then threw the body into the crowd. The horrified guests screamed and piled on top of each other trying to avoid his wrath.

Several men managed to escape through the side exit, but those who couldn't avoid his reach met violent death at the hands of an enraged rejected groom. Samson glanced one final time at the altar before leaving the tent and saw the woman who rejected him. She had dropped to her knees, crying uncontrollably over the body of her dead father.

Despite the carnage left behind at the wedding ceremony, Samson's anger was not quenched. He exited the temple grabbing every man he could find, killing them on the spot. Between the men he encountered inside the temple and the marketplace, Samson's rage led him to kill 1,000 Philistines in the town and on the road beyond the area. The townspeople were devastated.

Samson, turned his back on the scene. The only sounds were screams of pain from people left behind to rebuild their lives after the horrendous tragedy brought upon them by one man enraged because he had been insulted and embarrassed at a wedding.

Delilah placed fresh flowers on the patio table to accent decorations for her birthday celebration. Scheduled to begin within a few hours, she rechecked the tables, and ensured robes and drying cloth were accessible near the pool. For a brief moment, she paused and gazed at the road near the courtyard where her brother would appear on his return from Philistine.

Steffi observed her movements for several moments before speaking. "You know our Jared, ma'am. He'll be late, but he always comes home."

Delilah acknowledged her comment with a frown, then inspected the side tables. "I'm not entirely convinced my dear brother didn't end his travel and celebration in a drunken stupor, she responded. With a flash of anger, she shoved one of the chairs aside. "He's probably curled in the corner of a local tavern recuperating."

Steffi looked beyond her mistress, distracted by movement on the road. "Look. She shouted. "Someone's coming down the road, and he's walking very slow."

Delilah followed the direction her maid pointed. The man was too far to recognize facial features clearly, but Delilah studied his height and movements well enough to determine it was not her brother. The man limped along the road, pausing every few steps, while dragging a satchel. The more he walked the more pronounced his limp. Suddenly, he stumbled, grasped a tree trunk, the slid to the ground. Delilah dropped a linen bundle she was holding and lunged forward.

"Hurry, he needs help. Get a pail of water and cloths," she shouted over her shoulder. Pushing another maid toward the house, she pumped her fist in the air, "prepare a plate of food and bring some goat milk. Move!" She snapped, and continued toward the man on the road with two other maids running behind. Within a short distance, Delilah realized the young man was one of her brother's friends who traveled with him to the Philistine celebrations. He beckoned her with his free arm. In the other, he dragged a satchel.

"Help me," he said in a weak voice. "My name is Aaron. I'm Jared's friend. I need help."

The maids arrived and assisted him down the road to one of the patio chairs. Steffi sat next to him offering water and food, while the other maids cleaned his wounds.

"Tell us what happened, please," Delilah interrupted. Where is my brother?"

Aaron fell silent, a look of sorrow and pity crossed his face. "It was awful," he shouted, then crossed his arms across his chest and rocked back and forth. "So much screaming and shouting, and this man wielding a sword." He covered his eyes. Bodies dropping everywhere," he wailed. "He killed everyone in his path." The young man leaned forward, shook his head then looked at Delilah, speaking in a low soft voice. "He killed Jared."

Steffi groaned. Delilah jumped to her feet, lurched forward as if to run, then whirled around and faced the frightened young man withering in pain. She spread her hands wide, then made a steeple of her fingers. "What are you saying? She said in a low voice as a flash of anger shot through her. "Who killed Jared and why?"

Aaron cringed and responded with a quiver. "I'm unsure," he hesitated. I caught only a glimpse of him, but I heard his voice," he shuddered. "As he approached, everyone dropped in a pool of blood as the man with the sword slashed through the crowd. We tried to get out of the way, but there was nowhere to hide. There were too many people. We were like sheep in a corral--no way out." He looked around as party guests had begun to arrive for the birthday celebration.

Delilah ignored their presence while the maids seated them on nearby chairs.

Steffi approached and offered to take the young man to another area. "Madame, perhaps we should move Aaron to the side room," she whispered.

"No!" Delilah shouted. "Leave him here. Everyone needs to hear this story. Bring more covering and make him comfortable," she commanded and returned her attention Jared's friend.

"Please finish," she said gently. I must know every detail."

Aaron looked around, visibly distraught but continued his story. "While running from this madman, I felt a hard shove on my shoulder. I'm not sure, but I think it was Jared who pushed me forward." His eyes filled with tears. "I fell into one of the merchant stalls and crashed onto one of the tent posts. Everything caved around me. It may have been one of the posts that fell and knocked me out. I awoke early morning to sounds of women wailing and screaming." He wiped his eyes and trembled. "Someone helped me up, and that's when I saw Jared lying face down, several feet away, in a pool of blood. His body slashed several times, it was clear he was dead."

Steffi sobbed, and several of the party guests gasped. Delilah sat motionless for several seconds. Then, with slow, deliberate movement extended her index finger towards the young man.

"Who did it?" She said in a threatening tone. Who killed my brother?"

Aaron hesitated, then responded. "I can't be sure. They say it was the Nazarite Samson. They say he killed everyone in sight because of anger at what happened to him at the wedding event. It seems, when the girl refused to marry him, he decided everyone in the area was going to pay with their lives."

Trembling, Aaron put his face in his hands. "It was horrible."

Delilah, sank in the lounge chair, covered her face, and sobbed. Several guests surrounded and attempted to console her but to no avail.

After a few moments, Steffi interrupted and encouraged the guests to leave. "There will be no birthday celebration event today," she announced while pointing to the exit. "She needs time alone." With firm grip, Steffi lifted her from the chair and moved to the house entrance.

Before leaving, Delilah turned her attention to the weary young man, smiled, then directed the other maids to care for him. "Please, take him to one of the guest rooms and tend to his wounds," she whispered then dropped her head.

Aaron looked up. "I'm so sorry all this happened, he whispered," and reached for the satchel. He withdrew a small package and explained its contents. "Please receive this package," he announced trembling. "It's the gift your brother bought for your birthday. There was a ring, but I lost it somewhere."

Delilah stared at the package then placed both palms on her forehead, and fainted.

CHAPTER 14

S everal weeks passed since Delilah heard the news of her brother's death at the hands of the Nazarite Samson. Her attendants searched but could not find his body for days, because of the enormous number of body parts intermingled throughout and around the town. When finally discovered and returned home, he was buried in a plot of land near the house.

Delilah camped out near the site for days in mourning. During her grieving period, the maids were instructed to light candles and place them throughout the house, with orders that they remain lit until further notice. If not at the gravesite she retreated to her room, leaving only to sit on her private balcony overlooking the lush vegetation, the river, and the plot of land that now housed the body of her dead brother.

Shara entered her friends' home and was greeted by Steffi, holding a tray of untouched food she removed from Delilah's room. "Welcome, madame. So glad to see you again."

Steffi frowned and gazed at the staircase leading to the bedrooms. "Come," she waved. Holding the food tray, she escorted Shara to Delilah's suite. They climbed two short steps to the next level and walked the long corridor. "I'm very worried." Steffi continued. "She's in a very bad way. I have never seen her this depressed," she said, lip quivering. "I bring food three times a day that is barely touched." Steffi touched Shara's arm to slow their pace. "I'm afraid she's shut out the world, and withdrawn from all those connected with her. It's like she died with Jared, and all we need to do now is dig the grave next to him. Perhaps with you here she'll eat and things will be better."

Delilah opened her eyes, sat straight up in bed, and listened. In the quiet of the morning, she thought she heard Jared's voice beyond the balcony. Throwing covers aside, she jumped out of bed, and swung balcony doors open. In the silence, to her dismay, she realized it was only a dream. Disappointed, she dropped her head and returned to bed, pulling the covers close.

The early morning sunlight streamed through the large windows illuminating the brilliant color of her lamb skin chairs, and table decorated in stained glass and chipped stone. Her canopy white and blue sheer bed drapes moved gently from the soft warm breeze.

Shifting position, she laid flat on her back and gazed at the intricate designs on the canopy over her bed that Jared had directed constructing. Delilah chuckled when she saw the nicks and rugged areas, he promised workmen would repair before her birthday celebration. Her thoughts drifted as she recalled the unhappy events surrounding his death, and details about this stranger who killed her brother. Tears welled in her eyes. She covered her face with the bed pillow and wept. *I shouldn't have let him go.*

* * *

Shara and Steffi paused outside Delilah's bedroom door, glanced at each other with tight-lipped smiles. With a deep breath, Shara stepped forward, knocked, and walked in.

"Hey girl, aren't you awake yet?

Receiving no response, Shara waved Steffi forward to set up the tray, while she walked to the bed.

"Come on, sweetie. You have to get up now. It's time to face the new day and move on with your life. Jared would not want you to lie down and give up. Not the way he lived."

Delilah turned on her side, back to her friend, and curled in a fetal position. "I know you mean well, Shara, but go away. I don't want to hear this."

Shara ignored the response, sat on the edge of the bed, and smoothed the bedclothing using slow circular motions with the flat of her hand.

"Okay, so you don't want to hear about moving on with your life," she responded and hunched her shoulders. "Well then, do you want to hear the rumors about of plans to revenge for what happened to your brother and the 1,000 other Philistines who died that day?"

No response.

Shara crossed her legs and eyed her friend with concern. "Okay," she said with a shrug. "You can lie there and wallow in self-pity or join me, and others, to work on a plan to persecute this Nazarite for his evil deeds."

Delilah turned, sat up, grabbed several pillows, and leaned on the backboard. Her faint smile turned to a smirk. "Tell me more."

Steffi chuckled and moved forward with the tray loaded with bread, lamb, mixed vegetables, chicory, orange slices, and grapes. Laughing, almost giddy, she interrupted the conversation.

"Ma'am, you need a good meal before you start planning an act of revenge. Eat this, and let me draw a warm bath with your special oils."

Delilah acknowledged her maid with a nod and faint smile, selected several food items, then responded to Shara. "So, who's joining us in the plot against the man who killed my brother?"

Shifting position Shara smiled, grabbed one of the dried figs from her friend's tray and reviewed details of a brief meeting with several men from Philistine.

"It seems this Nazarite is one arrogant son of a pig's behind. He is stronger than any man alive, at least in this region. His weakness, however, is wine and women. He's a glutton for both."

Shara stood, stretched, adjusted her dress and walked to the balcony entrance.

"The night of Jared's death," she said with caution, "seems this Samson fellow was insulted by his bride-to-be. During the ceremony, she embarrassed him in front of the guest, ending with her refusal to marry him. It angered him so much that he went on a rampage, killing her father and other men at the ceremony."

Swallowing hard, she continued.

"This man Samson then left the wedding ceremony and entered a killing spree that included Jared," she exclaimed, fighting back tears. "There was no legitimate reason except he was drunk, embarrassed, and angry."

Shara sat next to Delilah, cut a slice of lamb and fed her friend. "Don't try to make sense of any of this. Eat. You will need your strength now more than ever. We have work to do."

She leaned close and lowered her voice.

"There's a meeting tonight. Several men approached me about speaking with you, and I invited them to the house. They learned of your loss and decided you were the best choice to assist in this plan." Shara walked to the closet, selected several dresses, layed across the bed.

"You don't live in Philistine, so the man Samson would not be suspicious of reprisals. It seems, despite the incident, he still frequents the area."

Remembering Steffi' presence, Shara rolled her eyes skyward, her expression sobered. "Enough said. I think it best we continue this conversation in private, once the representatives arrive. They want to discuss their plan in person. This select group must remain known only to those involved."

Steffi huffed and stepped forward.

"Surely the meeting includes me. I've always been part of my lady's plans."

Shara ignored the comment, and pulled several pairs of sandals from the closet. "Samson is a powerful warrior with supernatural strength, so the approach to his destruction must be planned in secret." Shara paused and glanced sideways. "They only want to know are you in?"

Delilah agreed to the meeting with Philistine representatives. Shara left to dictate reception details with staff leaving her friend with renewed strength, fueled by her eagerness for revenge.

"What do you think of this outfit," Steffi said while pulling *her* choice of attire from the closet. "You have several matching scarfs for this one."

Before Delilah could respond, Steffi rushed to the closet and returned with several sandals to match the outfit she chose.

"This a better choice than the ones Shara selected."

With hair in place and makeup perfected, Delilah approached her maid and smiled.

"You pick the outfit. I trust your choice. I'll select the arm jewelry and necklace to accent your choice, but let's hurry. I want to be in the guest area before the representatives arrive. I don't want to keep them waiting. This is an important meeting."

Delilah paused and touched Steffi's hand. "Thank you for your faithfulness. I couldn't have made it these last few weeks without you, but I am about to enter a dangerous zone, and you can't be part of it. If this man is as evil as he sounds, the only end to any plan is his death or mine. No one in this household can know what I am about to do. That way, should I fail, no one will be hurt but me."

Steffi opened her mouth to protest, but Delilah raised her hand for silence.

"This night, I need you to ensure the servants are kept busy, away from our meeting area." Steffi dropped her head and grunted disapproval.

Delilah took both hands and lifted her maid's chin.

"There must be no opportunity for anyone in the household to overhear any of these discussions. I don't even want them to see the men when they visit. I must assess the situation, the people, and ensure it's safe."

She jerked her thumb toward the door.

"Now, take the food tray down to the kitchen and check that the meeting room was prepared with fruit trays and wine as I directed. Shara and I will greet them on arrival."

Steffi's expression turned grim. She picked up the tray, nodded then left the room.

* * *

Delilah entered the guest receiving room, scanned the area, and smiled. The center table was decorated with three large white candles mounted on shiny brass holders that belonged to her mother. The sideboard, draped in white linen, included platters of cheese, dried fruit, and grapes, complimented with flasks of wine.

"Well, I'd say we're ready." She chuckled and waved at Shara. "Let's sit on the veranda. We can observe their arrival from that vantage point."

Shara breathed a sigh of relief. "It's good to see you smile, my friend."

As soon as they reached the entrance to the courtyard, Steffi rushed from behind shouting. "Ma'am, the men are coming. I was checking to make sure the courtyard was in order. I saw them," she stammered, "but they didn't see me." Avoiding the look of disapproval from her mistress, she bowed quickly and rushed from the room.

Delilah and Shara waited at the entrance and watched as five men in hooded travel garb approached, each carrying large satchels. As they neared the entrance, Delilah nudged her friend and whispered. "Look, see how they walk? These men aren't simple messengers, field workers or servants. These are soldiers or, at the least, high-ranking leaders."

The strangers noticed the women in the courtyard and approached. Without prompting, they bowed in unison, then the tallest representative stepped forward.

"I am Cobal." he offered while pointing to other members of the group. We represent five kings from Philistine and seek the one called Delilah."

Delilah stepped forward, "I am the one you seek, she responded and stepped back from the entrance. "Welcome. Please enter," she smiled.

After a few moments sharing fruit, bread, and wine, the group settled around the meeting table in the guest area. Cobal, cleared his throat, and addressed Delilah. "My companions and I each represent one of the five kings of Philistine. We are here with a challenge and a plan. A powerful enemy attacked our people and he must be apprehended and destroyed as soon as possible."

Delilah leaned forward, raised her hand and, using her index finger, counted each man at the table. She responded in a flat tone of voice. "With five kings represented at this meeting, each with military support, why don't you draw up a plan and destroy him?"

Cobal lifted his shoulder in a half shrug.

"He's no ordinary man, as you may have heard." The other men nodded, with somber looks.

Cobal tapped his fingers on the table. "We are here to request you join us in the plan we have to assassinate the Nazarite. He has unusual powers but one weakness. Beautiful women easily sway him." He leaned forward. "Your reputation not only for beauty but strength and intelligence is well-known in the region."

Delilah stood, walked to the side board, picked up a fig from the food tray with one hand, placed her other hand on one hip, and glared at the leader.

He held her gaze. Her eyes soften.

"Your charm, and mastery of entertainment, Delilah, are also recognized and can be very useful to us. We plan to ensure, through well planned strategies, this Nazarite learns of your reputation and beauty, becomes curious, and seeks you out."

Delilah sighed, closed her eyes, and smiled but didn't speak.

The visitors looked at one another then reached for their satchels. One by one, they pulled jewelry, silk, gold and silver trinkets, and expensive oils from their packages and laid them on the table. Cobal stood and pointed to the items.

"These are gifts for you with more to come. We have cattle, sheep, and food supplies to be delivered within the next few days, all as gifts for you to store, use, and share as you please."

Cobal spread his arms wide. "In addition to all you see here and the supplies promised, each of our kings has committed 1100 pieces of silver. There are five of us which means, for your efforts, you gain 5500 pieces of silver to do with as you please."

Shara, who had been quiet throughout the discussion, jumped from her seat and grabbed the wine flask. "Anyone for more wine," she chirped.

While the other representatives continued to pile the table with gifts, Cobal approached Delilah and touched her shoulder.

"The silver is our pledge when you discover the secret of his strength," he announced. "You are our secret weapon." Cobal smiled. "Details are set and your temporary home in Philistine secured. You will be a rich relative visiting on an extended stay while completing business in Philistine."

He took both her hands in his. "Do this, Delilah, and we will do the rest."

She slid him a guarded look, then nodded in agreement.

CHAPTER 15

It had been several weeks since the Philistine representatives visited. Before their departure, Delilah negotiated additional gifts and promises, including a massive extension to her home. Agreements in place, it was now time to prepare for her journey.

"Ma'am, what do you mean," Steffi said as she pressed her hands to her cheeks. "You want me to pack your things for a trip to the town of death?"

Delilah tossed several dresses on the bed then glared at her trusted servant.

"Steffi, for goodness' sake, be still. You were given orders to stay with the other servants during my meeting, but instead, chose to sneak and listen."

Delilah narrowed her eyes and clenched her jaw. "That was a private meeting, and you disobeyed my orders." She crossed her arms over her chest. "Now you challenge my decisions

Steffi bowed her head and whimpered. "I just wanted to be around in case you needed me. These were strangers from that evil town that took master Jared. I didn't want them to take you too."

Delilah put her arms around the old servant and hugged tight. "I appreciate you," she whispered, but dangerous times are ahead for us. I need assurance you will obey my orders, no matter what you think may happen in the future. My life may depend on your obedience." She tilted her servant's chin and studied her face with piercing scrutiny. "Do you understand?" She said in a soft, soothing tone.

Steffi wiped her eyes and nodded.

Shara, who had been rummaging through the closet, grabbed several other tunics and shawls and dropped them on the bed. She walked to Delilah's dressing table and gathered several necklaces, earrings, wrist bracelets, rings and pendants. Arms full, she searched for assistance.

"Steffi, please find another satchel. She may be gone for several weeks."

Steffi bowed and walked to the door.

"Wait!" Delilah shouted, then her throat thickened with sobs. "Check Jared's closet. I want to take one of his satchels with me. The one with the long gold tassel."

Steffi flinched, gave Shara a side glance, then left the room.

Shara flopped on the cushion chair, scanned the bed full of clothes and bit her bottom lip.

"I hope Steffi can handle what's coming. Secrecy is essential. If this man Samson discovers the plan, we're all dead. He has a bad temper and resolves issues by eliminating the enemy. If she shares any information, other servants may talk. That could be a disastrous.

Delilah gazed at the door.

"She'll be fine. I trust her with my life." She crossed her arms and tilted her head.

"I will definitely leave her here, however. This is her comfort zone. I'll give her a project that will be very useful to me near the end of this plan."

Shara chuckled, stood, and return to the closet. "I hope so, she shouted. Now, let's finish this packing; the caravan arrives tomorrow to take us to your temporary home in Philistine. Remember, you have a new family to meet."

Delilah spent most of the morning reviewing specific instructions with Steffi about final details of the new structure on her property. She had been placed in charge of overseeing a guest house to be built in the rear of the property, near Jared's grave. It was designed to be adorned with the lavish décor sent by the king's representatives and included items from the extravagant shopping spree to the marketplace by her mistress.

Shara arrived to inform Delilah the caravan was loaded and ready. She canvassed the foundation design of the new construction and the items already purchased.

"Whew! I hope you are paying close attention to what you're spending on this suite and adjacent chamber. At this rate, you'll have to increase *gentlemen favors* to cover the additional expenses."

Steffi followed her mistress on the path leading to the caravan, then grunted in agreement. "Yes, madame. It's is a bit much, don't you think" she commented.

Delilah jutted her chin; dissatisfaction plowed her brow.

"Your job isn't to question," she snapped. "It is to follow and obey. The cost is not your concern."

Steffi dropped her head.

Delilah sighed and hugged her tight. "It will be fine, just follow as I've instructed. I will see you again soon."

Shara smiled, walked away and waved for the two handmaids to board the caravan for the journey.

Delilah grabbed the small satchel and walked to the end of the path, with Steffi close at hand. As they walked, she hugged her faithful servant.

"Just do as I say, and don't worry," she shouted. I am not paying for this new structure. When the men arrive to complete the work, they will have been well paid. They will also bring additional funds you need to purchase items I listed in the instructions. Other than ensuring these men are fed and have a place to sleep, there's nothing for you to do."

Steffi rocked from side to side, brushed her hands together, but didn't speak.

Delilah smiled, "I will send a messenger when I am within a week of returning home. Be ready to do everything I tell you without hesitation. You must follow the instructions. My life may depend on your obedience." She hugged her handmaid then joined Shara and the others.

Steffi rushed back to the house, stood in the doorway, and watched the caravan until it was over the ridge out of sight. She closed the door, shook her head, and wept. *What has she gotten herself into? No good ever comes from hate and revenge.*

Delilah was quiet for most of the journey to Philistine. Despite the relative short distance, she had agreed with the king's representative to meet just outside city limits. A wealthy Philistine family agreed to be part of the scheme, donated living quarters on their estate, and promoted the pretense she was a relative visiting the area on business.

Having reached midway their trip, the caravan set up camp. While Delilah dressed for the evening, Shara rushed in the tent, followed by the maid servants with a flask of wine and several goblets.

"They're here," she announced while the maids prepared the table. "I told them to wait while I checked to see if you were prepared to receive them."

Delilah dismissed the comment with a chuckled. "Of course, I'm ready. Invite them into my temporary abode."

Shara looked down and swayed on her feet.

"I asked them to wait so I could have one more moment with you. I need to make sure you want to move forward with this plan. She hesitated then stepped forward. "You realize, even though I will be around as much as possible, you will be left alone to implement a plan not fully developed."

Shara grabbed Delilah's arm and anchored her attention on her friend's unemotional facial expression. "Look, just say the word, and we can get out of here and go home."

Delilah yanked from Shara's grip. A vicious leer growing on her lips.

"No, but perhaps you should go home," she snapped. I've got a job to do, and I'm getting well-paid for the service." She strolled to the tent opening. "Understand me," she shouted. "This opportunity gives me first-hand input on bringing down the man who killed my brother, so I need you to get onboard with this plan or get out of the way. I will never give up." She breathed deep and squeezed her eyes shut. In the moments of deafening silence that followed a gust of wind entered the tent, knocking the package holding the gift her brother bought on the floor.

Shara removed the package from the sand-covered floor, brushed it using gentle strokes, and placed it on the table near her friend.

Delilah, shoulders slumped, heaved a weary sigh, then laid her hand on the package. "I need you to either support me or go home and wait for my return. If you choose to stay, I need you confident and trust the plan."

Shara didn't speak. Instead, she picked up the large flask, poured wine in several goblets, placed them strategically on the table, and smoothed the white linen cloth covering to prepare for the meeting. She scanned the room to ensure all was in order, then walked to the tent entrance and lifted the flap. Before exiting, she turned and faced her friend.

"I'm not leaving you," she said, voice quivering.

"I will be here to the end, no matter what that looks like. I'm going now get the Philistine kings' representatives so we can get this tragedy started."

Before Delilah could respond, Shara lifted the tent flap and left the area.

The meeting with the kings' men went very well. Delilah received a formal commitment to completion of the structure built and furnished on her property in Sorek. She also received 1/3 of the 5,500 talents promised as payment for her deed, and confirmed the guarantee that several men would be assigned as guard during her stay in Philistine. They reviewed the agreed pretense for her visit to the area and assured it would be spread as a rumor throughout the Philistine area.

The kings' representatives rose to leave. The leader Cobal, paused, turned and emphasized a warning.

"You understand we cannot be visible once you connect with the Nazarite. It would only create hostility. We will, of course, have several of our servants assigned to attend to your needs while in Philistine. They will also be your communication source, keeping us informed when you need anything, and convey messages when necessary, but we cannot be with you all the time."

Shara, quiet during the discussion, she stepped forward and interrupted.

"So, tell me, what will you do if he attacks her? Is there a plan of escape?"

Cobal opened his mouth to respond but was interrupted.

"Let's be clear, Delilah replied, I have chosen this risk, and I am up to the challenge." She grabbed her friend around the waist and hugged tight. "The key to success is commitment to stick with our individual part of the plan, and that's what we'll do."

Shara's eyes sloped down at the corners like a sad pup. She turned, walked back to her chair, and sat down.

Delilah walked to the table, gathered the palpus with details of the plan, and waved them in the air. "We've outlined everything. Each one of us, if we stay true to the process, will be part of the victory over this enemy." She narrowed her eyes, smiled and beckoned Shara to stand by her side once again. "Shara is my true friend and I trust she will watch, wait and communicate messages to you, but this is my mission and my fight. I will live up to the pledge and complete the task."

Cobal smiled. "I believe good things will result from what we accomplish in the next few weeks." He turned, nodded to the representatives who gathered their belongings, bowed, and left.

Delilah placed the plans on the table and stood in silence.

Delilah was jolted awake by loud voices shouting outside her tent. Sounds of people laughing and cheering, followed by horses thumping around the campsite perimeter, forced her to rise, grab her robe and investigate. *My goodness. No one told us they had prepared to leave this early. Good gracious, this is a mess. Now I have to rush and no warm breakfast again. Where are the maidservants? I need to get things packed.*

She tied her hair with a ribbon, adjusted her loose-fitting robe and walked approached the tent entrance, but halted when Shara appeared, panic in her eyes.

"He's here, for God's sake. He's here," her voice just above a whisper. while pointing.

Delilah grabbed her friend.

"Calm down. What are you talking about? Who's here?"

Shara panted, voice trembling, "the man Samson."

Delilah fell silent, then flopped on a cushioned chair. She regained her composure, searched for appropriate clothing, but soon discovered she had no time. Without warning, the tent flap moved and standing before her was the tall, muscular man, head covered with long black locks. His smile was broad and welcoming. With striking deep-set eyes, he was one of the most attractive men Delilah had ever seen.

Their eyes met. His gaze cruised her body. She shivered and looked away.

"Forgive the intrusion," the man said. "I was told this was the tent of the caravan supervisor. I seek some items ordered and decided to retrieve them before arrival to town."

Delilah didn't acknowledge the question. Instead, she flashed a demurred smile and nodded. Suddenly, she realized her night wear was sheer, see-through and her robe was open. Moving slow, aware he was watching, she closed her robe, and responded. "The head merchant is lodged in another large tent. It shouldn't be hard to find."

Observing the situation, Shara stepped forward and shot him a disgusted glance. "Yes, he is several tents over. Shall I show you the way, Sir?"

Samson laughed. "No. I will find him." He bowed low, raised his head with a slight tilt in Delilah's direction, turned, and left.

Delilah grabbed a cloth, dipped it in the pale of water, and covered her face. Pressing firm, she breathed deep while fighting the uncomfortable nervous feeling in her stomach. Her mouth dry, she sipped water from the cup Shara handed her. "It wasn't supposed to happen this way," she muttered. "Where did he come from? And who the," she hesitated and squeezed her hands in a fist. "Who does he think he is?

Shara walked to the tent entrance, peered through the flap, breathed a sigh of relief, then dropped on the flat bed.

"He's Samson," Shara whispered as if he might be listening. "Just like we've been told, he moves in and out of towns like they are his kingdom. You, my dear, just met the man we're here to stop." With her eyes crossed in exasperation, she put her hand on her hips and tossed her head. "Well, now we can add survived premature meeting to our update."

Delilah didn't respond. She was well aware of the sarcasm that came with that statement. "Well, nothing has changed. I just met him a bit sooner than planned. The good thing is he knows I am in his territory. Based on the way he looked at me, I'm sure he will find a way to make our acquaintance again," she laughed. "Little does he know; it will be the worst mistake he ever made."

She grabbed her satchel and paused. "Enough said. Go. Direct the handmaids to confirm how much time before we break camp and start for the town?"

Shara jumped up. "I'm on it," she responded, and disappeared.

Delilah waited a few moments to be sure she was alone, then collapsed on the chair, still holding the satchel she realized belonged to Jared. *Help me, oh Dagan, god of the earth. Give me the strength I need to play my part in the demise of this enemy.*

"You never cease to amaze me, Samson," his close confidant, Abaddon, commented as they left the women's tent on the way to what they knew was the correct quarters of the caravan leader. "You couldn't wait until she arrived in town but had to see this beauty your way."

Samson chuckled. "You're just angry cause I won the bet. I told you I'd find the woman everybody is talking about. This stop was convenient since I was heading this way," he chided with a smirk growing on his face. "Besides, I like to see them when they aren't prepared for the visit. You can get a real sense of what you'll be dealing with."

He rubbed his beard and laughed. Now I see what everyone's been gossiping about around the town. Seems she's as pretty as she is rich."

Abaddon lifted his shoulder in a half shrug.

"Man, you're arrogant for sure. Now will demand the head merchant to look through all his stock for one package on delivery to you."

Samson laughed, walked in the merchant's tent, looked over his shoulder and shouted. "What did you say her name was?"

Abaddon frowned. "I didn't say a name. That's something you will have to discover on your own."

CHAPTER 16

After several weeks of rearranging household furnishings, establishing protocol with her hosts, and meeting several neighbors as the rich relative, Delilah settled in her new surroundings. Because of the fiasco at the caravan creating the unexpected and unwelcomed meeting with Samson, she sent word for the king's representative, Cobal, to visit as soon as possible.

While waiting, she strolled the gardens outside her temporary home enjoying the lush and expansive the vegetation covering bother sides of the cobblestone walkway, offering privacy and seclusion to complete the task at hand.

By mid-afternoon, while returning from a short walk to the pool area, Delilah recognized Cobal standing at the top of the garden path. Though relieved to see him, she didn't smile. Instead, chin jutted, she walked past him and sat down on one of the garden chairs, and crossed her legs.

"Well," she said with a smirk playing across her face, "now that the introductions are over, we need to plan the next phase of the trap."

Cobal had settled in one of the guest chairs but jolted forward, eyes wide, in response to Delilah's statement. "What do you mean? The end of what phase? I have only just finalized plans for the town's festivities that will enable an environment for you and the Nazarite to meet."

He pulled the chair closer and touched her hand. "Please, tell me what happened so I can help."

Delilah ignored the touch, stood and walked to the small sideboard table. She poured wine in one of the goblets, and moved her fingers around the rim in slow motion.

"I was left with the clear impression, I would be guarded during my trip from Sorek to Philistine," she said with a forced grin. "Instead, within 60 kilometers of the town, our caravan was interrupted early in the morning by a boisterous team of men led by your Nazarite."

Cobal leaned back in his chair, snapped his fingers, and smiled. "Okay, great, so you met. This is good. It will make enticing him to your welcome gathering that much easier. Having already seen you, he will attend, hoping to get better acquainted."

Delilah crossed her arms and glared at the king's representative.

"Do you and your people understand how important it is for me to be informed of this man's every movement? He is not one to be taken lightly, and his whereabouts are of primary importance to me. The last thing I needed yesterday was to be caught off guard. Besides, first impressions were crucial to our plan."

Throwing her hands in the air, she grabbed a flower and plucked it to the stem, then returned to sit with Cobal at the table, eyes intense.

"This man saw me at my weakest moment. He caught me off guard, and thoroughly enjoyed my reaction."

She placed on palms face down on the table surface and tapped her fingers. "I need to control of this situation. Your spies must notify me of this man's movements at all times. I don't need any more surprises, is that clear?"

Cobal stood, rubbed his hands together, and paced back and forth. "I apologize we were not prepared, and understand how this could have been most unfortunate for you. It will not happen again."

* * *

Shara stood in the patio corner observing the exchange between Delilah and Cobal. As directed, she maintained the position of frustrated silence while listening to the exchange. Once or twice she shifted from side to side or moved several fruit trays around the side board to remind her friend she was available if needed.

While in position, she noticed something moving in the shadows beyond the path leading to the front side of the house. Before she could step closer for a better look, one of the maids dropped a goblet of wine, distracting her attention.

"Your sloppiness is reprehensible," she shouted. "Clean it up and get another flask."

Irritated with the disruption, Delilah raised her hands.

"Enough, Shara. It's not that serious. No need to replace the wine. We've have concluded our meeting. I'm sure Cobal has other plans for the evening." She studied her visitor. "I think we've finished our little chat, don't you?"

Cobal arose from his seat; brows drawn together, conveying concern. "Certainly," he responded, then picked up his hooded travel robe, walked to the door and paused.

"I want to assure you, again, not to be concerned. We will maintain a better handle on the whereabouts of the man Samson. My sources informed me he is in the town right now, having arrived early for the festivities scheduled this week. We have several people assigned to his movements. No more surprises for you."

Shara desperately wanted to offer an opinion, but acknowledged Delilah's signal for silence. Ignored again, she mumbled.

* * *

Abaddon stood in the shadows opposite the roadway entrance of Delilah's guest home. A few moments earlier a tall stranger, riding a magnificent mahogany wood chariot, passed his hiding space and turned into the estate. At the request of Samson, Abaddon and his attendants rotated traveling around the region, investigating to determine the background and details of the newest lady of interest.

Tracking Abaddon's gaze, the attendant tugged at his robe. "Sir, just think, for the last four evenings, we've spent hours observing the activities around the home of this beautiful lady," he announced, waving his arms in the air. "Just when we thought there was nothing to see, the tall stranger in the chariot appeared. This is good, right?!" The attendant whispered.

Abaddon smiled, ruffled his hair, and shoved him forward. "Go," he commanded. "Move quick, follow the chariot, and investigate this visit. Hide well and, mind you, get caught, and I will strip you naked and drag you through the streets."

The attendant bowed and entered the roadway leading to Delilah's lodging, staying in the shadow of the trees. He passed the first building without incident and edged around the corner to the next structure and saw the visitor seated with two women in the garden.

Though he couldn't hear the conversation, body language of one of the women suggested that it wasn't a pleasant exchange. The attendant sat silent for several more minutes observing. Deciding there was nothing to report, he backed slowly from the area, missed judged a step, stumbled over several bricks, and grabbed a bush to prevent falling off balance. He froze.

One of the women looked in his direction and started to move, but was distracted by the sound. When she turned to investigate, he ran through the shrubbery and returned to the road. Keeping in the shadows, the attendant returned and shared his experience.

"She had a visitor, Sir, he said panting. I couldn't hear the conversation, but she didn't seem too pleased. I think he was making his intentions known, but I don't think it well received," he noted, then brushed his bruised palms. "Besides, a maid and another woman were right there all the time, so nothing was going on." *There, that's it. This should satisfy your buddy Samson. So, can we get out of here now? Easy for you out here safe from harm. I was the one in danger of death if caught.*"

Abaddon nodded, satisfied with the news. He tilted his head, stretched, and addressed the attendant. "Let's get moving," he said with an edge of impatience. "We must share these recent observations. This summary of events should satisfy Samson's curiosity."

After one final gaze at path, to ensure the chariot had not moved, Abaddon pressed his finger to his lips for silence, and motioned his attendant to follow. The two men moved in and out of the shadows on the cobblestone streets leading back to the tavern, eager to share the information discovered about the new lady in town.

Cobal left the meeting with Delilah, having reaffirmed the partnership commitment and next steps for the demise of the Nazarite, Samson. Scanning the area, he recognized several of her maids in the windows observing as he walked the pebble stone path leading to his chariot. With only a half-moon to light his path, he stumbled several times while maneuvering the roadway obstacle course. He boarded the chariot, grabbed the reins and moved the horses in a slow circle toward the exit.

In quick motion, Cobal lowered his head and tapped the floor of the vehicle.

"Shyam, are you awake?"

The small thin body of his attendant shifted in the far corner of the chariot. "Yes, Sir," he replied in a whisper. "I am awake, alert, and have an interesting report."

Cobal smiled. "Good, continue."

Shyam described the man who came out of the shadows and passed their chariot. "This stranger paused long enough near my position in the chariot, if he turned his head slightly, he might have seen me." The attendant paused, "but he didn't," he said then chuckled.

Cobal ignored the comment. "Get on with it man."

Uncomfortable, Shyam adjusted his position, and continued. "Though I couldn't see his final destination, I heard his footsteps moving in the same direction you traveled. It was some moments later before I saw yet another man on the street beyond the gate." Shyam leaned forward, so he was clearly seen under the moonlight, and jerked his thumb pointing to a building across the road. "The man stepped from the shadows and stood at the edge of the roadway leading to the house, but didn't approach. A few moments later, he returned to the shadows across the road."

Cobal pulled the reins, slowed the horses, and rubbed his chin.

"So, you say, there was yet another man? Interesting," he chuckled.

The attendant grinned and continued. "It wasn't long before the stranger rushed by the chariot and crossed the road, joining other man. They spoke for several minutes then left."

After completing his report, Shyam stretched his legs to relieve discomfort from the awkward sitting position.

Cobal noticed the movements and reached for his young attendant. "Come, stand with me." With quick motion, he put his hand under the attendant's arm and lifted him so that he was standing in the chariot next to his master." He smiled, cracked the whip, and the horses increased their pace. "You have done well. Let's go meet this Samson. One of his hangouts is close by. We'll start there."

They road along the well-lit streets, relaxed and chatting until the attendant tugged his master's robe with sudden jerking motions. "Sir, up ahead are the two men I saw outside the gates."

Cobal didn't slow the pace of the horses, but turn to his attendant with a penetrating gaze. "Are you certain of this?"

The attendant nodded.

"Interesting. Very interesting indeed," Cobal replied with a chuckle.

The chariot grew close, but the two spies ignored the sounds of approaching horses. Instead, they turned into a local tavern. The loud noise and number of patrons stumbling out the door suggested it was a lively establishment. It was also one of Samson's favorite locations.

Cobal stopped the chariot, and slapped his attendant on the back. "Come, we'll find Samson, eat and, have a closer look at our investigators."

Descending the chariot, he pretended to stretch while canvassing the immediate area. After the recent conversation, Cobal wanted to ensure they were no longer under observation. He waved to Shyam. "Secure the horses in the stable. I'll go ahead and find Samson or a table. We'll eat a hearty meal this night. You've earned it."

CHAPTER 17

Even with the congestion, Abaddon had no trouble finding his friend. Samson stood out in any crowd and controlled all situations. Because of his power and strength the townspeople tolerated his visits, despite his killing rampage several months earlier. Surrounded by women, competing for his attention, his friend was in good spirits.

"Abaddon, over here," Samson shouted, waving his hand in the air. For a brief moment the crowd grew silent, with several heading for an exit. Samson let out a hearty laugh, scanned the scene, and ordered, "continue on with your party, do you hear? I will spend time with my friend."

Samson shoved one of the women off his lap and waved his friend forward to take the nearest chair. "Sit," he commanded while taking a long drink. Share the news. What have you learned? Who's the competition for this my new love interest."

Abaddon laughed. "You mean to tell me you think there's a possibility that you may have competition. That's not possible, my friend? Look around. These people fear you. There's no competition."

Samson raised one of his massive hands, poked Abaddon on his arm, and laughed. "True, but I still like to know who surrounds my new interest."

Abaddon took the next few moments to share his observations of Delilah since her arrival. "She was introduced by her guest hosts to various people in the area. Several people have visited, but I have not identified any particular suitors." No sooner did he complete his report than the tavern door opened, and in walked the stranger who visited Delilah that very evening. He turned away to avoid eye contact. "There may be one suitor, however," Abaddon continued. "But I've only seen him twice. Once in the day and then this night. It could be nothing."

Samson's eyes narrowed.

"It is of no consequence to me, my friend. I will meet this woman and decide if she can hold my interest. I've been told there will be a gathering in a few days, and I will be there." Grabbing another woman to sit on his lap, he slammed his fist on the table. "But tonight, let's eat and enjoy the comforts of this place."

Abaddon shrugged, nodded, picked up his goblet, and scanned the room, searching for the tall stranger. He found him at a table in the corner eating. For a brief moment, their eyes met. Another man, smaller in stature, entered the tavern and slid next to the stranger, holding his head low. Though melting in the landscape, these men did not appear to belong to others in the town.

Draining his goblet, Abaddon waved it in the air for a refill, then studied the strangers. *These aren't local visitors. The tall one carries himself like royalty, one of means. What have I missed? Who are they, where are they from, and what's their connection to the woman Delilah? My man Samson is such a fool. He thought bringing a few trinkets as gifts and spending time laughing and joking with these people would help them forget about the Philistine men, their husbands, brothers, and fathers, who*

186

were massacred a few months ago. No point approaching him with my concerns, but something is wrong.

* * *

Delilah pressed her lips to smooth the plum colors she skillfully applied then stepped into her scarlet red double fold shear sleeveless dress, inlaid with silk to add modest coverage. She stared in the mirror and smiled. "What do you think of my armor, Shara? Will it do the trick tonight at the welcome reception?

Barely listening, her friend fumbled in the closet, searching through the travel satchels for the matching sandals to an outfit she selected to accompany Delilah on this first venture to entice the Nazarite. Frustrated with the search, Shara threw the satchel on the closet floor, walked to a cushioned chair and plopped down in silence.

Delilah approached, grabbed both arms of the chair and, with a flash of anger, leaned forward so their noses almost touched.

"Get a grip, Shara. Shake whatever it is you feel agitated or fearful about and get with this plan. Do you hear me!"

Shara shook her head but didn't speak.

Delilah stepped back and sighed. "Look, my Sis, everything is going to be alright. According to Cobal, Samson was curious enough about me that he has asked several people how he might be properly introduced." She returned to her night stand and added fragrances on her wrists and behind the ears. "I smell victory in the air," She laughed. "I feel like a soldier preparing for battle with a guarantee of success. Soon he will be captured and carried away knowing he was defeated by a woman who hated him from the depth of her soul." Dancing, she circled her friend and tossed her head from side to side. "Be happy for me, my friend, for tonight is the beginning of his demise, as I start my campaign to avenge my brother's death."

After a few moments of silence, Shara stood, wrapped her arms around Delilah and hugged tight. "You're right. This is a big night for us. Let's go get our revenge."

* * *

Positioned on a large guest estate, Delilah's guest house was located on the one side of the main residence, hidden by heavy shrubbery and trees. The event held in her honor, however, was located on the opposite end of the property. She and Shara entered the scene using a path aligned with torches mounted on large white columns.

Shara nudged her girlfriend. "My, my, look at this. I gotta say this is overwhelming." Tugging Delilah's arm, she pointed to the elaborate multi-color floral decorations on the architectural trim surrounding a vast pool area. At the center of each guest table were small gold trimmed platters filled with sliced apples, oranges, chicory, dried figs, nuts, and cheese. "My goodness," Shara continued. "With this layout, looks like they invited the whole town to this event."

They continued to walk beyond the pool to the garden.

Delilah gasped, "my goodness, this is too much," she giggled. "And, just think, it's all for me." Scanning the area, they saw rows of round tables covered with white linen accented with lighted candles surrounded by rose pedals. Soft music played as their hosts appeared.

Welcomed with genuine warm hugs, their hosts escorted them to the side board where several of the townspeople had already gathered, enjoying the wine and other beverages. Soon, more and more guests appeared, and the crowd grew thicker and more congested. Delilah engaged the group like a perfect hostess, staying close to the area where she could watch for the entrance of the Nazarite. The evening grew late, but her target had not appeared. Bewildered, she clenched her fists and turned to Shara.

"This is ridiculous. What an incredible waste of time and resources," Delilah snapped. "By the way, where the heck is Cobal? This was his doing," she said, eyes blazed with anger. "First, the man he was supposed to arrange for me to meet shows up, without warning, in my tent on the road to this place." She waved her arms in the air. "Then a no show from him tonight." She paced back and forth, still nodding and smiling at guest while seething with anger. "Look at this. Everyone who is anyone has been invited to this party, but he doesn't show up."

No sooner had those words escaped her mouth when she noticed a commotion at the event entrance.

"Good evening, please come in," her host announced with an elevated tone. In between several women gathered around, Delilah saw the tall, attractive, well-built man who had abruptly entered her tent many weeks earlier.

"Well, will you look at that," Shara blurted with excitement before nudging her friend to step forward so she could be seen. Resisting the pressure, Delilah flashed her an angry look.

"You are to control yourself, breathe, and be still. I move at my own pace. Your role is to stay in the shadows and watch my back. Either control your behavior or return to our quarters out of the way."

Shara rolled her eyes skyward, took two steps back and curtsied. "As you wish, I'll sink to the background." Gaining Delilah's attention, she added, "but before I go, I think you should know, he's heading your way."

Before Delilah could respond, she heard a deep, commanding voice close behind calling her name. "So, your name is Delilah."

With a warm smile, she turned and greeted the muscular man towering over her. "And you, as I understand, are Samson the Nazarite."

Samson bowed, took her hand, kissed her fingers, then offered a brilliant smile. "I have been curious to meet you, *officially that is.*"

Delilah blushed.

For a few moments, he appraised her with a look that was so intense that she felt she had been entirely undressed. She was unnerved and irritated at the same time.

Pointing to a nearby table, Samson asked, "shall we sit? I'd like to spend some time with you."

Delilah hesitated and looked around. She caught Shara's look of concern, then, gathering strength, tossed her hair and smiled demurely. "Of course, let's sit. I am curious to learn more about you, Samson the Nazarite."

With Delilah on his arm, Samson moved through the crowd of women that had formed for his attention, dismissing comments with a smile, and led his new love interest to a corner table.

Cobal stood in a far corner watching the interactions between the lady and the target. He frowned.

"Things are going well; don't you think, Sir?" His attendant asked.

Cobal pulled his hood close around his face and pointed his attendant to the exit. He walked several steps, then looked over his shoulder one last time. "Yes," he said with just a hint of sadness and concern. "Things are moving as planned. The hunter has been positioned to be captured by the prey." His shoulders slumped. "I only hope this process in deception doesn't leave her scarred," he responded.

Within moments, they disappeared in the shadows.

* * *

Shara burst into the bedroom carrying a bouquet of roses followed by handmaids with a tray of food, fresh towels, and water. "You must have made quite an impression," she quipped. Flowers delivered the first thing in the morning," she laughed and placed the floral display on the night table.

Delilah stretched, leaned on one elbow, and watched the flurry of activity taking place. Throwing the covers, she waved for her maids to bring the breakfast tray. "Move these flowers and set my food here." One of the maids took the flowers and moved them to a side table.

"No," she shouted. "Take them out of here. I have no interest in having them in my sight."

Shara signaled the maid to stop, and glared at her friend. "The Nazarite will be visiting you often. It is your plan, is it not?"

Delilah shrugged. "Yes, what of it?"

Shara threw her hands in the air. "Don't you think he will look for the flowers he sends to you? Get a grip, my girl. We need to ensure he feels loved and secure." She waved at one of the maids. "Take these flowers to the guest receiving area. Be sure they're placed on the center table near the lounge chair. She directed the other handmaid. "Go. Draw the bath for your mistress. She will need to refresh after she has eaten. Be sure to bring the fragrances and sweet oils and add them to the water."

With both maids out of the room, Shara sat on the edge of the bed. "Look, last night was a big win. The host and hostess had to kick him out." She spread her arms wide. "The world, and Samson, are at your feet. You've smiled your way into his heart. It was obvious to anyone observing." She nudged her friend. "Don't you see? You're in a great position to move to the next level, gaining his fondness and favor. Displaying these flowers provides a connection to you and helps establish his territory in the home environment of the woman he now desires."

Delilah nodded. "I know you're right, but this is going to more difficult than I thought." She rubbed her hands and stared into space. "He's a man, with a conflicted personality. Arrogant for sure, but behind that arrogance, there's something else. I just don't want to get so close that I expose a gentle, good side of him I don't want to see. Do you know what I mean?"

Shara crossed her arms and cocked her brow in surprise.

"Look, Sis, there are no shades of right or wrong in this situation. You don't have the luxury to second guess your choices. You have to stay the course. Hesitation could mean death for you and everyone connected to you. Do whatever you need to do but never forget why you're here."

Their conversation was interrupted by a soft knock and entrance of the handmaid carrying with a note on a tray. "You have a message, ma'am," she said with a bow. "The man is waiting for a reply."

Delilah ignored the comment and anchored her attention on the note. After reading it, she smiled. "Well, the courting process is in full swing." She arose from the bed, cross the floor to her night table, removed one of the flowers, and wrapped it in her soft pink sash. "My suitor has to leave the area for a few days but did not want me to think he had lost interest. He requests that I allow him to visit on his return in the next two evenings. Delilah smiled. I think I'll send my response using one of his flowers." She turned to her handmaid. "Here. Take this to the messenger. Say I look forward to his master's return and would have him join me for supper."

The maid bowed, took the flower, and left the room.

Shara lifted her skirts and whirled around laughing. "That's my girl. Welcome back."

Samson left the Philistine area and was gone for several weeks fighting a campaign, at the request of his people. Delilah was kept informed of his whereabouts through a periodic visit from Cobal, who had several spies monitoring his movements. The other kings also sent a representative as a follow-up to confirm their continued commitment to fulfilling their *monetary payment once she provides the information they need. Tired of waiting, Delilah had a change of plans, and shared this news with Cobal during his recent visit.*

"I will return home, Cobal. I think it strategically unwise for me to be found waiting for this man to return," Delilah said while tapping the wine goblet. She paced the upper balcony outside her room. "He uses the absences as part of his *love* game. He commands attention, then cools his target in an attempt to build expectation for his affection. I must do the unexpected and not be accessible on his return."

Cobal sat quiet, rubbing his beard.

"What if he doesn't follow you. What if he decides to wait for your return to Philistine?"

Delilah smiled and crinkled her nose. "Well, then I would say I didn't make as great an impression on this Nazarite as I thought." Moving closer to Cobal, she leaned forward. "But somehow, I don't think that is the case. He was very interested, very attracted to me." Their eyes connected, but she looked away and back off. "This Nazarite *is* interested, and *he will* come for me. Then I will have him."

Cobal reluctantly agreed and left to inform the others of the change in plans. Delilah informed her hosts she would be gone for a few days to check on status of her property in Sorek. For all inquiries, they should be informed it was unknown when her would return.

With Shara and one of her handmaids in tow, Delilah left for Sorek and arrived home greeted by her surprised, ecstatic personal attendant, Steffi. For two days, Delilah paced and waited, wondering if she made the right decision. The strategy was crucial. She could not return to Philistine without her suitor because it would appear as if she were chasing him. If he didn't come after her, she would be a failure, and the revenge she planned would be in jeopardy. Delilah realized much was riding on her decision, and each day of Samson's absence put her closer to a failed mission.

While waiting for her target to arrive, Delilah spent evenings relaxing in the new extension to her home, built by the kings as part of her payment. It was beautifully designed with lush silk curtains draped around a wide, deep, circular bed. The center of the area included a marble stone private pool fed by the nearby river. The windows faced a garden full of white lilies, roses, and other greenery.

One evening, too restless to sleep, Delilah strolled the property and ended standing in the bedroom of her new retreat space. The torchlights danced as the soft cool breeze flowed through the large windows. Delilah rubbed the nape of her neck, sighed, and let her thoughts drift to happy moments with her brother. Suddenly, she felt a presence behind her and turned to see Samson standing in the doorway. His skin glistened in the candlelight. He was even more handsome than she had remembered.

"I missed you, my Delilah," he whispered as he walked across the room and stood by her side. Before she could speak, he touched her lips with his fingers then swept a strand of hair from her face. She struggled to regain her composure, but it was too late. He covered her mouth with a long hard kiss. She responded. He then lifted and placed her gently on the bed. "Yes," he whispered. You are my Delilah."

CHAPTER 18

Samson and Delilah spent several days in her home in Sorek swimming, frolicking, eating, and most of all, being intimate. During their stay, Shara and Steffi were the only people allowed to see the two lovers and provide for their needs. Early one morning, Delilah appeared in the doorway of the main house kitchen. Shara and Steffi were engrossed in planning meals and delegating household instructions so her presence went unnoticed. She stepped forward, and grabbed an apple, then danced across the room.

"Well, I see you two have been keeping busy. Did you miss me?"

They both jumped, laughed, dropped what they were doing, and hugged. Shara pulled away quickly and nodded to Steffi who dismissed the maids. Taking a step back, Shara studied her friend's demeanor. "Are you alright? Is something wrong?"

Delilah fluffed her hair, stretched, then slid onto a nearby chair. "Nothing is wrong. Everything is proceeding as planned. He is taking a morning swim, so I told him I would visit with you guys to let you know our latest plans." Leaning forward, she looked around to ensure the other servants had left the area and couldn't overhear the conversation. "It's time to return to Philistine," she said while moving her hand over the deep cracks of the kitchen table—a place she spent many hours having late evening snacks with Jared."

Steffi poured a cup of water, set it before her mistress, then massaged her shoulder for comfort. Delilah smiled. "It's almost over."

With a deep sigh, she whispered to Shara. "I need you to send a message to Cobal that the Nazarite will be escorting me back to Philistine and I may have good news for him within days of my arrival. Standing, she walked to the window and looked in the direction of the new structure that housed her guest. "He belongs to me now."

Jumping to attention, Steffi shouted. "Great. When shall we leave?"

Delilah tapped her foot, eyes crossed in exasperation. "Now you know that's impossible. You are not going with me now or ever, so get that through your head. I need you here to maintain the place that will be my sanctuary when all this is over. She grabbed Steffi's hand and pulled her close. "Don't fight with me on this, please."

Before her trusted servant could object and plead her case, a loud voice came from the direction of the guest house.

"Delilah, my love. Come, see who has surprised us with a visit." Delilah flashed Shara a look of concern.

Samson, voice elevated, repeated the command. "Delilah, come!"

Delilah jumped up, waved for Shara to follow, and rush through the high shrubbery to the path leading to the guest house. Running down the path, she laughed aloud so Samson could hear. "Hurry Shara," she shouted. "Don't be such a slowpoke. My master calls," she chuckled, then hurried toward the beautiful structure she created for her prey.

"Coming," Shara shouted while tripping several times over stones on the path.

Delilah, still running, turned the curve leading to the steps of the guest house. Out of breath she stopped to gain her composure, and was surprised at what she saw. At the base of the steps stood Cobal, the king's representative. He was looking up at Samson, who towered over him, standing at the guest house entrance. Delilah froze.

"My love," Samson with contempt. "It appears you have a command to return to Philistine and complete your business, and this gentleman," he continued with an edge of agitation, "made a special trip to deliver the message."

With a bow of respect to Samson, Cobal turned his attention to Delilah. "My visit is certainly not a command, madame. I have been sent by request of your host that she might have clarity when you would return to settle the business matters. I manage the property in the Northern land. As we discussed on your last visit, there is a need for resolution so the escalation might begin before the drought season delays the plan.

Delilah strolled past Cobal, climbed the steps, took Samson's arm, and rested a hand on her hip. She flashed an angry look at the visitor. "Your visit has taken us by surprise. I would have preferred your sending a messenger." She snuggled close to Samson and sneered at Cobal. "I have been considering my return to Philistine. I am very much aware of the need to resolve business issues," she snapped. So, you see, she emphasized with a hostile glare, "there was no need for you to make a special trip to remind me of unfinished business."

An uncomfortable silence permeated the air.

Samson stepped forward; one heavy brow slanted in solid disapproval. "Perhaps, my love, the gentleman had other reasons for the visit."

Shara, who arrived in time to observe the intense situation, rushed forward and kissed Cobal passionately. Sensing her purpose, he returned the favor, giving her a passionate response.

Delilah stiffened, shifted from one foot to the other, and shot them a disgusted look. *What the heck is this?! She has to know he's attracted to me and that I'm attracted to him. What has that salty heifer been doing behind my back?*

Shara released the embrace. "You came, she laughed. I'm so sorry I didn't believe you when you said you would find me." Her eyes caressed his. "No more doubts, she laughed. No more crosswords."

With gentle strokes, Cobal brushed the loose strands of hair from Shara's face. "All is forgiven," he whispered.

Samson threw his head back and laughed loud and hard, then greeted Cobal with a hard slap on the shoulder.

"So, my man, I knew the reason for your visit was weak. Now I see. Good move. Come, let's all eat and relax. We shall make plans for my love to journey with me to Philistine with you and your woman to follow."

"Sir," Cobal smiled. That sounds great but, unfortunately, I cannot stay. I have business and need to continue my journey back to Philistine immediately. He hugged Shara close and caressed her with his eyes. I will take a few quiet moments with my lady, then take my leave. I brought, however, several additional camels and three of my attendants to ensure your comfort and travel accommodations.

Samson shrugged. "Suit yourself," lifted Delilah in one arm and waved. "We shall meet again." Then disappeared into the guest quarters.

Shara took Cobal's arm and guided him down the long path to the main house. "Well, that was close," she exclaimed. "What the heck were you thinking, showing up here unannounced? You could have set her back for weeks. This man is possessive and jealous." She stopped abruptly and stood in his path. "I'm sure you remember what he is capable of when he's embarrassed or jealous."

Cobal raised a brow and put his finger to his lips. Shara fell silent. He pointed in the direction of the far side of the main house. "You have been surrounded by spies for days, he said in a low tone. The man Samson never travels alone."

As they neared the main house, Cobal held Shara close until they entered the building. When the door closed, they move into the dining area for more privacy but found they weren't alone.

Taken by surprise, Steffi was speechless. Setting the tray of fish soup, bread, and vegetables prepared for Samson and Delilah aside, she approached the couple with a frosty look. "What's this all about? And Sir," she pointed, "why are you here? Don't you know you put my mistress in danger?"

Cobal grinned at Steffi, then looked at his partner. "Not anymore, thanks to Shara." He tossed his hooded robe on a chair, slapped his hands, and paced the floor. "The kings are restless and impatient. They want this issue resolved. As long as Samson roams the region, they are in danger. I was sent to assess the status of the situation and provide an update of the plans." He lifted his shoulders in a half shrug. "You must understand, ladies, the initial plans did not include returning to this place. So, when they discovered Delilah had left the area, they panicked."

Shara shoved Cobal hard and raised her voice. "You've got to be kidding me. Do you have any idea what it's been like these last few months with all the plans, travel, and sacrifice of privacy? Combined with the spies we've had to hide and lies we've told; this has been a dangerous disruption of our lives.

Cobal stepped back, brow furrowed, mouth turned grim. "Please forgive this unfortunate intrusion. You are exactly right in all that you've said." He looked at Shara. "I appreciate everything you've done. Your actions, saved our plans." He grabbed his travel robe and walked to the door. "I will leave now so not to create any further problems." Just before leaving, he paused and scanned the area. "Remember. You are being watched at all times, so be very careful." He touched Shara's hand. "It might be good if you walk with me to the caravan. It is a bit of a distance, but, after all, we are in love."

Shara laughed. "Sure. Let me grab my shawl."

The return to Philistine was much different from their first trip. Samson, not interested in the caravan accommodations for the return trip, made the excuse he had business to attend and went ahead. Delilah was quiet and reserved most of the journey, spending very little time with Shara. Ever since Cobal's visit, Delilah had very little exchange, no matter how often her friend attempted.

On the last evening before arriving in Philistine, Delilah entered Shara's tent unannounced. "Tell me one thing," she snapped as she leveled a glowered look in Shara's direction. "Just when did you become intimate with Cobal? Was it the same night I laid my trap for Samson? Behind the guest house? Or did you two find a place in town for your rendezvous?"

Shara leaned back on the evening bed, shook her head, and smiled. "So that's it. I was wondering what was bothering you these last few days." She grabbed her hand shook her head. "Sis, we are at war, and it is a war you declared that created a convenient partnership with others who want to kill your target."

Delilah breathed deep, stacked several large pillows on the oakwood plats covering the dirt floor, and flopped down in silence, covering her face with her hands.

Shara exhaled, sat, and leaned on her elbow. "I told you I would be with you no matter how this situation ends. You were in trouble the other day. There was no way you could cover for the unexpected arrival of Cobal. Because you changed the plan without communicating, he had to take the chance to ensure you understood the urgency that your return to Philistine was necessary and urgent."

Delilah sobbed. "Forgive me. I know you're right. I wasn't thinking."

Shara stood, walked to the tent entrance and searched to ensure no one was nearby listening, then returned and stood over her friend. "I knew, when Cobal arrived, Samson might have a negative reaction. A distraction was necessary." She forced a laugh. "So, I threw myself at Cobal praying he understood, and would play along." She threw her hands in the air. "As you could see, he did." Shara ruffled Delilah's hair, and shoved her over so she could share the pillows. "Look at you," she laughed. "Get over yourself, and never forget we are friends. Let's complete this mission so we can go home."

CHAPTER 19

Touring his usual Philistine hangouts, it was several days before Samson reappeared, since the trip from Sorek. In the meantime, Cobal visited Shara and passed messages to Delilah. During one his visits with Shara, Cobal warned he was being followed. "It appears I am being watched carefully. So far, the spies seem comfortable that you are the focus of my attention. However, let our lady know all messages from me will be sent through you. Let her know whenever she discovers his secret, and we will be ready to take charge."

Shara agreed and walked Cobal to the entrance gate, at the end of each visit, making a public display of their affection.

At a recent visit, he lowered his head, hugged Shara close, and whispered, "tell Delilah I care that she is well. Tell her I think of her." Before Shara could respond, he stepped back, bowed, and disappeared.

Delilah displayed the appropriate excitement when Samson appeared at the cottage late one evening, after several days' absence. She made a point not to complain about his lack of communication. He wrapped his arms around her waist, caressing her neck. "So, did you miss me?"

She whirled around, grabbed his neck, and returned the hug. "Was that your plan?" She smiled and moved closer to his embrace.

Samson laughed, "That's why I love you. One of a kind. You are the one I want by my side forever. I feel a special spiritual connection with you, my love. Have no doubt, I will take care of you. You will never again want for anything."

Delilah pushed him away and stared with piercing scrutiny. "You know what? She smiled. I think you mean what you're saying." She crossed the floor, poured a cup of wine, and sipped slowly while watching as the wind push the trees from side to side. In the silence, Samson joined her. Delilah placed her cup on the table and faced him. "There's a storm brewing Samson."

He placed his hands on her shoulders. "So be it. Whatever it is, we will face the future together."

Delilah smiled. "That's right, we'll handle the storm together. *And so, begins the final act.*

Weeks rolled by and the two lovers spent more and more time together. During one of his extended visits, that included numerous goblets of wine and long hours of intimacy, she snuggled close. "Samson, she whispered. So many stories you've told about how you conquered the enemies," she cooed and moved her hands over his hairy chest. "Tell me, my sweet, what's the secret of your strength?"

Samson stretched, then lifted his body so that he leaned on the back of the bed. "That's a curious question, he said with a smile."

Delilah lifted her head and blinked with feigned innocence. "You think so? You've spent days sharing details of your escapades. I was just curious about whether my man would trust me enough to share the secret."

Samson moved closer. She could feel his body stiffen. "Let's see; perhaps after we make love one more time, I'll share my secret." He covered her lips with his mouth, and they shared another moment of intimacy. Satisfied and relaxed, he rolled on his back and yawned. "So, now for the secret to my strength"

She smiled, nodded and cuddled close.

Samson kissed her forehead. "Well, my love, anyone should tie me with seven fresh bowstrings that have not been dried, I'll become weak as any other normal man." Full of much wine, he fell into a sound sleep.

When certain he wouldn't be disturbed, Delilah eased out of bed, grabbed her robe and sandals, eager to find Shara. Reaching the main house, she found her friend on the balcony. "Listen carefully," Delilah commanded. "Tell the messenger they are to bring seven undried bowstrings so that I may restrain this man and remove his power."

"Shara asked, eyes rolled skyward. "What are you guys drinking?" She laughed.

Delilah bolted forward; hands tightened into fists. "Get off your wide rump," she shouted and make haste. "Bring me what I need and bring it now. Samson is a sound sleeper, but I can't measure how long."

"Calm down," Shara admonished and grabbed her shawl. "I'm going. I'll be back as soon as I can." Moving in the shadows, Shara ran down the driveway and stood just outside the gate, in a prearranged area, which was a signal. One of the lookouts assigned to wait for instruction approached. She gave him the message then went back to the house and waited. Some time passed before the spy returned with Cobal and several Philistines with seven undried bowstrings requested.

Cobal stepped forward.

"Here's the plan," he said to Shara. You walk ahead of us and deliver these items Delilah requested," he directed while pointing up the roadway. "We will follow and wait in the chamber, outside the suite so we are close enough to respond when signaled that our enemy is ready for capture. Are we clear?"

Shara nodded in agreement, took a deep breath, and walked down the path, checking once or twice over her shoulder to determine to see if Cobal and the others were keeping pace. After a few minutes, she pointed the men to the side entrance, where they could enter the chamber and wait. Using slow deliberate steps, she moved in the opposite direction and climbed the steps where she found her friend, pacing back and forth, waiting at the entrance.

Without comment, Delilah grabbed the dried bowstrings and waved her away.

Shara hesitated, then hugged her tight. "Cobal and his men are waiting in the chamber. Be careful. Be very, very careful." Without another word, she disappeared into the shadows.

Delilah confident in Samson's usual gluttony when drinking wine, and was relieved to find him in a stupor on her return. She carefully tied the bowstrings around Samson's wrists and ankles together. Once complete, she lit several candles, then stood at the foot of the bed and shouted, "Samson, my love, get up. The Philistine's are here!"

Samson jolted awake and lurched forward. "What? Philistines, you say?" He swung both legs to the floor then noticed the bowstrings. With a laugh, he ripped the ties from his wrists and yanked the other strings from his legs and ankles, chuckling as they snapped and fell to the floor.

Delilah forced a laughed. "You lied to me. You told me seven undried bowstrings would strip your power but, since that didn't happen, I see you don't love me enough to share your secret."

Samson lifted her high above his head, then covered her with kisses. "Come back to bed, my sweet."

It wasn't long before Samson drifted back to sleep with his love wrapped securely in his arms. Delilah, her bottom lip jutting out, laid quiet, frustrated her plan didn't work. Beside her was the heavy breathing of the man she hated. *Another time. There will be another time.*

Cobal listened until he heard no movement in the bed-chamber, then waved his men to move to the exit. Once outside, they followed the path leading away from the cottage where they met Shara. Before Cobal could speak, she raised her hand.

"I heard enough to know the plan failed," Shara snapped, then pointed to the road. "Just go, please. I will contact your messenger when the next strategy is launched." Exhausted, Shara reached the main house and returned to the comfort of the cushioned lounge chair she left earlier. She was relieved the host family had been sent away until issues were resolved, leaving the house quiet. She covered her face with her hands. *This is a mess. Nothing is working. We need to find a way out of this deal. It's time to go home.*

Dressed in all black, Abaddon sat in the far corner of the tavern sipping wine while watching patrons move in and out of the crowded, smoke-filled room. Scanning the area, he noticed several familiar faces of men he saw around the guest home of the woman Delilah the last few days. He drained the goblet, stood, kicked his chair aside, and walked to the table where the men were huddled.

"Gentlemen," he shouted over the noise, "making plans for the evening?"

Cobal shifted his chair so he could face the stranger and eyed him boldly. "You have me at a disadvantage, Sir. Do I know you?"

Abaddon leaned forward with a fixed stare at the man he remembered seeing in the caravan with Delilah. "I'm a friend of a friend of yours. Just thought I'd stop by here before checking on *my* friend, Samson."

Cobal ignored the comment and looked across the room. Abaddon followed his gaze in time to see a man, small in stature, wearing a long-hooded robe, leaving the tavern. He gripped Cobal's arm. "I see plans have already been set for the evening." He sneered then released his grip. "It's of no matter to me. I was just about to visit my friend."

Standing erect, Abaddon rubbed his hands together. "Please continue with your conversation. Don't let me interrupt any further." He smiled, turned and pushed through the crowd. At the door, he looked over his shoulder, then exited. The men eyed each other. Cobal leaned forward. "We've got a problem and we need to handle it."

The two messengers stood outside the estate gates where Samson and Delilah were staying. Shara appeared out of the shadows. "I have another message. She needs new ropes. According to Samson, if she ties him in *new* ropes, he will become weak and lose his power."

The two men left Shara to report the new request. Midway between the house and the road, they ducked in the shadows when they saw a man on horseback approach. The rider paused, looked around, and then turned onto the roadway leading estate. One messenger nudged his partner. "Come, move quickly," and they disappeared out of sight.

CHAPTER 20

Abaddon, escorted by Shara, walked to the guest house. He entered the area bearing gifts for Delilah, and wine for his friend.

"My man, what a surprise. Come," Samson said with a grin and waved toward the dining area. "Join us." He slapped his friend on the shoulder. "Good to see you."

Abaddon hugged Samson, but greeted Delilah with a cold stare.

Laughing, Delilah ignored the cool reception. She slid her arms around Samson's neck, gave him a quick kiss, and ruffled his hair. With a wink at Shara, she walked to the door and paused. "Why don't we leave you gentlemen to enjoy the wine while we check to ensure you have a hearty meal," she announced.

"That's my lady," Samson shouted while grabbing two wine goblets. Seeing he was preoccupied, Delilah shot Abaddon a look designed to peel his hide and left.

Abaddon crossed his arms. "Man, what have you gotten yourself into," he asked while looking around to make sure the women had left the area.

"You've forgotten everything you have been destined to do. These are not your people." He punched his fists in the air. "Don't you see, they hate you, man. You need to come with me so we can head home before it's too late."

Samson sat on the high back lambskin chair at the head of the dining table, flexed his muscles, and tapped the wine goblet he was holding. "Relax my friend. Do you think I need a warning against anyone who would think to attack me?" He jabbed Abaddon's arm. "Don't worry about me, I have no fear of threats."

Abaddon pulled a chair close to his friend. "Listen. They are out to get you. This woman Delilah means you no good. I've been hearing stories and think you need to put some space between you and this woman so that you can clear your head."

Samson raised his hand. "Stop," he demanded while jamming a finger in Abaddon's chest. "Enough of this. Bring me no vicious lies. This is my woman you speak of with disrespect. Samson stood, walked to the window overlooking the garden, and chuckled. "Look my friend. We have known each other for years. Let's not damage the relationship over a woman, especially my woman."

Abaddon cleared his throat and waved his arm. "This is your tomb my friend. All preparations have been made, but you won't recognize the danger. The flood gates have opened, and the adversary is at your doorstep."

Samson laughed loud and hard. "I never heard marriage described quite that way." He leaned against the window sill, and looked heavenward. "I warn you, my friend, I will hear no more doom and gloom. Your attitude must change, or you must leave. I will not have my lady upset, and you will be held accountable if that happens. Do I make myself clear?"

Abaddon put his goblet on the table, walked to the door, turned, and faced his friend, a look of sadness in his eyes. "It's clear to me I've arrived too late. My staying would come to no good. You my friend, do not want to know the truth. Unfortunately, when you do, it may be too late." He crossed the doorsill and looked over his shoulder. "Please make excuses to the ladies for me."

Samson took one step forward, hands raised, palms up. "Will, you not stay and have a meal with us?"

Abaddon pinched the bridge of his nose and shook his head. "No, my friend. I'll return to the tavern, eat, rest, and make ready to return to our homeland tomorrow."

In the brief silence that followed, they heard sounds of chatter and laughter before Delilah, Shara, and two maids appeared with platters of fish, lamb, bread, cheese, fruit, and more wine. "I sent a messenger to invite a few of the neighbors to join us by the pool for a gathering," Delilah said with a smile and winked at Abaddon. "It's a hearty meal. I hope you enjoy it."

Once again, Abaddon glared at her, shook his head, and adjusted the hood of his travel robe. He gave Samson one last look, dropped his head, and left without another word.

"Well, that was a surprise," Delilah exclaimed. "Was it something I said?

The spies watch the stranger leave the gates and travel the roadway toward the center of town. Without speaking, the lead spy waved the other to follow. "Ensure he stays away from this place the rest of the evening. We need to defend the plan at all costs, do you understand?"

The spy nodded and disappeared into the shadows, running to keep pace with the stranger.

Abaddon reached the tavern stopped at the stable, removed his satchel, and turned his horse over for the evening. He crossed the road and re-entered the tavern he visited earlier. He checked into a room at the hotel desk, deposited his belongings, and returned to the tavern for a meal. Upon entering, he bumped into Cobal. Their eyes met, but they didn't speak. Abaddon took a seat in the corner.

Cobal and the others entered the deserted street.

The attendant, who followed Abaddon since he left Samson, rushed forward. "That man may be a problem. He just returned from the estate."

Cobal nodded. "If he becomes a problem, we will deal with him," and moved the group away from the doorway. "The plan is to capture and destroy Samson. We will not fail. One of you will stay here and monitor this man's movements. He is not allowed to return to the home of Delilah this night." He pointed to the largest man in the group. "You will stay and maintain order. Do you understand?"

The man nodded and pulled a dagger from his cloak. "He will not return, Sir. I can assure you of that."

Cobal nodded and adjusted his hood. "It's getting late. Let's get the new rope requested and return to the estate. Time is of the essence."

The gathering with the neighbors lasted well into the night. Delilah made sure Samson drank as much as he wanted while she teased and danced before him, with promises of an enjoyable evening when they were alone. As soon as the last guest had departed, Delilah led Samson to bed, disrobed, and joined him.

"My sweet," he said and dragged his hawkish gaze over her body. "Marry me." Delilah didn't answer but began to rub the hair on his chest. Moments later, he was heavy snoring. Based on Samson's information, the new ropes he said would affect his strength were close at hand, as were Cobal and his spies. Delilah lay very still to ensure her prey was deep asleep, then slid out of bed, grabbed her sheath dress and the new rope. It took several minutes to tie and tighten the rope around Samson's ankles and wrists. She even anchored the ends of the rope using the bedposts. Standing to one side, she called to him.

"Samson, by the gods, wake up! The Philistines are upon you." Eyes open, with jerking movements, Samson pulled the ropes and freed himself. Unchallenged, he sat in the middle of the bed roaring with laughter. "See baby," he shouted. "No restraints for me."

Rising from a squatting position in the chamber, just outside the room, Cobal put a finger to his lips with one hand, then waved his spies in the direction of the exit. Outside, he and his men traveled the path to the estate entrance without incident.

"No success again, Sir," one of the men mumbled.

Cobal didn't answer. He was watching a tall man approaching, moving at a slow pace. He recognized it was one of his men and quickened his pace. When they were within reach, the man Cobal recognized as one of his spies leaned his weight on the side of a building.

Panting and wincing in pain, the spy whispered. "He's dead. I took care of him. It is well, Sir," he smiled.

Cobal cradled the young man in his arms while searching for injuries. "Son, tell me what happened." The spy breathed deep and described his confrontation with Samson's friend, Abaddon.

"He followed you to the man, Samson. I got distracted and didn't see him leave. He was too far ahead for me stop, so I waited for his return. He was gone a long time and rushed by me, not looking. I confronted him, and we fought."

Cobal's spy raised his dagger to show blood on the blade. "He won't tell anybody about what he saw, Sir. He won't talk ever again."

Cobal waved the men forward. "Take him to the hotel, attend to his injuries, then get him out of sight. The tavern owner is aware of our plans, so he will help in this situation." Everything done in secret, he warned."

* * *

The following next night, Delilah sent word that Samson would allow her to weave seven braids of his hair into the fabric on the loom and secure it with a pin so that he will become weak like any other man. Receiving the message, Cobal and his men positioned themselves again in the chamber near Delilah and Samson and waited. Again, she was fooled, and Cobal and his men went back to the tavern.

Delilah was moody and silent the entire next day, avoiding Samson's attempt at affection. "It is clear you do not truly love me," she accused, with an increased pitch in her voice. "I am not the love of your life. I am just another woman to you. Why should I marry you? We are not one. Our souls have not connected."

She stood in the doorway of their bedroom. "I think I'll leave, return to Sorek and you will never see me again." Delilah grabbed the door handle. "You made a fool of me with your lies, and I'm sick of it." She stormed out of the house and slammed the door.

For the entire day, Samson was alone. Delilah refused to see him until he sent flowers with the message that he would share the secret she wants to hear. She smiled and sent Shara to find the spies. "Tell them they need to be prepared to visit the estate that night." She smiled. "Tell them I finally have the secret."

Delilah bathed using her best oils and, dressed in her most alluring attire, and entered the suite she shared with Samson.

Samson greeted her with open arms. "My love, I would not have you unhappy. I confess. My secret is my hair. Have you not noticed how well

I've maintained my seven braids at all times?" Delilah smiled and nodded. He guided her to the balcony, seated her on one of the cushioned chairs, then paced the area.

"I am a Nazarite with powers granted me by my God through my hair. If my seven braids are removed, I will surely lose my strength." He stopped pacing, and turned to face the woman he loved, and threw his hands in the air then sat quiet for several minutes. "This is the truth. My God granted me this strength, and you alone now have the secret to my power."

Delilah jumped from her chair, wrapped her arms around Samson's neck, and kissed him hard. "I'll go now and order our evening meal. We will then spend time planning our wedding." In the main house, she ordered an extravagant meal filled with all the delicacies she could find. "This must be a heavy meal," she directed. "I want him very full and very satisfied when it's over." She found Shara in her favorite location near the pool and directed her to take the message with details of the plan.

"Tell them I need instruments to cut Samson's hair tonight. They are to wait until they see me snuff out the candles, I will have on the side table. The chair will be position so that my back is to the chamber door, where they will enter. They must cut his hair and take him away this night." Shara hugged her friend and left.

After ensuring Samson enjoyed a good hearty meal with plenty of wine, Delilah positioned her chaise lounge near the balcony entrance with her back to the chamber next to the suite. A cool breeze entered, blowing the sheer curtains, so they seemed to be dancing. The lighting from the single candle provided the soft glow to the room. She laid several large pillows on the floor nearby and turned on her side. "Come, my love, relax your head in my lap."

Full of his normal overabundant intake of wine, Samson sat on the cushioned pillows, and placed his head on her lap. In a low rhythmic tone,

Delilah hummed an ancient song that was a favorite of her brother. Her voice was soft and soothing.

Samson lifted his head and squeezed her leg. "What a beautiful voice you have, my sweet. I look forward to many days listening to these sounds."

Delilah smiled and gently massaged the back of his head. It wasn't long before he breathed deep and relaxed confirming he had fallen into a deep sleep. Still pulling the braids and rubbing his head with one hand, she pinched the candle to signal Cobal's men could enter. After several moments, the door opened, and the men crossed the room at a slow, steady pace.

Once in position, they cutting began. Using a sweeping motion, one of the men lifted each braid and cut it close to Samson's scalp while Delilah continued to massage his head. This procedure continued until all seven braids were removed.

The process complete, Cobal and his men stepped back in the shadows and waited.

Delilah took a deep breath then shouted. "Samson, wake up. The Philistines are upon you!"

Samson opened his eyes, lifted his head from her lap, and jumped to the floor, prepared to deal with whoever would be bold enough to disturb him. However, this time, several men pounced on him, chained his feet, and tied his hands. While struggling, he looked at his braids lying on the floor. With an angry growl, he struggled to be free, and noticed Cobal observing, with Delilah standing nearby. Eyes glazed with anger, he shouted "Delilah, I truly loved you. Why did you deceive me?"

She stepped forward, faced Samson, and screamed, "I did it for my brother. You killed my Jared, she sobbed."

Samson looked sad and confused as several men dragged him out of the room. One attendant, who stayed behind with Delilah and Cobal, stepped forward. He handed Delilah the pouch with the balance of the 5,500 silver coins promised payment, smiled, then left. She put the coins on the side table and relit the candle. Its warm glow brightened the room.

Cobal stepped outside and dismissed the rest of the men, then returned, approached Delilah and wrapped his arms around her shoulder. At first, she stiffened, but seconds later, her knees buckled, and she fell in his arms crying. Holding tight, he picked her up, opened the door and placed her on one of the balcony chairs.

The night breeze was cool and refreshing. She could smell the roses from the garden. "I can breathe now," Delilah said with a sigh.

Cobal took her hand. "I'm here. I will always be here if you want me." She looked at him, smiled, and laid her head on his shoulder but didn't answer.

Shara appeared in the balcony doorway, smiled, and observed the exchange between her friend and Cobal. After a few moments, she leaned forward and asked, "Hey you two, can we go home now?"

COMMENTARY

Samson was a Nazarite consecrated to God from birth. He voluntarily took the vow that required him to abstain from drinking wine and anything made from grapes or shaving or cutting his hair. He was also required not leave the "holy place," his home, and mingle with those who did not follow his faith because he might become unclean, making God's holy place unclean upon his return.

In his arrogance and self-centered choices, Samson ignored the mandates of his sacred pledge. He entered the land of Philistine and mingled with people forbidden to him by God. His decisions resulted in actions that defiled his body and violated his sacred pledge all because of his need to suit his selfish pleasures. During imprisonment for murder of the Philistines, he suffered imprisonment, torture, loss of sight, and disgrace.

Delilah was a beautiful woman approached by the Philistines to entice Samson to share the secret of his powers. Though no details exist to confirm her as a harlot, it's suggested the Philistine Kings approached her because she was known for the ability to accentuate her body and charm to influence the behavior of men who came in contact with her. The fact that there was no record of her continued contact with Samson after he was captured suggests it was a business arrangement.

Strangely enough, the tragic end to their relationship opened doors of opportunity that enabled Samson to repent from his actions, seek forgiveness, and destroy the enemy in the name of the one true God he pledged to serve. This is also a story that serves as a reminder of the result when self-indulgent disobedience becomes the primary focus.

STORY FOUR: THE TEN VIRGINS: CHOICE AND CONSEQUENCES

CHAPTER 21

After a hot sun-kissed day, the gusty wind blowing through the terrace was a welcome relief. The workers arranged several chairs and tables, supervised by Eitan, the tall, muscular property overseer. His commands were never complete sentences, but the workmen understood his directions and followed without question. He stood back and appraised the area. "Good work. Remember, remain in readiness."

Shara, the head housekeeper in charge of the residence, gazed out the window and observed the workmen preparing the property before returning her attention to the maidservants. "Let's pick up the pace, ladies," she shouted and snapped her fingers. In response, several maids stumbled over each other as they hurried to complete final tasks in preparation for the arrival of the ten virgins.

"This is a mess," mumbled one of the workers while polishing the copper plates and cups for the second time in the same week. "We've been rushing around here for weeks scrubbing floors, washing dishes, and cleaning linen over and over again while waiting for a group of women to arrive for this bride celebration event he's planning."

Overhearing the comment, Shara paused and wagged a finger in their direction. "Ladies, the groom has left explicit instructions, and we need to remain vigilant; he is nearby," she warned while inspecting several plates, napkins, and cups that were positioned at each of the ten place settings in the dining area. "Stay focused on the task," she continued, offering a fake smile. "Too much chatter leads to distraction from your duties. Stay focused and get everything done."

Satisfied that they were following her instructions, Shara walked away and continued inspecting the dining area setting. Seldom used, it was a magnificent room with polished oakwood floors, complemented with a long mahogany table surrounded by high-back, cushioned chairs trimmed in leather bolted with small brass tacks. The base of each armrest was decorated with unique gold-speckled design. Every place setting included a blank name holder for each young lady expected to attend.

Having folded the last of the table linen, one of the maidservants nudged her friend, chuckled, and whispered, "Ten virgins selected to spend time here, and he will only pick five to join the ceremony in the marble house?" She put both hands across her chest and jerked her head toward the dining hall. "This ought to be good. I, for one, can't wait to see how this plays out."

They both laughed.

When Shara overheard the maidservants' conversation, a vein popped in her neck. She pressed both hands to her cheeks, and stood in the doorway. "Your commentary is unwelcomed, and slothfulness is even less desirable, so grab those buckets, brooms, and mops, and start cleaning this corridor." She clenched her fists and breathed deeply. "Better yet, begin with the second-floor corridor and work your way down." She jerked her thumb and opened the door to the back stairs. "Now go," she commanded. "I want every corridor swept and mopped corner to corner." She leaned forward; lips curled. "That means *everything*."

"When finished, report to me immediately." The two women bowed and walked out the door. Shara smoothed her longhair sprinkled with gray, adjusted her skirts, and continued checking details in preparation for the guests' arrival. *I've no time for idle chatter and foolishness.*

The reflection of the sky appeared in a puddle outside the earth tone, two-level, stone-trimmed building jutting out of the mountainside, overlooking beautiful terrain. A lone horse approached, reins pulled tight, and paused in front of the large structure. A petite young woman draped in a long travel robe dismounted, tucked her toffee-brown hair under her shawl, and brushed her cheeks.

Scanning the area, she noticed a building to her right. Much more pleasing to the eye than the one she faced; it was surrounded by eye-catching shrubbery with marble steps leading to its entrance. On either side of the white, gold-trimmed double doors two enormous torch lights highlighted the doorframe. To her left stood a weathered barn. She heard the sound of horses neighing while thumping on the ground and observed something, or someone, moving in the shadows near the barn's entrance.

Keep it together, ole girl. Your eyes are playing tricks. Don't let your imagination get the best of you. You're on assignment; stay focused. She ignored the urge to run and regained her composure. Brushing the dust from her skirts, she pulled two of the three satchels from her horse, dropped them to the ground, exhaled, approached the doors, knocked, and waited.

Within a few minutes, the oakwood doors of the building she faced opened, shaking the two brass door handles on the outside. Simultaneously, a flock of birds, perched high above on the sloped roof, flew away. She turned to gaze at a tall, stern-faced gentleman who stepped forward and bowed but did not smile. "Good evening," he said without expression. "Please enter," he continued and pointed to the doorway. "Many of the others have already arrived."

The young lady hesitated, took one step back, and scrunched up her face. "Well, hello, and I'm pleased to meet you too," she responded with a forced smile while stepping in front of him to slow his pace. "I know we haven't had much time together, but my name is Ikia."

The man barely acknowledged that she spoke and trained his eyes on her feet until she stepped aside.

"Follow me, he commanded. I will get your bags."

Ikia pursed her lips and gave him a frosty look. "I guess this is one way to start my new life." She shrugged and followed in silence.

They entered, and she was immediately directed to ascend the flight of stairs. The oakwood floors, banister, and steps shone and gave off the fragrance of fresh oil. Her guide moved quickly as if impatient to end his task.

They were welcomed by a maidservant at the top of the stairs, holding white linen and flowers. Flashing a bright smile, she led them down a long corridor flanked with large mahogany doors. On each door was an empty, gold-trimmed nameplate. The maidservant stopped midway through the passage and turned to Ikia with a cordial expression on her face. "We were informed of your instructions. All the young ladies have arrived and are gathered downstairs in the reception area, as directed."

The escort cleared his throat, moved from side to side, and stroked his beard while avoiding Ikia's eyes. "I, um, well, I'm Eitan. I didn't know you were in charge of this event. My apologies for the way I greeted you earlier."

Ikia gave a mirthless laugh and tugged her earlobe. "I think we can safely call that exchange more of a non-greeting, but thank you, and I accept your apology. Let's set a goal that you improve your methods, so future visitors have a better experience."

They proceeded down the hall with the maidservant pointing from room to room. "Which one would you like?"

Ikia slapped her forehead and laughed. "I'll take the one on the right, in the middle." The maidservant smiled, opened the door selected, and stepped inside.

Ikia entered and removed her sandals, while the maidservant motioned for the escort to leave the satchels on a bench. Without a word, he deposited the bundles as instructed, bowed, and left.

The maidservant waited at the closed door, listening to the escort's fading footsteps before speaking. When all was silent, she turned to Ikia and her eyes brightened.

"Welcome." She smiled. "I am Mira, sent to be of service to you during this preparation phase. No one knows of my true assignment in service to you, but I was assigned as your handmaid so my interaction with you would be viewed as normal." She clasped her hands behind her back. "As directed, I will be your eyes and ears and report any observations. so you can assess and guide as you see fit."

Mira waved her hand in the air. "This room has the best view of the white mansion, and it's a great location for the evening breeze. She crossed the room, picked up a beautiful clay pitcher, poured water into a basin, draped it with a cloth, and placed it on the side table near the canopied bed. "You have time to rest, refresh, and prepare to join the others at dinner," she offered, then grabbed Ikia's travel sandals and walked to the door. "I will be here to show you the way. In the meantime, I'll clean the mud from your sandals and return them later."

Ikia removed her travel clothes and lay down. She sank into the soft, goose feather pillow and closed her eyes, falling asleep to the sounds of birds chirping. Some time later, her sleep was disturbed by the sounds of footsteps, loud chatter, and laughter in the corridor. Startled, she grabbed her robe, jumped out of bed, cracked the door open, and peered into the hall.

Within several feet of her door, a group of young women stood close together in a circle, talking. Several large and small satchels surrounded them. Mira, her assigned handmaid, and guide stood in the group's center, nodding and responding to questions.

"Look, can't we just pick our room?" one young lady shouted.

"Right," another smirked, her eyes shot sparks.

Still, another stepped forward, grabbed her satchel, and announced, "If that's the case, I'll take this one." She grabbed the handle of the closest room door.

Another woman shouted, "Hey, that's not fair; what if somebody else wants that room? We should draw lots."

The noisy chatter and confusion continued until Ikia opened her door and stepped outside. The silence could be sliced with a knife. The maidservant lifted her eyebrows with a look of caution on her face.

Ikia ignored the signal and stepped forward. "Greetings, ladies." She smiled and entered the circle. "My apologies for interrupting. I could be wrong, but I thought this would be a good opportunity to introduce myself." She paused and pretended not to notice the hostile stares. "I'm your hostess."

After a brief moment of silence, one of the young ladies pressed through the crowd and faced Ikia.

"Hi, I'm Mia. So, I guess your announcement means, as the hostess, you get the first pick of rooms, huh?" She didn't wait for a response but crossed her arms and looked directly at Ikia, with sharp eyes that missed nothing. "My, my isn't that just great." She smirked and turned her back to Ikia to address the group. "Well, ladies, I guess the rest of us will have to draw straws. The one with the shortest straw can be the first to pick the next room, and we can keep going until all rooms are designated." Mia pointed to the maidservant. "Can you get us some straws from one of the brooms or even out of the barn?"

The maidservant nodded. "Yes, ma'am, and, by the way, the name is Mira." She smiled and walked out of the circle.

"No. Wait," Ikia objected and moved to the middle of the circle, with a hand raised. Wearing a cheerful smile, she swirled around, tilted her head to one side, and faced Mia. "Thank you so much for the suggestion, but I arranged room assignments before my arrival." She ignored the blank faces. "So, you see, I will direct the maids as to who goes where while you ladies are enjoying your evening meal."

Mia glared at the hostess but remained silent and stepped back into the circle.

Ikia rubbed her hands together and grinned. "Now, let's see if I remember all your names," she continued while fishing for a small sheet of paper tucked in her robe. "Though I have your names on this paper, let's test my memory." She tossed her hair, raised a brow, and walked around the circle. "We're going to have plenty of time to get to know one another but, for now, please let me know who you are when I call your name."

Several of the ladies gave her a side-eye and shifted position in the circle. Ikia moved with them. "If I recall, our ten *special* ladies selected to prepare for the groom include Nettie, Chloe, Jacomina, Salome, Vashti, Achazia, Eunice, Manya, Bina, and of course Mia." Moving from person to person, she paused in front of each young lady, giving each a special greeting by whispering a message only they could hear.

"Well, that's settled," she offered in a pleasant tone while pointing to the staircase. "Please, ladies, go enjoy dinner and on your return, just look for your name on the brass plate in the center of each room door." She nodded at Mira, who immediately walked ahead of the group and guided the young ladies down the staircase to the dining area.

Mia gave her hostess a fake smile and military salute before following the crowd.

"In my opinion, you have her all wrong," Nettie challenged. "Don't be so negative about our hostess. She was just trying to make it clear that we didn't need to be concerned about where we'll sleep because it's already been resolved."

"Oh, for goodness' sake," Manya responded and threw her fork on the plate. "Stop being such a goodie two shoes, Nettie. Mia's right. We should go up there and tell her we don't need her to select our rooms. We should have followed the plan Mia suggested and drawn straws. It's simple and easy." She rolled her eyes skyward. "Besides, we shouldn't just accept what she says."

Jacomina, concerned that she would have to break her routine of going to bed at her regular time, moved her food around the plate then paused. "You know, I don't usually eat this late. It's a change from my routine." She bit her bottom lip. "Now I'll have to stay up half the night to unpack and get settled," she shrugged. "I hope it's more organized for the rest of our visit. I just don't want to find myself in this predicament again. I just need a schedule. A little more order and preplanning, that's all I want."

Vashti wiped her hands and folded the napkin; a smile danced on her lips. "So, ladies," she interrupted, "what did you think about the introductions, with our hostess walking from person to person whispering?

THE BACHELORETTES OF THE BIBLE

Who wants to share what she said?" She continued while looking directly at her seat partner, Salome.

Salome slid her chair back, faced Vashti, and cleared her throat. "Listen, before we all start sharing information, let's make sure this is something our hostess, Ikia, would approve us doing. After all, she appears to have definite plans for how we are to proceed as we prepare for the groom. It doesn't seem wise to share details and take a chance on being out of order."

"Here, here!" Achazia shouted while raising her goblet in salute of Salome's response. "The ten of us have been invited here to receive instruction in preparing for the prenuptial party with the groom, and I, for one, have no intention of stepping out of line. There's a reason for structure, so I think we need to get clarification about what we can and cannot do, then follow as directed." Noticing the silence, she giggled nervously. "Of course, I'm open to other opinions."

"Well, I don't know about the rest of you, but I arrived here alone." Eunice blurted, her cat-like eyes moving from girl to girl. "I make my own decisions and intend to do whatever is necessary to make sure I remain part of the group that attends the pre-wedding party." She wagged her finger around the room. "You ladies do as you please. I'll make it my way."

Bina leaned forward and set her hands, palms down, on the table. "Well, looks like I'm the last one to give an opinion," she huffed. "I've listened and understood how everyone feels. We came to this from different areas, challenges, and home life experiences. Our only connection is that we are all virgins. Seems to me our best approach is to spend some time listening and learning, so we understand what's expected. I'm not in favor of making our own rules."

Ikia stood outside the dining area listening to the exchange. She then entered carrying a parchment tied with a gold ribbon. "I hope you ladies enjoyed your meal." Not waiting for an answer, she took the chair at the head of the table.

Mira walked to the sideboard, poured a cup of water, placed it in front of her mistress' place setting, and waited for instructions. After glancing around the room, Ikia, leaned back in her chair, squared her shoulders, and took a deep breath.

"I had a late afternoon meal, so I will skip dinner and use the time to review what you've all been waiting to hear." She opened the parchment and continued, "Before all of you made your journey here, you received the formal engagement offer, sealed with a ring through arrangements with your parents."

Smoothing the corners of the document, Ikia continued. "It is also the custom that the groom prepares a place for his bride, in this case, brides to be," she noted, eyebrows raised. "There will be a procession leading to a small party before the marriage ceremony and celebration feast."

Several of the young women started mumbling. Eunice quivered with indignation and her temples throbbed with rage. She raised one hand. "Excuse me. Do you think we might be able to get some more details on this processional pre-event?" She tossed her hair, then tapped her fingernails on the table. "You see, I wasn't aware there were additional requirements involved in this process. My parents accepted the arrangement, and I traveled here to relax, enjoy a pre-marital gathering with my fellow brides, and the groom then get married."

Ikia stretched out her legs and made herself more comfortable in the chair. "Your situation will be a little different, at the direction of the groom. Because we have several of you lovely ladies, we will spend additional time together reviewing other details, as part of your orientation, before making the short trip to the pre-wedding banquet the groom has prepared for you all."

Jacomina picked at her nails. "This is all fine, but I would like to have clarification of what we can expect by way of our routine for the next few days. I need to have a clear plan I can follow. All these unexpected changes are nerve-racking." Sitting next to her, Nettie patted Jacomina's hand. "Not to worry, dear. I'll help keep you organized so there's as little disturbance to your routine as possible. Just stick with me."

Ikia pushed away from the table, stood, and unrolled the parchment. "Before we break for the evening, I want to review some additional details you should keep in mind for the next few days that you must never forget. All of you were invited to the banquet, and the fact that you are here means you accepted the invitation. Isn't that correct?" She asked. Her penetrating hazel-brown eyes scanned the group as her annoyance flared.

"All of you understand the reason you were invited, and it's been confirmed to you that you are in the right place." In response to the silence, Ikia smiled, folded the parchment, and handed it to her handmaid, Mira, who bowed and left the room. "Tonight, I am here to reassure you that everyone will be equally prepared with whatever is needed in time for the event."

Excitement filled the air. The ten ladies chatted, laughed, and whispered in private conversations while sipping wine. Ikia ran her hands through her hair, brushed her skirts, then walked to the dining room entrance, directing Mira to follow as three other servants entered carrying lamps. The room fell silent once again while each of the virgins was handed one of the lamps.

"What's this for?" Manya snapped. "The stairs and corridors in this place are well lit. Why do we need lamps, and where's the oil?"

Ikia returned to sit, crossed her ankles, and nodded at Mira, who signaled the maidservants to retrieve the oil canisters from the sideboard. One by one, they filled each lamp to the rim while the ladies watched. "To ensure there was no doubt everyone received the same portion of oil, I ordered each lamp to be filled while you are together as a group."

She cocked her head and gave a half-smile.

"You will learn soon enough the reason for this lamp. In the meantime, take great care of this item as there are no replacements, if misplaced or broken." She brushed her hands together, made a steeple with her fingers, and puckered her lips. "I think that's enough information for one night." She pointed to the exit. "Your rooms are now available, and it's been a long day. Enjoy the rest of your evening."

CHAPTER 22

B ina tossed and turned most of the night. Today was the third day of this adventure. Despite the potential of a promising future, she missed home, and waking up to sounds of sheep in the corral and the rooster crowing once the sun rose over the horizon. Now, her mornings offered no sound whatsoever. She squeezed her eyes shut to fight back the tears.

What have I gotten myself into now? I'm a farmer's daughter. It's basic and straightforward for me. By now, I would have had most of my chores completed and found my favorite spot to take a break and enjoy those beautiful hills around my home. Bina buried her head in the goose feather pillow and let her thoughts drift to times at home.

The silence was interrupted by two soft taps at her door. Bina sat up and listened. Someone was tapping again. She grabbed her robe, slipped her feet into her sandals, and walked to the door. Ear to the door, she whispered, "who is it?" and grasped the handle.

"It's me, Eunice. Open the door."

Bina did as she was asked and glared at her uninvited guest. "What do you want? Is something wrong?" She backed away, leaving the door open for her to enter, and sat on the edge of the bed. "I think this is supposed to be a quiet time while preparing for any of the day's assignments." Eunice ignored the comments and joined her, sitting on the bed.

"Look, I was observing you last night and thought we may have a lot of things in common. You're not like most of the other girls," she chuckled. "You don't get riled or unnerved easily. I watched you studying the surroundings and taking it all in. Not like Mia," she frowned and jumped off the bed, walked around the room, then looked out the window. "Hey, I think your view is better than mine."

I can't believe this mess. Girl, please. Get out of my room.

Bina strolled to the bedroom door and gripped the handle. "You were there last night, Eunice, and know full well the hostess picked the rooms. All we had to do was show up and walk in. Just like you, I had no idea what view I'd have until I entered. We arrived so late last night there was barely anything to see. You're the first to have a look." She opened the door and stood to the side. "I need to get refreshed to start the day, and you need to do the same. It will be breakfast time before we know it."

Eunice moved toward the open door. "Okay, okay. I get it," she responded as her nostrils flared. "We'll have time to talk again. I just think we should stick together to ensure we both make it to the party."

Bina waited for Eunice to exit the room, then responded. "Don't pull your hair trying to create strategies to ensure you make it to the banquet. You'll only frustrate yourself. I've yet to hear that any one of us have a better chance of attending the groom's banquet than the other. We've all been invited."

Bina waved as Mira passed by with other maidservants, then ran her hand through her hair. "Don't read any more into last night than there is for the moment. Somehow, I think Ikia will provide specific steps we can take to safeguard our entry to the event, if that's necessary. In the meantime, relax. It will all work out."

* * *

Chloe closed the side door, keeping quiet as possible, and walked down the path leading to the road. While looking over her shoulders to be sure no one followed, she tripped over several dead branches lying on the path. She recovered, then continued walking with no specific direction in mind.

Needing a break from the ladies, she explored the surroundings and was drawn by a beautiful structure that appeared to float from the clouds on the hilltop. The closer she came to the magnificent building, the more peaceful the atmosphere. She entered the cobblestone path leading to the front door and was greeted by beautiful, well-manicured shrubbery sprinkled throughout with white lilies and pink and red roses.

Before she reached for the handle, Chloe looked over her shoulder one more time to ensure she was still alone. She opened the door and was shocked at the sight of a large room with old wooden benches on either side separated by an aisle leading to a large altar. Above the altar was a massive window with bright light streaming through and hitting a beautiful gold cross standing in the center of the room. Other than the sound of running water in a fountain to the right of the altar, it was quiet, almost serene.

"Come in, please," someone called from the front of the room. Chloe, eyes wide, looked up as a tall man stepped forward. His hooded white robe was secured with a silver belt. "You're welcome to enter to find the peace you seek." He walked to the altar. "I will only be here a short time. I'm the caretaker, you see, and once my duties are finished, will leave you alone to meditate." He stared at her intently for a moment, then proceeded to light several torches, pour wine into several goblets from a pitcher on a nearby stand, and place a small loaf of bread on a copper plate at the altar.

Chloe stiffened and tilted her head toward the condiments. "Is that supposed to be for me?"

The man turned, opened his arms, and smiled. "It is for anyone who feels the need to partake. I lay these items out here every day. It is one of my duties in service to the groom."

After several moments of silence, Chloe returned to the door and reached for the handle.

"You are overly rigid and self-disciplined," The man commented, his expression sobered. "Even at this moment, when you know you should stay and spend time in this solitude, you remain focused on a daily routine that has nothing to do with what the future may have in store."

She gasped. His voice washed over her like ripples of running water, easing her initial discomfort. Chloe moved away from the door and stood behind one of the benches. "How did you know my name, and what do you know about my future?" The caretaker folded his arms across his chest and smiled. "Sit, let us talk awhile."

"Let's see how she handles this." Vashti snapped as she took another bite of the honey bun that was one of the breakfast treats. "This is a real organized mess we have here. Instead of complying with the rules, several of us have decided not to arrive for breakfast at the appointed time." She threw a small chunk of bread on the plate and reached for a piece of fish. "I mean, really, I'm sure the maidservants gave everyone the wake-up call and instructions. You'd think people would do as they are told."

"Let's be patient," Nettie offered. "I'm sure they'll be here shortly. Jacomina had a rough time getting settled in last night. I checked on her before turning in, and she's had a challenge with the late evening routine. She'll be fine, though." She looked around the table at several empty chairs. "Besides, we really haven't been down here that long, and our hostess has yet to arrive, so everything will be fine."

Mia rolled her eyes and tensed her shoulders at Nettie's comment. "You're always protecting someone, aren't you?" She rubbed one shoulder. "I've spent a lifetime making excuses for why people didn't do something or why they are a certain way, and what did it get me? Here I am, a *privileged* virgin with nine other virgins preparing to attend the pre-marital party with a groom who promises a better life for those prepared to receive him."

Nettie shrugged and nodded. "I agree there are challenges to our faith in the plan. I'm not one hundred percent certain this story will have a happy ending, but we must stay positive."

Mia leaned back in her chair and chuckled. As bitterness filled her mouth, she continued, "There's more unknown than known in this situation. How can we be sure this isn't some game?" Before anyone could respond, the doors opened, and Salome, Achazia, Manya, and Bina burst into the room, giggling and chatting.

"So, you girls had a good morning?" Vashti asked while cutting her eyes over to Mia. "We've been waiting for you guys but decided, since breakfast was getting cold, to go ahead and start without you." After taking another bite of the bread, she dropped it on the plate, folded her arms, and stared at the new attendees as if waiting for a response.

"Look," Manya responded, her jaw clenched. "If you must know, we all kind of bumped into each other in the hall earlier. When we came down, it was too early for breakfast, and one of the maidservants mentioned there was a small lake behind the barn and several canoes, so we had a boat race." She pointed to the group. "Bina and me against Salome and Achazia. Of course, our group won."

Achazia scowled. "Yeah, right. Not to mention, you had a pretty good head start before shouting, *let's race*."

Everyone laughed while Manya blushed. "The goal was to win," she chuckled and served her plate.

Chloe eased into the room, grabbed a breakfast plate from the sideboard, and sat at the table. The girls continued bantering about their morning activities.

Salome gave her a side-eyed glance. "Where have you been? We do have rules, you know?" She waited for a response but Chloe smiled, moved the food around on her plate, and shifted in her chair.

"Give it a rest Salome," Nettie interrupted and winked at Chloe. "Girl, ignore her. If you haven't noticed already, Salome gets upset if the rules aren't followed exactly as demanded. Lord help us all if one thing is out of place," she said half-jokingly.

Everybody laughed and went back to eating and interrupting each other with their opinions about the schedule and instructions provided so far, projections on what would come next, and criticism of something each had or had not done, or could have done better.

Chloe was relieved to have their attention diverted from her. It allowed her to contemplate whether or not she was going to share her experiences that morning. The visit to the white mansion was like nothing she had ever experienced and, looking around the table, she wasn't sure who would understand anything she described. *Yep, I think I'll keep this to myself for the time being. Or share with Ikia. Yes, maybe I'll share my adventure with Ikia.*

* * *

Ikia entered with Mira following and carrying a wooden box with a gold-trimmed handle. She walked around the room, stopping to give personal greetings to everyone, then sat in her regular spot at the head of the table.

"Good Morning, ladies. I hope you all slept well."

Several of the ladies nodded, but Vashti heaved a heavy sigh and threw her hands in the air. "Seriously, are we going to have *another* mystery challenge?"

Ikia crossed her legs, and rubbed the back of her neck. "I think it's time for a reminder break. This is not a game. You are here for a purpose, and that is to prepare for the groom. This requires each of you to follow a specific process." She scanned the group, giving each an intense look. "The expectation is that everyone here will follow those rules, no matter what it takes." She waved her arms to include all the women. "I assume you're all planning to attend the banquet, right?" She asked, then waited.

They all nodded, and Ikia dipped her head in return as Mira opened the wooden box, and placed it on the table.

"Today, you each have assignments that require you to spend time alone. This challenge is one you must face in preparation for the banquet." Ikia pushed the box to the middle of the table. "To ensure there's no concern that any of you was given more of an advantage than the other, you each must pull your assignment from this box." The virgins looked at each other, but none of them reached toward the box.

"Oh, for goodness' sake," Mia snapped and jumped out of her seat to drag the wooden box within reach. She hesitated, then pulled a small piece of parchment from its interior. Before she could open and read the instructions, Ikia raised her hand and cautioned Mia to wait. "You must do exactly as you are told, no deviation."

"Of course," Mia responded, and proceeded to read the message in silence. When she finished, she gave Ikia a look of disgust and left the room without saying a word.

One by one, the remaining maidens reached into the wooden box and read their instructions. Each exited the room without comment.

Mira began clearing the used dishes with the other maidservants' assistance. Ikia remained seated, staring out the window to the garden overlooking the beautiful lake.

Then Mira spoke. "No one knows the hour of his arrival, yet they must be ready every day and at any time of day."

Ikia stroked the side of her cup. "True. They must all be prepared and ready to enter the banquet, or they will be left behind."

Mira raised her eyebrow and cocked her head to one side. "I don't understand. I thought they were all invited to the banquet. How could any one of them, therefore, be left behind?"

Ikia didn't answer but continued to gaze out the window. A soft breeze stirred the curtains. "I wonder if it will rain today. There was a dark cloud in the distance earlier." She half shrugged and turned her attention back to Mira. "Yes, all were invited, but it's still possible only a few will be chosen. It will all depend on the individual choices they make."

* * *

Mia left the dining room and stomped up the stairs to her room. *If she thinks I'm going to take a walk in the woods without covering and a lamp, she's crazy. Based on what she's given me to do, it will surely be nightfall before I return. This is ridiculous.* She grabbed her things, rushed down the hall to the rear staircase, and followed the corridor to the kitchen . She looked behind her several times to ensure no one was watching. At the kitchen entrance, she cleared her throat, and several servants looked up and smiled. "I have to make a short journey and may perhaps miss the midday meal or even supper," she said. "Please prepare a meal I may take along for this adventure."

Mira emerged from one corner of the room. "They'll be happy to prepare some refreshments for you," she offered. "It will only take a few moments."

Uncomfortable with being discovered, Mia shifted from side to side, avoiding eye contact. "I thought it would be good to have a meal in case my assignment takes me through the afternoon meal." She moved to the prep counter, picked up the food pack that had been prepared, and walked out the side door and down the trail that wound to the lake.

Mira stood in the doorway and watched the young virgin until she was out of sight. "Many are called, few are chosen," she whispered and returned to her duties.

When the house was out of sight, Mia slowed her pace and concentrated on the instructions listed on her parchment. They caused her to leave the path covered with pebbles and take a side opening covered with dead plants and broken branches. *This is ridiculous. She sends me on a venture to find a brown satchel tied with a yellow ribbon that holds five smooth stones.*

After a few more steps, the shrubbery became thicker, and the full coverage of the tall trees with gnarled tree roots blocked the light from the sun. Despite the struggle, Mia pressed forward. She breathed heavily from pushing aside the greenery and strained her eyes. Someone in the clearing ahead beckoned to her. Her heart pounded until she recognized the familiar figure.

"Ikia, is that you?" she shouted and hastened her pace. The person didn't respond but waved to beckon her forward. The surrounding shrubbery grew thicker. Focused on keeping sight of the individual, she stumbled over a tree trunk and stubbed her toe. Wincing in pain, she inspected her foot. Confirming no significant damage, she refocused her attention on reaching whoever was ahead on the path. She turned a slight curve in the road, and froze. The figure was gone. "Ikia!" Mia shouted and ran in the direction where she last saw the hostess. Tired and struggling to see, she stopped and lit her lamp. When she scanned the area, her eyes widened, and her mouth dropped open.

The clearing was transformed into one of the most beautiful scenes she could have conjured in her mind. The trees were an artist's dream; multi-colored green, orange, yellow, and red. At their base was every possible flower she could imagine, all interspersed with fresh greenery. Hummingbirds moved from flower to flower, sharing space with bees and other outdoor life.

"Sit and rest," came a warm, soft voice behind her. Mia whirled around to see Ikia smiling. "Come," Ikia repeated and pointed to several soft cushions on the ground. "Sit, and let's talk."

Mia made a wide circle in the dirt with her foot, then walked to the cushions and plopped down. "What's this all about," she snapped while adjusting the pillow seating. "If you wanted to have a conversation, we could have met back at the house and saved us both time and trouble."

Ikia sat on a set of pillows opposite Mia. "Yes, we could have met at the house, but somehow, I think I have more of your attention doing it this way." She reached into her satchel and pulled out a flask of wine and a loaf of fig bread wrapped in a white linen cloth. "You still have to find the satchel before your return. This is a time of refreshment, a break before you continue. It's also your time to focus on yourself in preparation for the groom."

Several moments of silence followed. Mia did a secondary inspection of her toe, that still throbbed while Ikia poured two cups of wine and placed them before her.

"You have a commanding spirit that, when used correctly, can serve well." Ikia reached for one of the cups and offered it to Mia. "If not under control, however, your behavior might be viewed as bitterness or as having an attitude of one who will force people, by commands, to your opinion."

Mia shrugged but didn't comment. The breeze flowed around them, causing the lamplight to flicker. Ikia picked up one of the cups and handed it to Mia. She then broke a piece of bread from the loaf and gave Mia her portion.

"Let's refresh for a moment while you think about what I've said. It might serve you well on your journey to meet the groom." Mia ate and drank the bread and wine without blinking, then placed the empty cup on the plate. She rose from her seat, and handed them both to Ikia.

"Of course, I appreciate you sharing your opinions and will certainly consider your recommendations, but now I must finish this exercise and find the satchel with the stones."

With that last comment, Mia returned to the cushions, and gathered her belongings. While adjusting her robe, she sighed and looked at the sky. "So, tell me, Ikia, are there any other activities like this planned that I should be prepared to complete. Also, don't you think it would have more impact if we worked on challenges like this as partners?"

Mia waited and when there was no response, she put both hands on her hips and turned around to repeat her question. She was shocked to find Ikia had disappeared. The wine, cups, and bread remained in place for only a moment before a gust of wind knocked them over.

Now isn't that just like her? What the heck? She pulled out the parchment and studied the notations, then picked up the lamp, gathered her things, and walked in the direction noted on the instructions.

In the shadows, Ikia stood silently watching. A figure nearby whispered.

"It is all about perspective, my hostess," Mira said. Had she listened and engaged, her assignment would have ended. Instead, she will go full circle only to return to find the satchel, with the five smooth stones she seeks, was here all the time."

Ikia nodded in agreement.

"Come," the kind voice commanded, "there's more work to do."

CHAPTER 23

J acomina rushed past Nettie with her face contorted and climbed
the staircase leading to the rooms.

"Hey girl." Nettie laughed. "You nearly knocked me over.
Slow down. Are you okay?"

"No, I'm not okay," she responded, her full lips curled into a pout.
"I'm so frustrated that dinner would be delayed again. I'm used to a
regular schedule, you know, consistency and balance."

She threw up her hands and pointed in the direction of the dining
room, then the piece of parchment in her hands. "Nothing is clear or
suggests a routine or flow you can depend on daily. From unexpected
instructions on this parchment to another change of schedule for the
evening meal, I feel nothing but confusion."

Jacomina, with Nettie following, stopped at the top of the staircase,
rubbed her temples, and gazed out the window. "Tell me, just what does it
take to stick to a simple meal schedule? There are too many unknowns in
these constantly changing details."

Nettie rubbed Jacomina's shoulders. "Calm down, my friend. We'll get through this together." Nettie and Jacomina became companions, meeting on the upper-level balcony near their rooms after everyone was sleep in the evenings. They shared thoughts about the day's assignments and their past experiences. Nettie felt Jacomina needed support until she was more comfortable with their routines and could get a firm footing as to what was expected of them.

"It'll be fine, Jacomina," Nettie commented. "Just take a few deep breaths, and enjoy the view." She continued in a soothing tone, "we'll be able to eat soon, just be patient. After that, the new evening routine you planned and adapted to will continue uninterrupted."

Ignoring the encouraging words, Jacomina freed herself from her friend's embrace, and pointed out the window. "Yeah, right. I don't see how we'll be eating any time soon. Look, isn't that Mia coming out of the woods? She's a mess. Now, we'll have to wait until she's cleaned up before we can eat." She whirled around and faced Nettie, both arms across her chest. "Yet another delay."

Nettie fell silent as Jacomina gave a dismissive wave, and smirked. "See you at dinner," she said, then marched a short distance to her room.

Turning back to the window, Nettie stared outside. She couldn't help noticing how slow Mia was moving, as if she were tired or in pain. *"Maybe she needs help."*

Without a second thought, Nettie ran down the stairs. At the bottom, she paused, looking both ways, then took the long corridor leading to the side entrance. *"The way she looks, I'm sure she'll enter from this side, so she can walk through the back garden to the patio area. That way, she can take the back stairs unnoticed. I wonder what happened to her?"*

Jacomina closed her bedroom door, leaned on the frame, and scanned the room. *My head is spinning with too many changes and new instructions every other day. No time to process and prepare before something new happens. I'm not cut out for this.*

She decided to spend some time selecting outfits and matching jewelry for the next day. While making selections, she paused, went to the dresser, and picked up the instructions she'd been given earlier. With a sigh, she closed her eyes, and leaned against the door massaging her arms.

After several moments, she inhaled then opened her eyes. Stricken with fright, her mouth dropped open. She was no longer in her room. Instead, she stood in a chapel surrounded by beautiful torch lights mounted on long-stemmed gold posts. The base of the benches were also made of gold and covered with rich red cushions.

Frightened, Jacomina closed her eyes then opened them again, only to discover she was standing in the same place. A tall, dark, strikingly handsome stranger stepped in front of the chapel's altar, followed by two beautiful women, each dressed in long white hooded robes tied with gold tasseled belts. They acknowledged Jacomina with a smile then, heads bowed, clasped their hands forming a steeple. The man did not approach but spoke to Jacomina as if they had known each other all their lives.

"Your focus needs adjusting. It is the reason for your parchment assignment," the stranger offered with a smile. Remembering the paper she still clutched, Jacomina opened her hand and unrolled the parchment note that contained a list of ten items. Every other instruction was a command to stop and redo the previous instruction. Exhausted by the thought of what she was expected to do, Jacomina sank on one of the benches and shook her head as tears streamed down her face.

The man took several steps forward, stopped, then called her name.

When she looked up, he continued, "Wipe your face and look at your instructions again. What does it state? Read them out loud."

Moving in slow motion, she wiped her eyes, and opened the parchment and read aloud.

"Before you do anything, the instructions directed, *read everything first."*

Jacomina looked at the man, "I did read most of it, which says the same thing, and that's to start one thing, then stop and start another."

The man shook his head, smiled, and waved his hand then Ikia appeared. "What does the last line say, Jacomina?" she asked.

Jacomina looked at her parchment again, and read the last line of the instructions aloud. *"After you have read these instructions, you are to do nothing but discard the parchment and spend some time before dinner walking in the garden."*

After reading,, Jacomina laughed, punched the air, and jumped from her seat. She hugged Ikia, then closed her eyes and leaned on the back wall, continuing to laugh. A few moments later, she inhaled then scanned her surroundings again. To her disappointment, she was back in her room, leaning against the door and clutching the parchment. She rubbed her forehead, then closed and opened her eyes a second time. Nothing had changed.

Accepting her fate, Jacomina sighed and re-read the instructions. The words lifted her mood and joy filled her spirit like warm sunshine. She walked to the bedroom window, gazed at the sky, and scratched her head. *"I don't know what just happened, but I sure feel better. Thank you, Lord God."*

Vashti strutted around the garden patio where she, Nettie, Manya, and Salome gathered before the evening meal. Although the others sat in the shade, the slight breeze did nothing to cool the patio. The atmosphere was tense, which did not improve the situation.

"Well, I can certainly tell you this, I, for one, wouldn't go dragging myself around the woods chasing some dreamed-up instructions just to test my worthiness to be one of the brides. Mia should have put her foot down, stopped, and called it a day."

One of the maidservants arrived with a tray of fruit. Before she could place it on the sideboard, Vashti stopped her and held the display aloft. "Look at this variety of beautiful, appealing fruit, all shapes and sizes. This platter is us! We're the beautiful, delectable fruit selected for the groom." She handed the platter back to the maidservant and waved her on, then continued to stroll around the patio.

"In my opinion, this is all just busy work because they want to make us think there's more to it." She danced around the table and laughed. "Seriously, I don't know about you, but I'm already worthy." She waved her arms in a wild circle and twirled like a graceful ballerina. "We're all worthy, otherwise why were we invited? Think about it."

Nettie shifted in her seat. "Well, I just think Mia, like the rest of us, decided to complete a task assigned to her. Frankly, I think she did a great job."

Vashti paused in front of Nettie's chair and leaned forward. Disapproval gleamed in her eyes. "Of course, you would say that, oh protector of everyone."

While observing Vashti's performance, Manya chuckled and twirled her hair while reflecting on her adventure moments before joining the group. Deciding this virgin could be a serious competitor, she lingered before joining the ladies on the patio. When certain the coast was clear, she entered Vashti's room to explore how her rival lived to determine if any secrets could be uncovered.

Once inside, she inspected several items, none of which held her interest. While looking inside one of her satchels, she heard footsteps in the hall. Manya froze in place and listened. Whoever it was, stopped at each room before moving to another, coming closer and closer to her location. When the footsteps stopped at Vashti's room, there was a long pause before the door handle moved.

Beads of sweat formed on Manya's forehead. She held her breath and waited for someone to enter. Instead of opening the door, however, the person put an object outside the door then moved on.

Manya waited until the footsteps faded down the hall and immediately threw the satchel to the floor and walked to the exit. Eyes focused on the door, she tripped over a sandal and stooped to return it to its position. She then realized a note written on parchment was wedged into the sandal. She read the message, then smiled as she returned the paper to its position.

After shutting Nettie down, Vashti continued pacing back and forth, dictating how they should respond and what actions they should take when certain things occurred or directions are given. "You know I'm always available to talk, so don't feel pressured to respond each time you're given an instruction." She smiled and opened her arms. "I'm here. You can stop by my room any time for a chat."

Manya pushed her chair away from the table, stretched, then cleared her throat to interrupt Vashti's performance and gain the group's attention.

"Tell us, Vashti," she said while crossing her legs. "What about you? How did you complete your assignment? What did your parchment say?"

Vashti recoiled, cocked her head to one side, and studied Manya, eyes blazing. "You're kidding, right? I didn't expect any instructions to be written on my parchment, and there wasn't."

She waggled her hips and walked closer to Manya, her attitude combative. *This little heifer asking me a question like that in front of everyone.* "I would wager there are several of us who weren't assigned to complete these foolish exercises."

The women looked at each another, but no one spoke.

"That's right, ladies," came a familiar voice. All the ladies turned their attention to Ikia who leaned against one of the white archway pillars leading from the patio to the house. "It's not necessary or permitted to share individual assignments."

Strolling around the patio, she stopped next to Vashti. "Everyone who has instructions should follow them." She smiled, eyes penetrating as she scanned the group. "As for you, Vashti, like you said, if you didn't see any specific instructions on your parchment, then there's nothing left for you to do."

Vashti forced a smile then sat at the table with the rest of the women.

In the silence, Ikia's handmaid, Mira, appeared and announced dinner was ready and waiting. Several of the ladies stood immediately and walked down the path leading to the house behind Mira. After a few moments, the only people remaining on the patio were Ikia and Vashti. Ikia sat across the table from Vashti and leaned forward with her chin resting on her palm. She cocked her head to one side and gazed at the sky for a few seconds. "So, your parchment was blank, was it?"

Vashti bit her lip and shifted in her seat. "Well, maybe not blank, but there weren't any specific instructions that I could see."

Ikia pushed her chair away from the table and walked to the edge of the patio before she turned and glanced at Vashti. "I suggest you take a look at your message one more time before joining us for dinner. It may give you fresh insight," Ikia turned away and walked down the path toward the house.

Vashti pulled the parchment from the pocket of her skirt, smoothed the edges, and read the message. This time instead of folding the parchment, she crumpled and shoved it deep into her pocket. Tossing her hair to one side, she walked down the path to join the others for dinner.

* * *

Achazia was the last to arrive for dinner, fearful of being questioned about whether she was carrying the parchment, which she had forgotten. Weighing the consequences of being without her instructions, she ran from the patio area up the back stairs to her room. She grabbed the note, then rushed to the main stairway leading to the dining room. Before she descended the first step, someone called her name.

"Achazia, there's something much bigger at stake than making sure you have a set of instructions."

Achazia whirled to see Ikia standing behind her, not far from her room.

"You spend so much time weighing possible consequences of your actions, or over-researching issues, it often creates hesitation in your making important decisions that could lead to your missing the point of the exercise or an event."

Ikia stepped closer, pointing at Achazia. "Look at you," she continued, "instead of being part of the gathering in the dining room, you're up here because you weighed the decision about whether or not to keep the instructions with you earlier."

Achazia didn't speak but fingered the note in her pocket.

Ikia put her arm around Achazia's shoulder and reached for the young woman's chin. "Be careful not to overthink issues or hesitate to make decisions. Doing so could derail your plans at a most crucial time."

Walking ahead of Achazia, Ikia grasped the rails and smiled. "Take heed to my words not to overthink your decisions. They could serve you well in the days ahead." Ikia extended her hand. "Come, let's join the others."

Achazia hesitated and scrutinized her guide, then took her hand.

Ikia shook her head. "Later, when you return to your room, review the instructions, focus on making a decision and act on that choice without hesitation."

Achazia and Ikia reached the opening to the dining room just in time to hear Eunice complain, "So we are to count one to ten and be identified by numbers from this point forward? Are you kidding me?"

The other women murmured while Mira stood at the head of the table with a large round jar.

Ikia cleared her throat to gain their attention and escorted Achazia into the room. "Is there a problem?" She offered with a smile. "I instructed Mira that you all are to reach into the jar and pull a number. You are not to share the number, but place it face down on the table." In slow motion, she surveyed the room. "Does anyone recall Mira instructing you that I said you were now to be addressed by the number drawn from the jar?"

Several of the women shifted in their seats, but no one answered.

"Great," Ikia continued, "then the jar will be passed around, as directed. Please retrieve a tab and accept the number assigned. When the time is right, I will let you know the assignment connected to this exercise."

Mira moved at a slow, deliberate pace and stopped next to each chair and waited. Each young woman pulled a round tab from the jar, read the number, and placed it face down on the table.

"Now," Ikia directed, "when you leave the dining hall, stop at the table before ascending the staircase and take one of the clay jars filled with oil. This will be used to refill your lamps, when and if needed."

Ikia dismissed Mira then addressed the group. "Tomorrow may be the day you'll travel the required distance to meet the groom," she chuckled. "Of course, it might not happen until the following day. One never knows, but we want you prepared." She paused, took a deep breath, and smiled as she made eye contact with each young woman. "In the meantime, enjoy your dinner," she said, then left the room.

Bina grabbed her tab, squeezed her palms into a fist, and held it high. "It's amazing that all of us have been living here for the last few days doing the same thing, yet have expressed different opinions about what we've experienced. I think you'll agree tonight is different. It's become clear this whole journey is about choices or selections—our choices and the groom's selections."

Eunice grunted, "Or it's about how our choices about what to do or how we react will create or prevent opportunities for us to be more favored by the groom."

Vashti slammed her hands on the table. "You ladies still don't understand. It's all a game, don't you see? We're all in. They just created the groom's delay to make us eager and ready when he arrives."

"Well," Nettie offered, while rising to leave. "If anyone needs help or feels anxious about anything and just wants to talk, my door is always open."

During the exchange of side-eyed looks, several maidservants appeared with decanters. One of them asked, "Would anyone like a cup of wine?"

"Well, that's one way to relieve anxiety, Eunice commented."

After a moment's silence, the room exploded in laughter.

CHAPTER 24

F ull of chatter about the evening's events, the ten virgins left the dining area and stopped at the table below the staircase, as directed. Mira was on hand to provide details of their next steps. "Good evening, ladies. Please notice the slits at the bottom of your jar. This is where you will insert the tab you were provided with earlier. Please ensure the tab is inserted securely."

Without comment, each of the young ladies took one of the small jars of oil then proceeded up the stairs to their rooms. Midway up the staircase, Chloe stopped abruptly. Mia, following close behind, fumbled to keep her balance as she avoided crashing into her back.

"What on earth are you doing?" she shouted. "If you aren't careful, we could all land on top of each other on the floor below."

Chloe ignored the comment and raised her jar high above her head. "Now, don't forget, ladies," she smirked. "Find the slit at the base and insert your tab. Not following these instructions may cause you to miss the wedding banquet, because we still don't yet know when and where it will be held."

"Stop it, Chloe." Salome admonished. "These are the rules, and they have a purpose. If we are patient, it will all come together. Now move on or move over so the rest of us may get to our rooms and follow instructions for preparing the jars. It will all look better in the morning."

Hearing laughter behind them, they turned to find Ikia, dressed in a travel robe, beckoning to them. "Go, cover yourselves for warmth, deposit your jars and retrieve your lanterns, then join me again in the garden patio."

"See what I mean," Jacomina whispered. "Another unplanned event. Another unscheduled change in routine."

Nettie grabbed her hand. "Come on, you can do it. Get your things, meet me outside your door, and we will walk down together."

Nettie and Jacomina met several women who gathered at the bottom of the staircase on their way to the garden patio. Laughter and chatter filled the area, creating a festive atmosphere.

Vashti, always wanting to make a grand appearance, was the last to arrive. At the bottom of the stairs, she slapped her forehead. "Oh, for goodness sake," she announced for everyone to hear. "I forgot my lamp. When I opened my door, the corridor was so bright, I left before grabbing it." Flashing a brilliant smile, she put her arm around Nettie's shoulders. "Rather than waste time going back, I'll walk with you ole' helpful one."

Nettie hunched her shoulders and shook her head. "Well, as long as you keep pace with the rest of us, I guess there should be enough light."

Shouting from the rear of the group, Mia chimed in. "What bright light? When we left our rooms, the corridor was dark, and we had to light our lamps to descend the stairs." She pressed her cheeks with both hands.

"Oh, that's right. I forgot. You're special, so, of course, the corridor would be lit for you."

When everyone laughed, Vashti quivered with indignation. She glared at Mia, tossed her hair, and pushed ahead of the group onto the patio.

Ikia observed the young ladies as they entered. She clapped her hands. "Well, this is great. I see most of you came prepared with your lamps. Yes, this is very good." She opened her stone tablet. "You are about to partake in a sacred ceremony that will bound you to an individual for life. Your time here was deliberately planned that you might be prepared for any known and unexpected circumstances. Your openness and willingness to adhere to the requirements placed on you up to this point are appreciated." She paused, then added, "The groom is on his way."

The room exploded with applause, with everyone speaking at the same time.

Ikia raised her hand for silence. "Ladies, Ladies, hear me. The exact day of his arrival is still unclear, but we have you down here this evening to review details of the next steps." She returned to the stone tablet and detailed the new arrangements. "Initially, the celebration was to be held at the white mansion nearby. However, plans have changed."

Jacomina groaned. "My goodness, another change?"

Nettie patted her arm. "You'll be fine."

Mia whispered to Eunice, while Manya raised her hand to interrupt. "Excuse me, but haven't we had enough of this. I mean, we're all familiar with these surroundings. Why must we have to travel yet to another location for the festivities?"

Ikia eyes twinkled as she gave Manya a knowing glance. "Yes, I am fully aware of how familiar these surroundings have become. I'm sure one or two of you could move about these grounds and the white mansion itself with your eyes closed, having spent a great deal of time exploring, even when you should have been completing other duties. However, instead of celebrating here, you will travel to another location."

She pulled several documents from the satchel that sat near her chair. Her expression sobered. "If you haven't already noticed, this is a unique experience that is much different from any other. For this event, you are required to give this experience more serious attention than normal."

Vashti adjusted her chair, cringed, and nudged Eunice. "Here we go again, another *best advice* lecture."

Ikia looked at Vashti with a half-smile. "For instance," she continued. "All of you were required to bring your lamps to this session. Following those simple instructions was an example of what can be expected as you participate in the final details of your journey to join the groom and enjoy the celebration planned for you."

Mira walked ahead of several maidservants carrying trays of fruit, sweet bread, and a flask of red wine. Once each young lady held a full cup of wine, Ikia stood and nodded to dismiss the servants. A sudden gust of wind moved through the garden. Lamp lights flickered, and several of the women secured their shawls against the breeze.

Ikia rose from her seat and picked up a cup. "Ladies, you are in a *pause moment* planned to allow you to download information and guidance needed before moving to the next phase." Her face contorted. "Don't waste the time." The wind slowed to a gentle breeze, but the air turned chilly.

Ikia picked up her robe and draped it over her shoulders, chuckling. "When invited to gatherings, it's always good to come prepared for the unexpected. Please, enjoy this brief period of refreshment and relaxation." She sipped the wine, raised the cup high, then placed it in the center of the table. Before she stepped onto the path leading to the house, Ikia turned and smiled. "Rest well, ladies. You have a busy schedule ahead, and there's no room to correct a failure. Pay attention so you can choose wisely."

Mira waited in the shadows for the garden event to end. The torch lights posted at the house' entrance flickered under the cool breeze. When Ikia approached, Mira stepped into her path. "Ma'am, I think you should be cautioned not to give the ladies too much information. The groom, our master, forbids it."

Ikia took one step back and glared at Mira. Within seconds of that response, her shoulders sagged, and she nodded. "You are right, of course," she whispered, "I meant no harm. I was focused on giving them one last chance to hear and understand that though all were invited, it does not mean everyone will enter the celebration. Tonight, was simply a focus on the importance of preparation."

Mira hugged her companion. "I understand but for this assignment, our role is to present, not guide. Requiring that they bring their lamps to the meeting is one thing, but mentioning its possible importance to their tasks is another." Mira folded her arms, and lifted her eyebrows. "I agree it's a fine line, but a line we should not cross."

Ikia surveyed their surroundings. "We must leave this area. The ladies will be returning from the patio soon, and they shouldn't see us."

Mira nodded and walked away, then stopped short, causing Ikia to bump into her. They both laughed, creating a relaxed atmosphere as they continued through the doors to the main hall.

Maidservants were dismissed for the night, and room torch lights extinguished; only their lamps provided lighting.

"I ensured the scriptures were placed in their rooms as directed," Mira announced while resting her hands on the double doors leading to the servants' living quarters. "If they are observant," she continued, eyebrow raised, "all the ladies should have read the personal message before going to sleep."

Ikia walked up several steps, stopped, and whirled around.

"Listen, they're coming. We'll talk again in the morning," she announced, gathered the hem of her sheath dress, and rushed up the staircase. "My room is at the far end of the corridor, and I don't want them to see me when they arrive." At the top of the staircase, she turned and smiled before disappearing into the shadows.

* * *

Nettie waved at Achazia, Bina, Salome, and Eunice, then entered her room and fell across the bed exhausted. With her face planted firmly in the goose feather pillow, she prepared for sleep. She had placed her lamp on the side table when she entered but forgot to snuff the flame. Turning to one side, she clutched her pillow. Still in bed focused on mustering the energy to attend to her lamp, she raised her head when someone knocked. She threw her pillow aside and scrambled to get to the door.

"For goodness sake, who is it? Don't you know ..." She stopped speaking in mid-sentence and also froze. From the flickering lamplight glow, she noticed something written inside the door. "Just a minute," she shouted, then grabbed her lamp and held it high. She saw her name and a message.

"Open the door Nettie," came a frantic voice on the other side. She did as requested.

Bina, wide-eyed and frantic, rushed past Nettie, throwing her off balance, and rushed into the room. "I got a message," she almost screamed. "When I entered my room, I walked over to the window to widen the curtains for more air. There on the ledge was a message inscribed in the wood." She pulled Nettie's arm. "Come with me, and I'll show you."

Nettie took a few steps, hesitated, then blew out the lamplight so Bina would not see the writing on the back of the door. The only light in the room streamed from the moon. She took her friend's hand. "Listen, Bina, I cannot see your message."

She guided Bina to the door, turned the handle, and let it open. "Remember what Ikia said tonight? We are being prepared for the banquet with the groom. If I was meant to know the contents of your message, then it would have been revealed to us all." She hugged Bina then shoved her gently into the passage. "Go now, read *your* message and meditate on what it means for you."

Bina bit her bottom lip, forced a smile, then left without saying another word.

Nettie closed the door, re-lit the lamp, and held it up to the inscription inside the door. *"You can triumph in the work set before you. Remember how short the time, conserve your resources, but be wise and make haste in preparation."*

Nettie extinguished the flame of her lamp, sat on the edge of her bed, exhaled, and looked out the window. The moon was still bright enough to illuminate the space around her. She put both hands over her face and whispered, *"Lord God, help me know what to do."*

Bina returned to her room and slammed the door with tears running down her cheeks. She placed the lamp on her bedside table and curled in a fetal position on her bed. After a few moments lying still, she prayed, let out a harsh breath, and lay flat on her back. She then mumbled the message inscribed on her window sill. *"Have you learned to see in the dark?"*

Eyes wide, Bina stared into the darkness and repeated the message, seeking clarity.

"Thanks, Salome," Vashti announced as they reached her door. "I appreciate your taking this detour to my room before turning in. I realize it was a bit out of your way." She unstrapped her sandals and dropped them outside her door. "You're such a dear," Vashti continued and turned the door handle. "I don't know what I was thinking when I left my room earlier."

Salome tapped her lamp and looked over her shoulder, impatient to leave. She would have to retrace her steps and turn the curve at the end of the corridor to reach her room at the far corner. "Look, I've got to get moving. They were very clear with instructions that we go to our rooms. No detours," she offered, while shifting from one foot to the other.

Vashti, eyebrows raised, gave a dismissive wave and chuckled. "Yes, Yes. I get it. Another set of rules that we can manage or tweak to fit our needs." She opened her door, then waved at Salome. "Come in if you like. I have some fruit and sweet bread left from earlier today. You can have a quick snack before going to your room."

Salome shook her head and backed away. "No thanks, my friend. I have no interest in breaking the rules. I have my heart set on attending the banquet and have no intention of endangering that opportunity because I violated instructions. It's pretty dark in there, so grab your shoes and, for goodness' sake, hurry up and light your lamp so I can get started to my room."

Vashti walked to her night table, and lit her lamp. "Now that's done, and please don't worry about my sandals. I usually leave them outside the door for one of the maids to clean in the morning." She grabbed the tray of fruit and sweet bread from her side table. "Are you sure you won't join me in a late snack?"

When Salome didn't respond, she looked over her shoulder to the entrance.

The doorway was empty. Salome had left. Still holding the tray,

Vashti kicked the door closed and returned to the side table. The lamp's light flickered, exposing the inscription printed above the wood frame of the door. Still holding the tray, she leaned forward and studied the words. *"There are many ways to describe the actions that lead to completion of all endeavors. The key will be found in what you choose."*

She dropped the tray on the table and sat with her chin in both hands, and stared into space. The light continued to flicker, casting shadows on the wall and ceiling. Vashti didn't move, confounded by the mystery of the message she just read. Outside her window, the sounds of horses' hooves clattered on the cobblestone.

Salome moved in a fast pace toward the bedroom door, anxious not to be seen as not adhering to the rules. Breathing a sigh of relief, she secured the lamp then pulled sleepwear from the closet. While removing her sandals, her gaze went to the odd markings on the floor near the bed, and someone called her name. Peering out the window, she saw a bright light and movement inside the barn.

A sudden gust of wind blew the curtains and covered her face. She grabbed the lamp to look closer but someone had closed the barn door and the swaying movement of the trees obstructed her view. Salome stepped away from the window, still holding her lamp high, and studied the wording scribbled on the floor. *"Be careful not to surround yourself with predetermined conclusions. Don't assume things will happen according to your preplanned schedule. The groom controls the time."*

Inside the barn, Eitan, the property overseer, issued orders for the attendants to prepare the coaches. "We have work to do this night. Make haste."

* * *

Manya snickered over how she had stood in the shadows, watching the exchange between Salome and Vashti. This was one of many times she lingered to observe the behavior and movements of her fellow virgins, hoping to discover information that would put her at top of the list of those favored by the groom. Manya spent many nights creating situations, hoping to rattle the participants' nerves by throwing them off guard so they felt uncertain and anxious. Even this night she crept onto the patio below Salome's room and called out her name, hoping to rattle her nerves.

Despite instructions to get a good night's rest and ensure her things were in order, Manya closed her bedroom door, extinguished her lamplight, then paced the room.. After several moments, she crossed the floor opposite to her closet and stopped. She heard movement and turned her head toward the sound. A bright glow emanated just inside the closet opening.

In slow motion, she peered inside. On the corner wall of the small enclosure, a bright warm light shined over a message that read, *"You will not have control over every outcome, but all will be revealed if you let go of the need to have all information."*

Manya's eyes flooded with tears. She dropped to her knees, threw her hands in the air, and looked heavenward as she prayed.

Mira kept both arms at her side, revealing little emotion in her cool eyes. "Mia, I understand you have a concern and want to talk to Ikia, but you were given specific instructions to return to your room, ensure your items were in order, and rest in preparation for upcoming activities." She raised her hands, palms open. "I cannot allow you to disturb her at this hour."

268

Mia paced the corridor outside Ikia's door.

Mira observed her movements in silence.

After a few moments, Mia stopped pacing and glared at Mira. "Look," she shouted with a look of disgust on her face. "You're the maidservant, right? You're supposed to serve." She put her hands on both hips. "Well, servant, I am directing you to let your mistress know I need to speak with her."

Mira took one step forward, gave Mia a look intended to skin her hide, and tossed her hair. "You have yet to meet the one whom I serve," she said through clenched teeth.

In the moment's silence, Ikia opened her door and stepped into the hallway. "Well, Mia, I see you are not only wasting precious oil but time at this late hour. Midnight will be here before you know it. Then the dawn of a new day with new adventures." She crossed both arms across her chest. "What brings you to my suite at this time, in violation of the directive to prepare and rest?"

"Madame," Mira interrupted. "She insisted on disturbing you, but I'm happy to escort her back to her room."

Mia recoiled. "I can find my way, thank you," she retorted. "I want to discuss the message that was pinned inside the canopy of my bed."

Ikia smiled. "The message was written *to you* and is for *you*. Review it when you return to your room. You will find nothing that suggests you meet with me for additional discussion or explanation."

Mia tapped her foot but said nothing.

Ikia continued. "I realize you are more accustomed to giving rather than receiving instructions, but all of you ladies receive the same courtesy and attention. I don't intend on breaking the pattern by entertaining your need to talk about an issue I have not discussed with the other ladies." Ikia moved closer to Mia.

For a moment, she seemed taller and more threatening than at any other time since her visit.

"You have been given a message. I advise you to return to your room, meditate, then rest." Her voice softened as she pointed in the direction from where Mia had come. "Go now, return to your room."

Mia dropped her head and walked back down the winding corridor, holding her lamp high. She walked on her toes to avoid disturbing the others, not wanting them to see her tears. As soon as she climbed into bed and pressed the message back in place, she lay staring at the words. The lamplight was positioned on the nightstand, illuminating the message that appeared to float across the canopy like a wave in the river. *"When you hang on to the logic of your truths, you are in danger of losing sight of the true meaning of the goal."*

Jacomina bolted from the bed, stood in the middle of the floor, and listened. Moments earlier, a series of taps awoke her, but she couldn't identify the location they came from. The longer she lay in bed, the more intense the sound. Now, standing still with her body rigid and ears on alert, she was able to concentrate. She closed her eyes, but the sound was amplified, as if it emanated from several areas of the room at the same time. When she opened her eyes, she was drawn to the shelf above the window. Perched on the ledge was a beautiful dove surrounded by a bright white and yellow light, holding an object in its beak. The moment Jacomina nodded, the dove flapped its wings, dropped the item, and flew in a circle for several minutes before escaping through the window.

Jacomina scooped up the item. Made of lamb's skin, it was smooth to the touch. She unrolled the skin and read the message inscribed. *"You will be given the destination without the clarity. Only preparation will get you there."*

With a broad smile, this virgin pulled her satchel from the closet and packed a change of clothing and other necessary items for a journey—including the lamb's skin. When finished, she placed the satchel near the door, brushed her hair, and climbed into bed feeling at peace.

Eunice walked with Achazia as far as her room, smiled and waved, then proceeded in the direction of her bedroom. When Achazia was out of sight, Eunice, lamp in hand, doubled back and detoured down the rear corridor to the outer court, determined to find out more about the next event. For weeks, she noticed that Ikia spent hours in a library near the dining room before joining the others for dinner. and decided to explore without the others watching.

She opened the tall oakwood doors and was surprised that the room was lit by torchlight as if visitors were expected. In the silence, the sound of the running water from the fountain in the garden just beyond the window created a peaceful atmosphere. Eunice approached the mahogany desk in the far corner with a high-back leather chair behind it. Its seat faced a beautiful, floor-length tapestry with an array of soft colors. She looked closer at the tapestry and noticed a manseated on a large rock holding a lamb. Eunice gasped as panic ran through her. With the torchlight flickering, she was almost certain the man in the tapestry was smiling at he.

"You are constantly searching, Eunice, determined to do it your way," a familiar voice announced.

Eunice shuddered as the high back chair moved, and Ikia stood holding a small parchment note. "This is for you," she said, and stretched her hand for Eunice to take the message. "This is what you seek."

Eunice accepted the parchment, then rushed from the room, clutching the lamp. She ran down the corridor and up the staircase, panting with every step, and embarrassed at having been discovered. After she closed her bedroom door, holding the lamp high, she read the message. "*People are often separated by their choices based on whether they are, by nature, wise or foolish.*"

Achazia closed the door to her room and breathed a sigh of relief, more than happy that Eunice didn't want to have "girl talk" again this night. She had already missed recording her thoughts for several evenings and looked forward to jotting down her observations of this day. After hearing about one of the girls entering a bedroom and moving items around, she secured her writings by hiding them under one of the loose boards in her closet, covering it with her satchel.

Securing the lamp on the side table, she removed the wood covering to retrieve her materials from the hiding place. When she reached below the board, something hard had replaced the soft parchment sheets. She discovered a beautiful gold-covered box. When she opened it, all the sheets she had been writing on were folded neatly and covered by a scroll tied with a gold ribbon. Achazia smiled as she untied the scroll and read the message. "*Your world is about to shift. Don't let delay reduce your efforts.*"

THE BACHELORETTES OF THE BIBLE

"Trust in him who has all things in order. Set your understanding aside." Chloe repeated this phrase over and over the moment she read it. When she opened her drawer to prepare for bed, there it was, written on a smooth stone. She placed it beside her lamp, studied the message, and repeated the line so often it had almost become a chant that could be put to music.

After a few minutes, she extinguished her light and shouted, "Trust him. Trust who? The groom?" She threw her hands in the air, and spun around the room until she was too dizzy to stand. She fell face forward on the bed, mumbling the message into her pillow until she drifted into a deep sleep.

CHAPTER 25

At midnight, ten maidservants followed Ikia and Mira up the long staircase to the corridor leading to the bedrooms. One by one, the maidservants stood by the entrance of their assigned virgin's door and awaited the signal to enter. Each maid carried an hourglass, measured and synchronized to the exact level so that each young woman had the same amount of time to make ready for her journey.

Ikia stood at the end of the corridor, waiting for all maids to be in position. Mira, holding a lamp, stood by her side. At Ikia's signal, Mira grabbed the lamp by its handle, raised her arm high, and moved the light from left to right three times. The ten maidservants, holding the hourglass with one hand and grasping the door handle with another, entered the room shouting, "Awake! Awake! The hour has come. Get up and prepare for your journey to meet the groom." As instructed, each maidservant lit the virgin's lamp and placed the hourglass on the bedside table.

The maidservants were given specific instructions on what to say or not say in response to any questions. No one could provide additional details or comments to their assigned virgin. Once the hourglass was positioned on the side table, the maidservant addressed her designated virgin. "Madame, take heed to the movement of this instrument. When the sand runs out, you must leave your room immediately and join the others downstairs at the front entrance, prepared to travel, awaiting further instruction." The maidservant walked to the door and paused to ensure her virgin arose from bed. They then curtsied, and left their charge to prepare for the journey.

At the appointed time, the virgins left their rooms and congregated at the bottom of the staircase near the front entrance, and were greeted by Eitan and Shara, the head housekeeper.

"Where's Ikia and Mia?" Vashti asked while scanning the area. "Are they not going to be here when we leave?"

Eitan ignored the question and instead provided additional instruction. "The celebration banquet, as you've already been told, will be held at another location. The groom is on the way. It's a long journey, and it will begin now." He paced back and forth, elevating his voice to ensure all would hear.

"Listen carefully. Each of you was given a number to insert in the slot provided at the base of your lamp. Look at that number."

Following the instructions, each virgin raised her lamp to confirm the assigned number while whispering comments about the process. Eitan clapped his hands to gain attention from the group.

"Hear me," he shouted and pointed to the door. "When you leave this house, you will no longer address each other by name. You will be identified only by the number assigned."

Several women laughed, others murmured and snickered, but no one responded.

Eitan opened the door, beckoning the virgins to file outside. Since it was still dark, each virgin held their lamp aloft to be sure of their footing.

With Shara's assistance, they then gathered their satchels and any other items they chose to bring, and stepped into the night.

Two coaches, pulled by four horses each, awaited their passengers. Eitan stood next to one coach and waved the virgins forward. "This coach is for virgins one, three, five, six, and seven." He pointed to the attendant standing next to the other coach waiting behind. "Virgins two, four, eight, nine, and ten are to board the other coach." Snapping his fingers, he shouted, "Move now. We must be on our way."

The women piled into their respective coaches, after which the attendant and Eitan grabbed the reins and cracked their whips. The horses lurched forward, tumbling several virgins to the floors of the coaches.

While passing the large white mansion, Virgin #4, with a firm grip on the handle in the coach ceiling, looked at the rest of the group. "Hey, look at that. I wonder why the banquet wasn't held at the mansion?"

The coach hit a bump, and everyone shifted. Virgin #2 shook her head and responded, "You can't have a ceremony there. No matter what it looks like on the outside, the interior is full of old benches lining the room, with a pulpit at the front.

"What do you mean?" Virgin #4 snapped. "When I peeped inside the other day, I saw a large space with a beautiful, long mahogany table in the center of the room surrounded by leather chairs. The window drapes accented the shiny wood floors. It was a perfect place for a celebration."

The other virgins looked at each other but kept silent.

In the other carriage, adjusting in her seat, Virgin #5 bumped a container near her foot. "Hey, who else brought extra oil?"

The women exchanged glances, but no one responded. Virgin #3 picked up the jar of oil, stuffed it next to the other items in her satchel, and tucked it between her feet.

They rode a few more miles before the coaches veered off to a side road and stopped. Eitan and the attendant dismounted and opened the doors. "You must walk from here," he commanded and pointed ahead. "Hurry, follow this road. There will be guides along the way to ensure you reach the appointed destination."

Most of the virgins dismounted and moved forward without hesitation, leaving two or three behind to argue the reasoning for having to walk the rest of the way. Panting as they caught up with the rest, Virgins #1 and #3 shouted, "Listen, we stayed back to try to convince the attendants to take all of us farther, in the coach. While we tried to help everyone, you guys just left us."

Waving her arms, Virgin #1 rushed forward. "If we had all stayed together back there, we might have been able to convince them to take us farther."

Virgin #9 shook her fists, and confronted the boisterous Virgin. "You're always giving orders, always deciding what's best for the group." She squared her shoulders. "Not this time. Our instructions didn't include the choice to pick your partner or to work as a group." Virgin #9 picked up her belongings, and took long strides as she walked down the road into the darkness with only the movement of the lamplight recognizable.

The others followed.

The road was straight in some areas, then winding and full of overgrowth in others. Their lamps were crucial for this part of the journey. After a time, the virgins noticed two figures , in long white robes, approaching from the other direction accompanied by several attendants carrying food and flasks. Smiling and nodding, one of the women pointed to a clearing. "Please, refresh yourselves. The groom has been delayed, and there is time for a brief rest. The attendants laid food platters and utensils on a white, linen table covering.

"Eat and rest," one of the women in white repeated. "We will return in a moment to assist so that you may continue the journey."

The Virgins sat, ate, and refreshed themselves with water. "I hope our destination isn't going to be much further," Virgin #9 exclaimed. "My lamp oil is getting low."

Checking her container, Virgin #5 breathed deep and exhaled. "Yeah, I've been thinking that same thing."

No one else commented, and they continued eating.

Several minutes later, one of the ladies in white appeared. "Ladies, arise, gather your things, and continue your journey," she announced while pointing to the road ahead.

"My goodness, Virgin #10 announced as they left the clearing and walked onto the path. "If we weren't deep in these woods under the covering of these trees, we could preserve the oil in our lamps. As it is, I might run out soon," she shouted to no one in particular. Being ignored, she ran back to the clearing to ask one of the women if they could spare some oil. To her surprise, the area where they had been sitting looked as if no one had ever visited. The women in white and the attendants had disappeared. She hurried to catch up with the group, deciding not to mention what she discovered.

Some time passed and the virgins pressed forward in their travels. Virgin #3 checked her lamp and panicked. The light flickered because the oil was low. She rushed to catch up with Virgin #2, whom she noticed had opened the extra jar of oil she brought to replenish her lamp.

"Sister!" Virgin #3 shouted as she pushed past the other women. "Please, give me some of your oil. I don't need much."

Virgin #2 gave her companion traveler a side-eyed glance and continued to fill her lamp. "Sorry, my sister, we haven't reached the destination, and we don't know how far we have yet to travel. I can't afford to share my oil and take the chance of running empty so close to the end of the challenges we've faced on this journey to meet the groom." Having filled her lamp, she closed the jar and returned it to the satchel. She paused and faced Virgin #3 with a look of pity. "We were all given the same resources and guidance on what was expected. It was up to us to choose our course of action." She picked up her satchel, shifted its weight, and continued to walk the assigned path. Virgin #3 grunted and followed close behind.

* * *

The heaviness of the growth surrounding the wooded area thickened, but the virgins pressed forward, as instructed. A virgin stopped to replenish the oil several times while others moaned, muttered, and complained about the limited oil they had remaining.

One of the virgins with extra oil, drifted back to walk with the small group of three virgins with little oil who had gathered to console one another.

"I cannot share my oil," said Virgin #6, but I suggest that you walk with me so you do not stumble in this darkness because of your dim light. We will reach our destination together. No sooner had she spoken these words when they heard a squeal of joy.

"Look!" came a voice from the front of the line. "Over there! It's a house, a beautiful large mansion."

The virgins in the back row pushed the other ladies out of the way, and stumbled forward. All could see daylight appearing over the horizon as they left the heavy covering of the trees and entered the field full of white lilies leading to the mansion on the hill. The sound of heavenly music flowed from the inner rooms of the mansion, and the flowers of the field they walked through swayed to the tune.

Laughing, the ten virgins increased their pace until all had entered the cobblestone path leading to the front of the building. They paused below marble stone steps leading to double doors where two men, dressed in pristine white suits, stood on either side. Several ladies climbed the steps, talking, laughing, and hugging one another. When they reached the door, one of the attendants announced, "Only those whose lamps are filled with oil are permitted entrance. Please present your lamps."

The virgins looked around, checking to see who had lamps full of oil.

"Excuse me," Virgin #2 said and walked past the others to the door. She raised her lamp. The attendant smiled and nodded, and Virgin#2 entered the mansion. Moments later, Virgins #4, #6, #7, and #8 came forward, lamps filled with oil, and passed through the doors to the banquet. The virgins with empty lamps stood on the marble steps in silence, watching their companions disappear behind the doors.

"What about us?" Virgin #5 demanded as she stood before the attendant, eyes bulging. "Answer me!" she sobbed.

The attendant crossed his arms over his chest and responded, "Access denied."

Humiliation overcame her and she dropped to her knees, rocking from side to side. "My lamp," she cried. "Access denied because my lamp was empty. I didn't bring the extra oil, so I was turned away from joining the groom and the banquet," she shouted and pointed to the door attendant. "One small missing item, and all you can say is *access denied.*"

Stunned at hearing the news, the five remaining virgins looked at their empty lamps and, one by one, turned, and walked back down the marble steps to the cobblestone path.

"What the heck just happened?" Virgin #9 whispered as she surreptitiously glanced at the mansion guards stationed at the door. "Amazing," she then shouted. "We were refused entry because of lack of oil? This just can't be."

Virgin #1 held her head low and whispered, "maybe it was more than we thought. Maybe the oil was just a symbol of something else." No one acknowledged her comment. Instead, they continued to lament and console each other while complaining about how they had been treated.

At first, no one paid attention to the horses galloping in their direction, coach in tow.

"Look." Virgin #3 shouted and pointed in the direction of the sound. When they recognized Eitan from their former residence, they ran to greet him. He pulled the reins and halted in front of the five virgins, dismounted, and opened the doors to the coach. Without saying a word, virgins #1, #3, #5, #9, and #10 climbed aboard.

Before Eitan closed the door, he offered them a flask with water, fish, bread, and fruit. "You are required to continue to address each other by number, not name," he instructed. "I am here to return you to the house, where you will refresh yourselves before your journey home."

Virgin #9 protested. "Can't we go back up there and see if there is any way we can enter? I mean, this just doesn't make sense."

Eitan raised one hand. "Silence," he commanded. "Decisions have been made based on what was acceptable by the groom for entrance to the banquet. You did not meet the requirements, and it is time to leave." He closed the coach door, climb aboard the driver's box, released the brake, and the coach lurched forward.

The rejected virgins were on their way back to the residence.

Informed of their arrival, Ikia and Mira stood at the door awaiting the coach carrying the five rejected virgins. "They'll be full of questions," Mira stated as she waved the maids forward to continue their duties.

Ikia nodded. "But they will only receive what we are permitted to offer. The goal is to make them comfortable, help them refresh, and send them home to continue their lives. The groom offered no other concessions."

The coach stopped in front of the door, and Eitan assisted the virgins to dismount. They grabbed their satchels and entered the house.

Ikia greeted the ladies. "I realize returning here was not what you expected or wanted, but we are here to ensure you are rested and refreshed before you return home." Ikia ascended the staircase with the virgins following.

"Are we going to find out what we did wrong and why we didn't enter the banquet?" Virgin #1 asked.

Ikia paused midway, turned, and faced the group. "You will have a few hours to rest and think about your activities here, and your journey to meet the groom. If you concentrate and give yourself time to meditate on all that has occurred, you will come to the right decision about why you are here today." In the meantime, please rest. One of the maids will notify you when dinner is available."

"Which room shall we choose?" One of the virgins asked, her voice laced with sarcasm.

Ikia whirled, eyes intense. "Feel free to select whichever room suits your needs. They are all available.

Silence fell upon the group. Several avoided eye contact and walked down the corridor, pausing only long enough to open the room selected and close the door.

Dinner was uneventful. Neither Ikia nor Mira made an appearance. The number of maidservants was reduced, and the area surrounding the house —usually well-lit, leading the garden patio—was dark.

"I guess we are to eat and return to our rooms," Virgin #5 commented.

The remaining meal was eaten in silence. No one started any discussion about the events leading to their failure.

One of the maidservants entered with a flask to replenish the wine. "I've been instructed to let you ladies know your families have been contacted and are expected to arrive early in the morning. You will be awakened in time to take care of your personal needs and have breakfast. As your families arrive, you will be notified. In the meantime, the hour is late, and your rooms have been prepared for the evening." The maidservant bowed and prepared to leave.

Virgin #5 placed her cup on the table and extended her hand to interrupt. "What about Ikia and Mira? Are we not to see them this evening? We have questions."

The maidservant walked to the exit and paused. "I'm sorry, but Ikia and Mira left some time ago. I do not expect their return." She placed the wine flask on the sideboard and smiled. "Please, enjoy your evening and have a pleasant night's rest."

"Virgin #9 was the first to rise from the table. "The evening is late, and this event, for us, is over. I, for one, am going to bed. If I don't see you in the morning, it was a pleasure meeting all of you, and I bid you good night."

It was late morning before Ikia and Mira met in the dining room. The decision to have the virgins believe they had left the premises followed the groom's requirement to avoid further disappointment and unhappiness by describing what created their failures during the preparation phase. All the virgins who were rejected and refused entry into the banquet were returned to their respective homes. The maidservants prepared the house for closing while Eitan and his attendants waited to return Ikia and Mira to the mansion to continue serving in the groom's household.

COMMENTARY

The story of The Ten Virgins can be found in the Gospel of Matthew, Chapter 24. It speaks to Jesus sharing a parable about how our earthly actions have heavenly meanings. Its message is a reminder to consider our ways and examine our actions. Though all are invited, access to the Kingdom of God could be denied. The oil and the lamps were significant examples of how people can seem altogether ready and prepared, by appearance, yet lack what is needed for spiritual fulfilment.

As an example, I recently participated in a training program covering the use of personal protective equipment. The instructor emphasized the importance of reviewing the owner's manual because each part has a distinctive quality, requiring understanding of how it would apply to the user. Malfunctions occur because people don't take time to review, or fail to observe, procedures that may keep them from progressing to the next steps or create a false sense of confidence that gives the impression they have achieved the stated goal.

This parable is part of a powerful teaching by Jesus, in love, warning us to examine ourselves and not assume, when you reach the "woken up" stage of the revelation of who He is, that you are automatically ready for the wedding banquet with the Groom. "Many are invited, few are chosen," is a message we all should keep to memory.

You may have noticed that this fictional narrative concluded with the virgins starting their final journey to join the groom, having names replaced with numbers. This was decided because the message of this story was not focused on the names or physical description of the individuals. It was more about addressing what *might have been* the sum of an individual's actions and behaviors *that might have* led to decisions for them to enter, or be prohibited access to the banquet.

As a reminder, below are the quotes each virgin discovered before being awakened at the midnight call. It is for you to decide which virgin had an assigned number and was selected for the banquet.

- "Your world is about to shift. Don't let delay reduce your efforts." *Achazia*

- "Trust in him who has all things in order." *Chloe*

- "You can triumph in the work set before you. Remember how short the time, conserve your resources, but be wise and make haste in preparation." *Nettie*

- "People are often separated by their choices based on whether they are, by nature, wise or foolish." Eunice

- "Be careful not to surround yourself with predetermined conclusions. Don't assume it will happen according to your preplanned schedule. The groom controls the time." *Salome*

- "When you hang on to the logic of your truths, you are in danger of losing sight of the true meaning of the goal." *Mia*

- "Have you learned to see in the dark?" *Bina*

- "You will be given the destination without the clarity. Only preparation will get you there." *Jacomina*

- There are many ways to describe the actions that lead to the completion of all endeavors. The key will be found in what you choose." *Vashti*

- "You will not have control over every outcome, but all will be revealed if you let go of the need to have all information." *Manya*

AUTHOR BIO

Theresa V. Wilson, M.Ed., CPBA is an award-winning author, suspense/thriller Screenplay Writer, Indie Book Entrepreneur and fiction and non-fiction author.

An ordained minister, former educator and nonprofit executive, Theresa has been involved in her writing passion for over twenty-five years. Her experiences include serving as faculty member and newsletter editor for the American Christian Writers Association, and founder/coach of a writers' group. Always exploring, she has written and published poetry, created an audio CD, and achieved several awards for her screenplays. As one of TBN's latest authors, Theresa expanded horizons to include television commercial advertisement, under the Trinity Broadcast Network.

Theresa's fiction title, *The Real Housewives of the Bible*, received the Christian Indie Award for Historical Fiction. Her nonfiction titles include: *When Your Normal Is Upset: Living Secure in Uncertain Times*, *The Writers' Guide to Achieving Success: A Workbook for Implementing the Plan*, and *Reaching, Searching, and Seeking: Letting the Spirit Lead*.

Her screenplay, *Out of the Mist: The Battle in the Middle Realm* received Award Winner status from Los Angeles Motion Picture Festival,

Independent Shorts and Global Shorts, and Award-Winning status at ScreenPower Film Festival, United Kingdom, Independent Shorts and 13Horror.com Film Festival, and placed finalist in the California Women's Screenplay Festival. Theresa lives with her husband, Doug, in Owings Mills, Maryland.

For All Media Inquiries: theresa@theresawilsonbooks.com

facebook.com/theresavfacebook

twitter.com/twittertheresavwilson

instagram.com/theresawilson

CPSIA information can be obtained
at www.ICGtesting.com
Printed in the USA
LVHW011026310821
696548LV00008B/253